JOHN MARSDEN DESCRIBES HIS APPROACH TO WRITING:

'Writing is not a job or activity. Nor do I sit at a desk waiting for inspiration to strike. Writing is like a different kind of existence. In my life, for some of the time, I am in an alternative world, which I enter through day-dreaming or imagination. That world seems as real to me as the more tangible one of relationships and work, cars and taxes. I don't know that they're much different to each other.

'However, I write about these alternative worlds because it helps to preserve them. I'm their historian, their geographer, their sociologist, their storyteller. I write them into being. I have to say I don't care whether this is a good thing to do or not; this is just the way I am and the way I live my life.'

Also by John Marsden

So Much to Tell You
The Journey
The Great Gatenby
Staying Alive in Year 5
Out of Time
Letters from the Inside
Take My Word for It
Looking for Trouble
Tomorrow . . . (Ed.)
Cool School
Creep Street
Checkers
For Weddings and a Funeral (Ed.)
This I Believe (Ed.)
Dear Miffy
Prayer for the 21st Century
Everything I Know About Writing
Secret Men's Business
The *Tomorrow* Series 1999 Diary
The Rabbits
Norton's Hut
Marsden on Marsden
Winter
The Head Book
The Boy You Brought Home
The Magic Rainforest
Millie
A Roomful of Magic

The *Tomorrow* Series
Tomorrow, When the War Began
The Dead of the Night
The Third Day, the Frost
Darkness, Be My Friend
Burning for Revenge
The Night is for Hunting
The Other Side of Dawn

The Ellie Chronicles
While I Live
Incurable
Circle of Flight

THE TOMORROW SERIES

JOHN MARSDEN

THE DEAD OF THE NIGHT

PAN
Pan Macmillan Australia

John Marsden's website can be visited at:
www.johnmarsden.com.au

First published 1994 in Macmillan Hardback by Macmillan Publishers Australia
This Pan edition published 1995 by Pan Macmillan Australia
1 Market Street, Sydney

Reprinted 1995 (twice), 1996 (three times), 1997 (four times), 1998 (twice),
1999 (six times), 2000 (four times), 2001 (twice), 2002, 2003 (twice), 2004,
2005 (twice), 2006, 2007, 2008, 2009

National Library of Australia
cataloguing-in-publication data:

Marsden, John, 1950– .
The dead of the night.

ISBN 978-0-330-35647-3.

I. Title.

A823.3

Printed in Australia by McPherson's Printing Group

Papers used by Pan Macmillan Australia Pty Ltd are natural,
recyclable products made from wood grown in sustainable forests. The
manufacturing processes conform to the environmental regulations
of the country of origin.

Acknowledgements

Many thanks to: Sean McSullea, Rosalind Alexander, Melanie Smith, Laurie Jacob, Jessica Russell, John Welford, Rob Wingad, Charlotte Austin, Eric Rolls, Gabrielle Farran, Mary Edmonston, Felicity Robb, Frank Austin, Rachel O'Connor, and apologies to those whose names I've forgotten, or didn't record.

To my brother Sam, a loved and loving man.

Chapter One

Damn this writing. I'd rather sleep. God how I'd love to sleep. But I can't. It's been a long time since I had a peaceful night's sleep. Not since I went to Hell. Since I went to that complicated place called Hell.

When I get a chance to lie down I try everything. I count Border Leicesters, Merinos, Corriedales, South Suffolks. I think about my parents. I think about Lee. I think about Corrie and Kevin and all my other friends. I think a lot about Chris. Sometimes I try closing my eyes hard and ordering myself to go to sleep, and when that doesn't work I order myself to stay awake. Reverse psychology.

I read a lot, when there's daylight left, or when I think it's worth wasting a bit more of the batteries. After a while my eyes get tired and heavy, and I move to turn off the torch or put down the book. And that little movement so often jerks me back into consciousness. It's like I go all the way down the corridor of sleep, and just as I get to the door, it slams in my face.

So I've started writing again. It passes the time. No, I'll be honest, it does more than that. It gets stuff out of my head and heart and puts it on paper. That doesn't mean it's no longer in my head and heart. It's still there. But once I've written about it, seems like there's more room inside me again. More room for other things. I don't think it helps me get to sleep but it's better than lying in the tent waiting for sleep to come.

Before, everyone was so keen for me to write. It was going to be our record, our history. We were so excited about getting it all down. Now, I don't think they care if I do it or not. That's partly because they didn't like some of what I wrote last time. I told them I was going to be honest and I was, and they said that was fine, but they weren't too pleased when they read it. Chris especially.

It's very dark tonight. Autumn's creeping through the bush, dropping a few leaves here and there, colouring the blackberries, giving the breeze a sharp touch. It's cold, and I'm finding it hard to write and keep warm at the same time. I'm crouched inside my sleeping bag like a hunchback, trying to balance the torch, my pen, and the paper without exposing too much skin to the night air.

'My pen.' Funny, I wrote that without noticing. 'The torch', 'the paper', but 'my pen'. That shows what writing means to me, I guess. My pen is a pipe from my heart to the paper. It's about the most important thing I own.

Even so, the last writing I did was ages ago, after the night Kevin drove away from us in the dark Mercedes, with Corrie wounded and unconscious in the back seat. I remember thinking afterwards that if I'd had one wish, it would be to know that they'd made it to the Hospital and were well-treated. If I'd

2

had two wishes, it would be to know that my parents were still OK, locked up in the Cattle Pavilion at the Showground. If I'd had three, it'd be for everyone in the world to be OK, including me.

A lot has happened since Kevin and Corrie left. A couple of weeks afterwards, Homer called us together. We were still edgy and maybe it wasn't a good time for a meeting, but then maybe we'd been sitting around for long enough. I thought we'd be too depressed to talk much, or to make plans, but once again I'd underestimated Homer. He did so much thinking – not that he ever said so himself, but it was obvious from the way he spoke in our meetings. There'd been a time when a thinking Homer would have seemed as likely as a flying platypus, and I was still kind of slow adjusting to the change. But from his words that day, when we gathered again at the creek, it was obvious that he hadn't stayed in a slump like some of us.

He stood there, leaning against a boulder, his hands pushed into the pockets of his jeans. His dark, serious face was scanning us, his brown eyes resting on each one for a moment, as though considering carefully what he saw. He first looked at Lee, who sat along the creek a few metres, gazing down at the water. Lee had a stick in his hands and was slowly breaking off little pieces, letting the bits drift away with the current. As each bit disappeared into the tumbling gurgling water among the rocks he repeated the process. He didn't look up, and even if he had, I knew I'd see only sadness in his eyes. I found that almost unbearable. I wished I could drive it away, but I hadn't figured out how.

Opposite Lee was Chris. He had a notebook on his

3

knees and was writing in it constantly. He seemed to live more in that notebook than he did with us. He didn't talk to it – well, not out loud – but he slept with it, took it to meals, and guarded it jealously from snoops like me. He was writing mainly poems still, I think. There was a time when he used to show me all his stuff, but he'd been seriously offended by what I'd written about him, and he'd hardly talked to me since. I didn't think I'd said anything too bad, but that's not the way he saw it. I'd liked his poems too, even if they baffled me. But I'd liked the sound of the words.

Trucks grumble in the dark cold,
On the road to despair.
There's no sun, no clouds,
No flags anywhere.
The men walk with bowed heads.
They have no love to spare.

That was one bit I remembered.

Next to me sat Robyn, the strongest person I knew. A funny thing seemed to have happened with Robyn. The longer this terrible thing lasted, the more relaxed she became. Like all of us, she'd been devastated by what happened to Corrie and Kevin, but that hadn't stopped Robyn getting calmer with each passing day. She smiled a lot. She smiled at me a lot, which I appreciated. Not everybody smiled at me. Robyn was so brave that in the middle of one of our toughest times, driving a truck through a bullet storm at ninety k's, she'd kept me sane. Left to myself I think I might have pulled over to the slow lane, to let all the enemy vehicles overtake. Or stopped at a pedestrian crossing, to give way to a soldier with a machine gun. I drew a lot of courage from Robyn that night, and other times too. I just hoped I didn't leave her leeched dry.

Opposite Homer, sitting with her slender feet and her perfect ankles and her ballerina legs dangling in the water, was Fi. She still looked like she'd always done: ready to pour tea for your grandmother, and hand it over in a Royal Doulton cup. Or ready to step onto the cover of a Western Rose clothes catalogue. Ready to break another guy's heart or make another girl jealous or make your own father go red and laugh and chatter away like he was twenty years younger. Yes, that was Fi: cute, pretty and fragile. That was Fi, walking alone through the dark night looking for enemy patrols, lighting a petrol-soaked fuse to blow up a bridge, riding a motorbike across country in a wild scramble to escape bullets.

I'd been awfully wrong about Fi.

And I still hadn't got her figured out. After we'd blown up the bridge she'd been giggling, saying, 'I can't believe I did that! Let's do some more!' After Kevin drove away with Corrie unconscious in the back seat she cried for a week.

More than anyone, it was Fi who was hurt by what I'd written about our experiences. Chris had been angriest, but Fi had been hurt. She said I'd broken confidences, made her and Homer sound like dorks, like children, and that I'd cheated her by not telling her how I felt about Homer. I know what I wrote had a bad effect on their relationship. They got really self-conscious with each other, really awkward. I should have realised that would happen. I dumbed out.

Homer had been upset too, although he hadn't said anything directly to me. That was a bad sign, because we'd always been able to talk so easily. But he'd become self-conscious with me too. If we found ourselves alone together he mumbled some excuse and quickly went off somewhere else. I was very upset about that, maybe even more upset than I was about Fi.

Oh, the power of the written word.

But things had improved again. In such a small group we couldn't stay enemies for long. We needed each other too badly. Half the problem, I think, was that we were tired, and strained like wire in a new fence, so we twanged at any little thing that happened. I just desperately wished for everything to get back to what it had been. Only Lee and Robyn had been pretty much unaffected by what I'd written. They treated me the same all the way through. My problem with Lee was different – it was how he kept disappearing inside himself, fading away in front of my eyes. It was getting harder to get him back when that happened.

Well, we started our meeting, though I don't know why I call them meetings. They were much less formal than that. Although Homer seemed to run them most of the time, we were all pretty equal and we said what we wanted.

But this was our slowest start. It was obvious that Homer was the only one with much to say. And he seemed nervous. It was a while before he pulled the choke out. We didn't help much, gazing into the creek as he talked, Lee still breaking bits off his stick, Chris still writing in his notebook. I was scratching at a rock with a bit of bone, but not making any great impression.

'Guys, it's time we got our brains back into gear. We can either sit here and wait for something to happen to us, or we can get out and make things happen. We can either be like Lee's bits of wood, getting chucked around and battered and drowned by the creek, or we can get in and redesign the creek, rip the rocks out of it till there's no more rapids. The longer we wait, the harder it'll get, and the more danger we'll be in. I know sometimes everything's seemed a big mess. We're all way out of our league, but at the same time, we've got to remember, we haven't done that badly. We knocked off a few soldiers, got Lee out of town when he had a bullet wound, then blew up the whole damn bridge. For a bunch of amateurs, that's worth a few points.

'I don't know about you guys, but I've been sitting around here feeling depressed, only that's not going to get us anywhere. I think it's the shock of losing Corrie and Kevin, right at the moment when the four of us were coming back feeling so up and proud and happy. Wrecking the bridge felt good, and it was a shock to go straight from that into a disaster. It's no wonder we all feel sick and unhappy and angry. It's no wonder we've all been biting each other's heads off, though there's no logical reason why we should. The fact is, no one's made any terrible blunders. We've made mistakes, but nothing worth slashing wrists over. Corrie getting shot – no one could have picked that. We'll never be able to cut out all risks. The way Kevin told it, these turkeys just came from nowhere. We can't protect ourselves from all possible attacks, twenty-four hours a day.

'Anyway.' Homer shook his head. He looked tired, and sad. 'That's not what I wanted to talk about. We've all thrashed these things out among ourselves often enough since it happened. I want to talk about

7

the future. And by that, I don't mean we forget the past. No way. In fact, one of the things I want to say will show that, but I'll come to it. First, I want to tell you what I've been thinking about most. And that's courage. Guts. That's what I've been thinking about.'

He squatted, and picked up a dry old twig and started chewing on it. He was looking down at the ground, and even though you could see he was self-conscious, he kept talking. More quietly but with a lot of feeling.

'Maybe this stuff is obvious to everyone else. Maybe you all figured it out when you were knee-high to grasshoppers, and I'm just struggling along in the distance trying to catch up. But you know, it's only occurred to me the last week or so how this courage business works. It's all in your head. You're not born with it, you don't learn it in school, you don't get it out of a book. It's a way of thinking, that's what it is. It's something you train your mind to do. I've just started to realise that. When something happens, something that could be dangerous, your mind can go crazy with fear. It starts galloping into wild territory, into the bush. It sees snakes and crocodiles and men with machine guns. That's your imagination. And your imagination's not doing you any favours when it pulls those stunts. What you have to do is to put a bridle on it, rein it in. It's a mind game. You've got to be strict with your own head. Being brave is a choice you make. You've got to say to yourself: I'm going to think brave. I refuse to think fear or panic.'

Homer, pale-faced and eager to convince us, was talking earnestly at the ground, only glancing up occasionally.

'We've spun our wheels for weeks. We've been

8

upset and we've been scared. It's time for us to take charge of our heads again, to be brave, to do the things we have to do. That's the only way we can hold our heads up, walk proud. We've got to block out those thoughts of bullets and blood and pain. What happens, happens. But every time we panic, we weaken ourselves. Every time we think brave, we make ourselves stronger.

'There's a few things we ought to be doing. We're heading into autumn; the days are getting shorter already, and the nights are sure as hell colder. We've got to keep building up our food supplies, stockpiling for winter. Come spring we can plant a lot more vegetables and stuff. We need more livestock, and we have to work out what's practical to keep down here, given that there's no pasture. We've got enough warm clothes, and we'll never run out of firewood, even though it's not easy to get sometimes. But they're only the basic things, the survival things. What I'm talking about is not just hiding in here like a snake in a log but getting out and acting with courage. And there's two things in particular I think we should do. One is to go and find some other people. There's got to be other groups like us, and all those radio reports keep talking about guerilla activity, and resistance in the occupied areas. We should try to link up with them and work together. We're operating in such ignorance: we don't know where anything is or what's happening or what we should be doing.

'But before we go looking for them I want to look for someone else. I think we should go find Kevin and Corrie.'

To anyone watching (I hope there wasn't anyone) it must have resembled an outdoors ballet class. We all slowly began to unfurl and turn towards Homer. Lee dropped his piece of wood. Chris put down his pad and pen and stretched out. I stood and moved to a higher rock. Find Kevin and Corrie? Of course. The idea infused us with hope and excitement and boldness. None of us had thought anything about it because it had seemed impossible. But Homer's saying it had brought it within the realms of possibility, till suddenly it seemed like the only thing to do. In fact, his saying it made it seem so possible that it was almost as if it had happened already. That was the power of the spoken word. Homer had put us back on our feet and got us dancing again. Words began to pour from all of us. No one doubted that we should do it. For once there was no argument, no debate about the morality of it. All the talk was about how, not whether.

Suddenly we'd forgotten about food and livestock and firewood. All we could think about was Corrie and Kevin. We realised that we might actually be able to do something about them. I felt stupid that it hadn't occurred to us before.

Chapter Two

Already, just a couple of months since the invasion, the landscape looked different. There were the obvious changes: crops not harvested, houses lifeless, more dead stock in the paddocks. Fruit rotting on trees and on the ground. Another farmhouse, the Blackmores', had been destroyed, maybe by accidental fire, maybe by soldiers' shells. A tree had fallen onto the roof of the Wilsons' shearing shed and still lay there in a cradle of galvanised iron and broken rafters. There were more rabbits around, and we saw three foxes, which is unusual in daylight.

Some of the changes weren't so obvious. A gap in a fence here, a broken windmill there. A tendril of ivy curling in through a window of a house.

There was something else too, an atmosphere, a change in the feel of the land. It felt wilder, stranger, more ancient. I was still comfortable travelling through it, but I felt less important. I felt that I wasn't much more significant than a rabbit or a fox myself. As the bush took back the farmlands, I would become just another little bush creature, scurrying through the undergrowth, barely disturbing the land. In some

11

strange sort of way I didn't particularly mind that. It felt more natural.

We took our time, keeping well away from the road, walking across paddocks in the shadow of the hills, using the trees for cover. We didn't talk, but there was a new mood in all of us, a new energy pumping through our blood. We walked all the way to the ruins of Corrie's house, then took a break there, raiding their little orchard for afternoon tea. A lot of the apples were nibbled by possums and parrots but there were enough whole ones for us to stuff ourselves, and we did. But we paid a price an hour later when we all started ducking behind trees; the apples had gone through our alimentary canals like a flood in Venice.

Still, it was worth it.

We hung around the Mackenzies' place until well after dark. We figured we were pretty safe there, because with the house just a pile of rubble there was nothing much left to attract the soldiers. I'd thought I'd feel depressed at the sight of the wreckage, but I was too nervous at the thought of what lay ahead. To be honest (there I go again) I'd already stopped dreaming noble dreams of rescuing Corrie and Kevin; instead I was thinking more about keeping myself alive. I even had the grim idea that my body might soon be looking like Corrie's house, splattered across the landscape.

The worst thought of all though – the one I stamped on every time it reared its dark filthy head – was that Corrie might be dead. I didn't think I'd be able to cope with that. I was scared that finding Corrie dead would be the end of me. I didn't know how it would finish me; I just had this deep belief that I could not continue living if my mate Corrie had been killed by a bullet fired by an invading army in the middle of a war. Surely I couldn't survive that? Surely no one could survive that. It was too far beyond normal.

From the moment Homer had suggested we go into town and find Kevin and Corrie we'd banished the thought that either or both of them might have been killed. The quest for them had given our lives meaning again; we weren't in a hurry to rip that up and throw it away.

At eleven o'clock we started out for Wirrawee, walking in pairs on the grass verge of the road, about fifty metres between each pair. We'd hardly left the Mackenzies' when Lee, to my surprise, took my hand and held it in his warm grasp. That was the first time in weeks he'd taken any initiative with me. I'd been making the running, and although he'd responded OK most of the time, it had made me feel insecure, as though maybe he didn't care all that much. So it felt good to be walking along hand in hand, under the thick black sky.

I was keen to say something, any trivial little thing, just to let Lee know how happy I felt to be wanted again. I gave his hand a squeeze and said, 'We could have used the bikes, to the Mackenzies' at least.'

'Mmm. But not knowing how much things might have changed... Better to play it safe.'

'Are you nervous?'

'Nervous! It wasn't just the apples that had me dropping my daks.'

I laughed. 'Do you know, that's the first joke you've made in weeks.'

'Is it? Have you been counting?'

'No. But you've seemed so sad.'

13

'Sad? I suppose I have been. Still am. I suppose we all are.'

'Yes... But with you it goes so deep, and I can't reach you.'

'Sorry.'

'It's not something to be sorry about. It's just the way you are. You can't help that.'

'OK, I'm not sorry then.'

'Hey, that's two jokes. At this rate you'll be doing stand-ups at the Wirrawee nightclub.'

'Wirrawee nightclub? I think I missed that. Our restaurant's the nearest thing to a nightclub in Wirrawee.'

'Remember how everyone at school kept complaining that there was never anything to do in Wirrawee? Definitely no nightclubs. We had that Year 9 disco but we never got around to having another one. It was good fun, but.'

'Yes. You and I had a dance.'

'We did? I don't remember that.'

'I do.'

He said it with such feeling, and his hand tightened so hard on mine that I was startled. I tried to look at his face, but couldn't make out his expression in the darkness.

'You remember it that well?'

'You were sitting with Corrie, under the premiership flag. You were holding a drink with one hand and fanning yourself with the other. You were red in the face and laughing. It was pretty hot in there and you'd been dancing with Steve. I'd been wanting to ask you since I'd got there – that was the only reason I went in the first place – but I didn't have the guts. Then suddenly I found myself walking towards you without

14

even knowing how I'd started. It was like I'd become a robot. I asked you and you just looked at me for a sec while I felt like a complete idiot, and wondered which tactful way you'd find to say no. Then without saying anything you gave Corrie the can of drink and you got up and we had our dance. I was hoping for a long slow song but it was "Convicted of Love". Not too romantic. Then at the end Corrie dragged you off to the dunnies and that was the end of it.'

My hand had become damp and sweaty, but so had Lee's I think. It was hard to tell whose hand was providing the damp. I just couldn't believe what I was hearing. Had Lee really felt that way about me for so long? Unbelievable, wonderful.

'Lee! You're so... Why didn't you tell me all this ages ago?'

'I don't know,' he mumbled, shutting all his words in again, as quickly as he'd let them out.

'You've seemed so... I never know whether you really care or not.'

'I care, Ellie. It's just that I care about other things too; mainly my family. I get so exhausted thinking about them that there's no room for anything else.'

'I know. Do I ever know. But we can't deep-freeze our lives until our families get out. We have to keep living, and that means thinking and feeling and... and just advancing! Do you know what I mean?'

'I know it. Only it's hard to do it sometimes.'

We were passing the Church of Christ at the edge of Wirrawee. Homer and Robyn, who were ahead, had stopped and we waited with them for Fi and Chris, who'd fallen a little behind. From now on there would be no more talk of emotions, and liking each other. I had to put away my amazement at the

15

strength and depth of Lee's feelings. We had to be completely alert, concentrating. This was a war zone, and we were going into the heart of it. There must have been a hundred or more soldiers just in little Wirrawee, and every one of them would want to kill us if they could, especially after what we had done to their buddies.

Each of our three pairs separated, one person to each side of the street. I was on the right, Lee on the left. We waited until the dark figures of Homer and Robyn had been gone sixty seconds, then we followed. We went along Warrigle Road, with the Mathers' house on the ridge above us. I wondered how Robyn would feel as she passed it. We turned into Honey Street, as we'd agreed, and crept along the footpath. There were still no lights in this part of Wirrawee and I caught only occasional glimpses of Lee. I saw nothing of the other four, and could only hope that we were all going at the same speed. Honey Street at least seemed normal enough, except for a wrecked car crushed up against a telegraph pole. It was a dark blue car, which made it hard to see, and I nearly walked into it myself. As usual my mind started wandering: I began wondering how I'd explain it to the cops if I had a collision with a parked car... 'Well Sergeant, I was going east along Honey Street, doing about four k's, when I suddenly saw the car right in front of me. I hit the brakes and veered to the right, but I struck the vehicle a glancing blow on its right-hand side...'

I had so many different daydreams for when I was walking anywhere. My favourite was counting things, like the number of electrical appliances we had at home (sixty-four, I'm ashamed to say), the number of songs I could remember with a weekday in the title (like 'Let's Make it Saturday'), the number of mozzies who'd never be born because of the one I'd just killed (sixty billion in six months, if every female laid a thousand eggs).

My problem was to stop thinking about stuff like that when I was walking through a town crawling with soldiers wanting to kill me. It amazed me that even in those situations I still found it hard to concentrate. I was OK for ten minutes or so, but then something would distract me and my mind would drift out in the rip again. Incredible but true. It was the same in this battlefield as it was in Geography classes at school. I was scared I'd dream myself to death one day.

From Honey Street we cut across a little park with no name, into Barrabool Avenue. We met, as agreed, in the front garden of Robyn's music teacher's house, and had a quick conference under the peppercorn tree.

'It's quiet,' Homer said.

'Too quiet,' Lee said, with a little smile. He'd watched a few war movies in his time, Lee.

'Maybe they've all left,' Robyn said.

'We're a block and a half away,' Homer said. 'Let's keep going, just the way we planned. Everybody happy?'

'Laughing hysterically,' Chris said.

Robyn and Homer tiptoed away through the trees. A few moments later we heard the little thuds of their feet on the gravel as they jumped from the garden back on to the footpath.

'Can we go next?' Fi whispered.

'OK. Why?'

17

'I can't stand the waiting.' She looked too thin in the darkness, like a ghost. I touched her cold cheek and she gave a little sob. I hadn't realised how scared she was. All the time we'd spent holed up in Hell had preyed on her mind. But we had to be tough when we were out here in the streets. We needed Fi if we were going to check the Hospital thoroughly.

So all I said was, 'Think brave, Fi.'

'Yes, that's right.'

She turned and followed Chris, as Lee took my hand again.

'I wish Fi and I were as good friends as we were before,' I said to him. He didn't answer, just squeezed my hand.

We made our way back out to Barrabool Avenue, separating again to left and right. Now at last I had no trouble concentrating. Logically, the area around the Hospital shouldn't have been more dangerous than any other part of town – one of the points we'd been sure of was that the Hospital wouldn't be heavily guarded – but because it was our target, our goal, I was now alert and watchful and nervous.

Wirrawee Hospital is on the left side of Barrabool, near the crest of the hill. It's a single-storey building that's been added to over the years, with lots of different wings, so that now it's like a letter H next to a letter T. Between us we'd had enough experience of the place to work out quite a good map. We had information from everyone. Lee had visited it when each of his little brothers had been born. Robyn had been admitted for a few days when she broke her ankle cross-country running; Fi's grandmother had been there for months before she died; I'd had my shoulder X-rayed, picked up tablets for Dad at the dispensary, visited friends when they were in there. Yes, we all knew the Hospital.

The trouble was that we didn't know how much things had changed since the invasion. The adult prisoners we'd talked to once had told us that our people were still being treated at the Hospital, but we had to expect that they wouldn't be in the best private rooms. In the car park, more likely. Before the invasion the entrance foyer was in the crossbar of the H, with Casualty and Outpatients and X-Ray and all that stuff on the right, and the wards on the left. In the crossbar of the T were the offices, and in the long row behind them were the wards for the old people.

See, our Hospital was as much an old people's home as it was a hospital: we didn't get a lot of open-heart surgery and kidney transplants in Wirrawee.

It was 1.35 am when we got there. The electricity was on in this part of town, as it had been every time we'd visited Wirrawee. There were no streetlights, but there was a big security light shining on the car park. The Hospital was lit, but mainly just the corridors and the foyer. There weren't many rooms with lights on.

At 1.45, as we'd agreed, Homer and Robyn made the first move. From a belt of trees across the road from the car park Lee and I saw the two dark figures moving towards the far end of the Outpatients section. Robyn was in the lead, Homer was peering around more as he followed. I was surprised at how small they looked. There was a door near that end of the building which we'd figured was the least conspicuous entry, and we were hoping it would be unlocked. But Robyn was only at it a moment before she turned away and began checking the windows along the side nearest us, while Homer disappeared around the other side. A few minutes later Homer reappeared, Robyn rejoined him, and they moved quickly back to the trees. So that was one failed option.

Five minutes later, Fi and Chris came out of their hiding place, behind some sheds a little further up the hill. Their target was the T-shaped building – the offices and old people's wing. It took them ten minutes, or close enough, but the result was the same: the place was tight as a Vacola. Chris looked in our direction and held out his arms, palms up. He couldn't see us, or so I hoped, but he knew approximately where we'd be. Then he and Fi retreated to safety, leaving the field to us. Lee looked at me and rolled his eyes; I grinned back, hoping I didn't look as frightened as I felt.

We waited the agreed five minutes. It was 2.09 am. I tapped Lee's arm, he nodded, and off we went. Across the crunchy gravel, up a small bank planted with straggly red wallflowers, and towards a side door in the main wing. We walked slowly, about three metres apart. I was breathing hard, as though I'd run a crossie, and I was sweating all over. The sweat felt so cold on my skin, like it was turning to ice. My throat had a lump so big I felt I'd swallowed a chicken bone. Basically, I felt sick. I was very scared. I'd almost forgotten the emotion that had brought us there: my love for Corrie and Kev. I just wanted to do the job, find them or not find them, and then get out of there. That was all.

I reached the door, which was in shadows but had an illuminated green exit sign above it. I turned the handle slowly and pushed, then pulled. The result was the same: the door was tightly locked.

As the others had done, we separated and began checking the windows. The ones on the corridor side were all closed, but on the other side quite a few were open. But they were up high, beyond our reach without a ladder. I was getting too close to the lights of the entrance foyer, so I went back, meeting up with Lee again near the locked exit door. It was too dangerous to talk there, so we went over to a shed about forty metres away – a small locked wooden hut – and hid behind it.

'What do you think?' Lee asked.

'I don't know. Those open windows would be for wards. I don't see how we could just drop into a ward.'

'Plus they're so high up.'

'Yes.'

There was a pause. I had no idea where to go from there.

'I wish the others were here. They might know what to do.'

'It's only ten minutes before our pull-out time.'

'Mmm.'

Another minute passed. I sighed and started to stand. I couldn't see any point hanging around there, in such a dangerous place. But as I began to move, Lee grabbed my arm.

'Shh. Wait. There's something...'

I heard it too, at that moment. It was the sound of a door opening. I peeped around one corner of the shed; Lee looked around the other. It was the door that we'd been hoping to find unlocked. A man in military uniform was coming out. We could see him easily, backlit by the dull light from the corridor. He didn't even look around, just walked along the bank, pulling things out of his pocket. Only when his hand went to his mouth did I realise what he was doing. It was a cigarette. He'd come outside for a smoke. Just like us, these people weren't allowed to smoke in hospitals. I got quite a shock. I'd been thinking of them as animals, monsters, but they had rules, codes of conduct, too. I guess it sounds naive, but it was the first time I felt any common ground with them. It was odd.

It was frustrating to crouch where we were and look at that open door. The yellow light from the corridor made it seem as if I was peering into a gold mine. I desperately searched my mind for some way to get in there. Then my thoughts were interrupted. From away to our left, in among the trees, came a cry, a groan, like a bunyip having a baby. My skin goosebumped all over. I turned and grabbed Lee and looked at him in horror. I know my eyebrows were somewhere up above my hairline, and still rising. The cry came again, even worse, and more prolonged. The bunyip was going to need stitches.

Lee whispered in my ear, 'It's Homer.'

As soon as he said it, I realised everything. Homer was trying to get the soldier away, leaving us a wide open door to stroll through. Lee and I let go each other and turned back to our lookout points. We got a shock. Instead of rushing heroically into the trees the soldier was bolting towards the door. He got there and skidded through it, pulling it shut behind him. Even at such a distance we could hear him deadlocking it, slamming a couple of bolts home for good measure.

'Bloody Homer,' Lee said. 'He thinks it's a game.'

'Hope there's not a fire in the Hospital tonight,' I said. 'It'll take them half an hour to get out.'

'I thought soldiers were meant to be tough, fully trained professionals.'

'Remember what we heard? That they had professionals, but they also had a lot of draftees? Amateurs. Unwilling amateurs, too, by the look of it.'

'We'd better get out.'

We withdrew, meeting the others twenty minutes later at the music teacher's house. Homer looked a bit embarrassed, a bit defensive. He hadn't become totally mature and responsible overnight. There was still a bit of the wild and crazy guy lurking inside.

'OK, go on, everyone have a go at me,' he said, before I could get out more than half a sentence. 'It seemed like a good idea at the time, that's all. If he had come looking for us, Lee and Ellie could have gone straight in and you guys'd now be kissing me on both cheeks and buying me beers.'

'We ought to be kicking you on both cheeks,' Lee mumbled. 'And you know which cheeks.'

'It was pretty dumb,' Chris said. 'If he'd had a gun he could have shot you. If he didn't have a gun there was no way he was going to charge off into the bush in the middle of the night to investigate. Either way it was pretty dumb.'

There didn't seem to be much to add. We were all tired, and at our worst. We nominated Homer for first sentry duty and the rest of us bedded down on the first floor of the house. It was the safest house we knew, because there were so many exit points out of upstairs windows, along tree branches. And it gave such good views of the road. No one could approach without the sentry seeing them.

I got a real charge out of being in a bed, in a bedroom again. It was a beautiful, secure, comfortable luxury. I did sentry from six till eight, then slept again till lunchtime.

Chapter Three

 W e spent the afternoon lounging around trying to think of brilliant ways to get into the Hospital. I was on the floor most of the time, wrapped in a tartan rug. I remember laughing at Chris, who was pretending to watch television. He was reacting to the flat grey screen as though there were game shows and sitcoms and action movies on it. It was strange how TV had been such a major part of our lives, and now, without electricity, the TV had become about the most useless thing in the house.

Most of all I felt pretty happy that day. It was because we were starting to get on well again. It only showed in little ways, but those little ways were my food, my drink, my air, my life. The others thought I was tough and independent, but I needed those five people more than I'd ever needed anyone or anything in my entire existence.

For all that though, we still couldn't think of a way to get into the Hospital. Night started to fall, then it fell, till it was lying all over the ground. And we still hadn't thought of anything. But I'll take a lot of the credit for the inspiration we finally had. I'd been idly thinking about Homer's crazy distraction tactic. It seemed to me that there were possibilities in the idea. He just hadn't done it right. Something was nibbling at my brain, like there was a tiny mouse trapped in there. If I could find the key I could let him out.

'Lee,' I said, when he was relieved by Fi from sentry duty.

'Yes, my beautiful sexy caterpillar?'

'Caterpillar?'

'That's what you look like, wrapped up in your rug.'

'Thanks a lot. Listen, you remember that very quick conversation behind the shed, after Homer finished wailing?'

'And frightened a poor innocent soldier out of his wits? Yes.'

'What did we say? There's something from that conversation that's bugging me.'

'Caterpillars are always bugged. That's what makes them caterpillars.'

'Very funny. But I'm serious.'

'What did we say? I don't know. We were talking about how it was probably Homer who was making the noise.'

'Yes. And then?'

'I can't remember. Just watching the guy running in and shutting the door. Locking it so tight.'

'Yes. Something about... The way he was locking it.'

'You said something...'

'Yes, I did.'

I sat there, frustrated.

'Is this really important?' Lee said presently.

'I don't know. I'm probably being stupid. I just

25

think there's something there, if I can remember it and let it out. It's like watching a heifer calving. I can see the head of the damn thing but I don't know what it's going to look like.'

I got up and started walking around. We were in an upstairs sitting room, which Ms Lim must have used as a practice room. There was a beautiful black baby grand piano facing the window. Homer had written *Heavy Metal* across it in the dust with his fingers. But I had seen Lee with the lid raised, running his hands across the keys. His fingers were trembling and there was a look on his face even more passionate, more intense than when he looked at me. I'd been standing in the doorway watching. When he noticed me he lowered the lid quickly, almost guiltily, and said, 'I ought to play the 1812. Get the soldiers to provide the cannons.'

I didn't answer; just wondered why he tried to turn something that he felt so strongly about into a joke. There were times when I got sick of jokes.

But now I did a tour of the room, swatting the blind cord, spinning the piano stool, rubbing out Homer's graffiti, straightening the books, opening the front of the grandfather clock, then closing it again.

'Let's have an instant replay,' Lee said, watching me.

'Not very instant,' I said, sitting on the piano stool and facing him. 'But OK, let's.'

'All right. I don't think we said much till the guy was back through the door and closing it. We abused Homer a bit, that's all.'

'Then we talked about how tightly he was locking it.'

'And how they must have professionals and amateurs, like we thought. And how this guy must be…'

'Wait.' I sat there with my hands gripping my head. Suddenly it was there. I stood. 'I've got it. Let's go find the others.'

That night, as Lee and I watched Homer from our hiding place, I thought again how there were advantages to being the wildest guy in the school. Homer knew some amazing stuff. While the rest of us had been studying product differentiation and price discrimination in Economics, Homer and his mates at the back of the room had been training in urban terrorism. I don't know how they learnt some of the things they did.

Homer was creeping towards the Outpatients' section again, this time with Robyn fifty metres behind, on the lookout. He got to the door at the end of the building that he and Robyn had tried before. This time he didn't bother with it, but went instead to the little metre-high door under the building, about halfway along. He had to grope his way through the lavender bushes to reach it, but from the angle we were watching we had a good view. I saw him pull on the door but it must have been locked, as we'd expected. He used a chisel then, to try to lever it open, but that didn't work, although the door seemed flimsy enough. It consisted only of four vertical white slats nailed to two crossbars.

Homer was undeterred, however, and he was well-prepared. His hand went to his bag of tools again and pulled out the screwdriver. He set to work on the hinges. It took five or six minutes, then at last he took a firm hold on the door and lifted it gently off. Without a backward glance he wriggled – he's a big guy, Homer – through the opening.

We couldn't see him any more but I knew exactly what he'd be doing. Lee and I both tensed, knowing that it was nearly time for us to go into action. I could picture Homer, undulating through the cold dark underworld like a big worm. He'd seemed so certain that his plan would work, once I'd given him the initial idea. But after all, he was just recreating one of his more outrageous school stunts. He'd had a dress rehearsal.

He had to find a place to make a hole in the floor. The building he was in, being rickety and old, seemed a good choice for that, and he had a keyhole saw and a brace and bit with him. We'd thought this through very carefully. We didn't want to leave any evidence of our visit: that's why we wanted to do it through a hole in the floor, rather than the easier method of breaking a window and throwing Homer's bomb through. So we watched and waited and shivered, glancing at our watches, then at each other, then anxiously back at the Outpatients' Department.

When the action did happen it happened with knobs on. We hadn't wasted our evening, sneaking into house after house in Barrabool Avenue to find ping-pong balls. Homer had promised us a worthwhile result, as he wrapped the balls in foil. We'd watched, fascinated, not prepared to cast doubts as we thought back to the evacuation of the AC Heron High School just six months earlier. It had certainly worked then. And it worked now. Suddenly, sharp loud beeps started to emerge from Homer's end of the building, and almost immediately, through the clear night air, came a series of announcements. These were in English and loud enough for us to hear. They seemed to come from all over the Hospital; I

28

think they were prerecorded and came on automatically. The first one was 'Code two, code two, code two', repeated every fifteen or twenty seconds. After a minute or so came the next message: 'Zone four, zone four, zone four'. Then: 'Level three. Level three'. By now the Hospital was stirring into life. Lights were coming on everywhere and we could hear people calling out. A second round of announcements began; the same as the first I think, but by then I'd stopped concentrating on them. Instead, Lee and I were creeping forward, looking for our chance. I couldn't see any smoke actually emerging from the end of Outpatients' but the people coming out of the wards were all heading in that direction. There were two soldiers, running, then a few men and women in ordinary clothes, then a woman in a nurse's uniform, and three or four people in pyjamas. I couldn't see their faces, so couldn't tell which ones were friends, if any. But it was quite a party for two o'clock in the morning.

We didn't want to do any harm to sick people. Homer's smoke bomb was guaranteed not to start a fire, and we were hoping that the staff wouldn't rush around evacuating patients. We had gambled that the Hospital would have a fire detection system that could be triggered by smoke, and that it would still be working. It wasn't a very big gamble: pretty much a certainty. And the staff had reacted as we hoped they would. They hurried to the site of the alarm. And they left doors open everywhere.

We didn't have much time. Out of the corner of my eye I saw Fi and Chris moving quickly to the door into the main wards. Lee and I had the old people's wing as our target, in the long section of the T-shaped building. Only one person had come from there, a soldier, and he or she had flung the door shut, but so hard that it bounced open again.

I set off, half a stride ahead of Lee. I was hoping we could sneak across the car park, not being noticed, but once we entered that great bare black desert I realised our only chance was speed. I put my head down and sprinted, hoping the footsteps behind me were Lee's. The night air was cold on my face, but colder was the chill down my neck and back; the fear of the ripping bullets. I got to the door puffing, gasping, and grateful to be alive.

Time was so short. All I could do was stick my head through the door and look to left and right. The old wooden corridor was empty of people so in I went, trusting to Lee to follow me. He did, so closely that I could feel his breath around my ears.

Although the corridor was empty you could sense that the building was full of people. I don't know what it is: the little sounds maybe, the creaks, the shuffling noises. Or maybe it's the smell of human bodies and breath, or the warmth that fills the place, the close humid warmth that heaters and fireplaces can never generate. So I knew right away that there were people everywhere, behind all the closed doors along the corridor. I made an instant decision to turn right, not for any reason in particular; I just did it, walking quickly along, trying to decide which door to go through, wishing for X-ray vision. We passed a small kitchen with an open door. It was empty and in darkness. The next room was labelled B7. No light showed under the door. I stopped, looked around at Lee, and indicated the door by raising my eyebrows and pointing to it. He shrugged and nodded. I took a deep breath, hunched my shoulders, squeezed the handle tight, turned it and opened the door.

Inside all was dark. Not only were the lights off but the curtains were drawn too. Yet again I knew it was full of people. It seemed such a small room, but so full of people. There was a lot of heavy breathing, some slow and deep, some quavery and long. I stood there, trying to get used to the darkness, not knowing whether to risk speaking or not. But Lee tapped me on the shoulder and I followed him back into the corridor.

'This is bloody risky,' he said. He was sweating heavily. We heard a noise down the corridor and turned quickly towards it. The door from the car park was being opened again. Suddenly we had no choice. We made a dash for the nearest door, which was B8. I tried to open the door as quietly as possible, but there wasn't much time for subtlety. We fell into the room together, making a fair bit of noise. Lee shut the door quickly behind us as a voice asked aggressively, 'Who is it?'

I felt such relief that she spoke in English. It was a woman's voice, someone quite young, twenty-five or thirty maybe.

'We're looking for a friend,' I said quickly.

This was the first conversation I'd had with an adult since the invasion.

'Who are you?' she asked again.

I hesitated, and finally answered honestly. 'I don't know if it's safe to say.'

There was a pause, then in a voice quivering with astonishment she said, 'Do you mean you aren't prisoners?'

'That's right.'

'Well bloody hell. I didn't think there was anyone left.'

'Are we safe in here?' Lee asked.

'How many of you are there?'

'Only two,' I said.

'Well, you're probably safe till morning. Sorry I growled at you when you came in, but you never know round here. Sometimes attack's the best method of defence. Look, old Mrs Simpson next to me, she's in a proper bed – the only one who is – hop under there and you'll be hidden if anyone turns the light on. Gawd, I can't believe this.'

We groped our way to the bed and wriggled under it. Mrs Simpson smelt pretty bad, but we tried to ignore that.

'What's happening?' I asked. 'Who are you? Who else is in here?'

'Well, I'm Nell Ford, used to work at the hairdressers. My husband's Stewart, worked for Jack Culvenor. We were building that new brick place out on Sherlock Road, past the truck yard.'

'Are you a patient?'

'Gawd yeah. You've got to be pretty sick to get in here. But I'm out tomorrow or the next day. Back to the Showground.'

'So are all the patients in here prisoners?'

'In this building, yeah. They've shoved us in here like sardines and they've given themselves the good wards, over in the main section.'

'Do you have nurses? And doctors?'

She laughed, but bitterly. 'We get one nurse. Phyllis de Steiger. Do you know her? And the doctors are allowed to come over occasionally, when they're not treating the soldiers. If we get them for half an hour every second day we're lucky. We have to look after ourselves, basically. It's pretty rough.'

'How many people are in this room?'

'Seven. It's a bugger for infections. Anyway, what are you kids doing here? Did you say you were looking for somebody?'

Under the dusty bed, lying next to Lee, talking in whispers, I tensed myself, pressing my fingernails hard into my palms.

'Do you know Corrie Mackenzie?' I asked. 'And Kevin Holmes?'

'Oh, so you were with them, were you?' she said. 'Well, that all fits together. I know who you are now. You're the ones who blew up the bridge.'

I was sweating furiously. I didn't know we were so notorious. I didn't answer, and Nell laughed. 'Don't worry,' she said. 'I'm not a talker. Well, I suppose you want to know how your mates are.'

'Yes please,' I whispered.

'Kevin's all right now. He's back at the Show-ground. Poor little Corrie...'

She paused. I felt an awful, impossible weight inside my chest. My heart.

'Well, love...'

'What? What?'

'Look, she's pretty crook, love.'

All I could think was that she was alive.

'Where is she?'

'Oh, she's in here. Two doors down. But like I said, she's pretty crook.'

'How do you mean?'

'Well love, she's still out to it, you know what I mean? Unconscious. She's been that way since she got here. She's not too good.'

'Can we go and see her?'

'Course you can, love. But just wait a bit longer. The guards are due to come round soon. They only do one patrol a night, but there was a fire alarm before, so they might be late.'

'That was us,' Lee said. 'It was the only way we could distract them, so we could get in here.'

'Mmm. They say you kids have been pretty smart.'

'Tell me more about Corrie,' I begged. 'Tell me everything.'

Nell sighed. 'Oh dear. I wish I could think of some good news. But you know, they've been pretty rough with her. Young Kev drove her right into Casualty, and at first they let the doctor have a look at her, but when they found it was a bullet wound they turned nasty. They locked her in a room and wouldn't let anyone see her, till the doctors jacked up. But even then it was ages before she got any proper treatment, and a lot longer before they moved her over here for us to take care of her. The soldiers kept saying she was a "bad girl, bad girl". Maybe she was lucky, being unconscious. You know, better off. But the poor kid, she just lies there. They finally got a drip into her, but she doesn't seem to be getting any better. We do everything we can. She's the only one here in a room on her own, but someone always sits with her. It's Mrs Slater tonight. You know her.'

There was a long silence. For the first time I felt real hatred for the soldiers. It was such a dark evil force that it frightened me. It was as though black vomit was filling me – as though a demon inside was spewing black stuff into my guts. I was frightened, frightened at everything: the hatred I felt; the state Corrie was in; the risks Lee and I were running by being there.

'Do you know how our families are?' Lee asked.

Nell gave a little gurgle. 'I'll have to know who you are before I can answer that,' she said. 'Was I right, what I said before?'

So we told her. We didn't know if she was trustworthy or not, but our need to know was greater than our sense of caution.

Nell, like all hairdressers, knew everything about everyone. My parents were OK, although my father had had a rifle shoved into his guts the first day of the invasion, when he got too aggressive, and he'd been knocked down a couple of times since for the same reason. I'd always been afraid of that. Farmers are so used to being their own bosses. They don't like being told what to do by anyone, including their daughters. Dad would have been purple in the face when he realised that these guys from another country were going to lock him up and order him around for the next few years – or for the rest of his life.

Lee's family were all right too, though again they'd had a rough time at first. They'd put up a fight when the soldiers arrived and hauled them out of their restaurant. Maybe, too, they were given a harder time because they were Asian. Anyway, Lee's father got a broken arm and his mother got two black eyes, but the little kids were OK, just shocked.

Most of the others seemed well enough, except for Homer's brother, George, slicing his hand open when he was cutting vegetables for a meal, and Fi's little sister getting some bad asthma attacks. But life at the Showground sounded terrible. Nell said they were too crowded; the sewerage system couldn't cope; often there wasn't enough food to go around. There were a couple of showers in the horse pavilion for the grooms, but no one was allowed to use them, so they all stank and itched. Scratches and cuts got infected easily, and there were epidemics all the time. The current one was chickenpox; the last one had been mumps. People were depressed and bad-tempered and tired. There were fights all the time; some people not talking to other people; a few attempts at suicide; a dozen deaths. Most of these were old people, some who'd been kicked out of the Hospital, but one had been a baby, and one a girl of twenty, named Angela Bates, who'd been murdered. No one knew much about it: they'd found her body dumped outside the dunnies one morning. Everyone was sure it was the soldiers of course, but complaining to them was a waste of time. The murder remained unsolved.

There had been some rapes while people were being rounded up and brought in to the Showground, but none since. Nell said the soldiers there were well disciplined most of the time, but they'd bashed dozens of people who'd disobeyed orders. A guy called Spike Faraday, a young cockie from out near Champion Hill, had been shot in the kneecap for assaulting a soldier, and six people who'd tried to escape had been bashed, and dragged off to the Wirrawee lock-up. Another Spike, a guy called Spike Florance, a jackaroo, had been beaten up repeatedly because he just wouldn't back down, kept antagonising the guards.

It was all much worse than we'd thought. The little information we'd picked up from prisoners' work parties, and the comments on the radio about a 'clean' invasion, had lulled us into a false sense of optimism. Things seemed to be deteriorating. There was nothing clean about all this. I wanted to go and wash my hands.

There were two things Nell said from her mattress on the floor that really shocked me. One was when she told us that a lot of people were cooperating with the soldiers. I didn't know what to think when I heard that. I hadn't read a lot of war books or seen a lot of war movies, but I'd always had the impression that the goodies in them were all heroes. You were on one side or the other – either a goodie or a baddie – and you stayed that way from start to finish. Nell said that some people were sucking up to the soldiers, real brown-nosers, and what's more, some of them were actively helping, offering to do jobs for the guards, and going out of their way to support them. Others were spending the night with them.

We were both bewildered. 'Why?' Lee asked. 'Why are they doing that?'

Nell laughed her little bitter laugh, that I was getting used to. 'Listen love,' she whispered, 'I'm a hairdresser, and hairdressers are all amateur psychologists. We reckon we know everything there is to know about people. But I've seen stuff at that Showground that I'll never figure out, not if I live to be a million. Who knows what goes on in the brains of those bastards? Some of them do it because they're scared. Some do it for food or cigarettes or grog, or even for a shower and a bottle of shampoo. Some do it because they want to get power for themselves, I reckon. Some are such sheep they like being told what to do. They don't care who's giving the orders, as long as there's someone doing it. Personally I reckon they're mad. Things are going to get worse before they get better.'

There was another silence, while we digested all this. I didn't seem able to focus on anything except the

37

word 'sheep'. Most people are so rude about them, but you won't find many farmers talking that way. So I said, 'You're wrong about sheep, Nell. They don't like obeying orders. And they're not as stupid as people make out. They have a good set of survival instincts...'

'Oh shut up Ellie,' came Lee's tired voice.

I can't help it if I like sheep.

Nell started telling us the second thing that shocked us. She said lots of people – our people – were looking forward to what the soldiers called the 'colonisation'. What this meant was that when the soldiers were satisfied they had the country under control they would bring in millions of their own people. Each family would get some acres of land and they'd farm that, using us as slave labour, to do all the crap jobs: crutching sheep, digging spuds, cleaning houses.

'Why are they looking forward to that?' I whispered. I was getting thoroughly scared, deep down. It seemed that everything was becoming too bad, too awful, and there was no hope for any of us.

'Oh well,' Nell said. She was getting vague, and was tired too. 'They just... if you were in the Showground you'd understand. It's so awful in there, so crowded. We just want to get out. Fresh air, being able to walk around. That's why people volunteer for the work parties now. Seems like any change'd be a good change.'

It was while she was telling us this that the soldiers did their check. We heard them easily enough – they weren't making any special effort to be quiet. They opened the door to the room and flashed the lights on, then turned them off again, a second later. It was so long since I'd been in a room with electric lighting that I felt like I'd been bashed over the head. It was so powerful. Lee and I flattened ourselves, breathing in dust and the smell of old wood.

'They don't normally turn the lights on,' Nell whispered after they'd gone. 'Your fire alarm might have spooked them a bit.'

Still, I was sure they couldn't have worked out the source of the smoke, or there would have been a much more frenzied search. Homer had carried a sack to throw over the smoke bomb when they burst into the room above him. All they would have found was a room full of smoke, with no obvious cause. He'd been aiming for the X-Ray Department, because with its complicated electrical equipment they wouldn't have known what to blame.

We heard the tread of the soldiers' footsteps as they returned down the corridor to their post. At last the moment I'd prayed for had arrived. I wanted it so badly, but why did I feel so frightened? I suppose I didn't know what I'd see in B10: my best friend, my oldest mate, Corrie... or some kind of unrecognisable monster, a vegetable.

'You ought to be safe now,' Nell was whispering. 'Just be careful.'

I didn't really need that advice. I wasn't about to go cooeeing down the corridor, or playing Demolition Derby with the trolleys.

We slithered out from under our bed, like snakes from a blackberry bush.

'Good luck,' Nell said.

'We'll come and see you before we go.'

'Righto love.'

I opened the door gingerly, and peered out. The passageway was quite dark, and empty. It was cold, after the close warm human smell of B8. As lightly as possible I fled along the corridor, knowing Lee was with me. But when we got to Corrie's door I didn't have the courage to open it. Since the invasion I'd had to reach for courage many times. Surprisingly to myself, it had always been there, even if sometimes I'd had to dredge deeply, even if sometimes there hadn't been much left to draw on.

Now I just leaned weakly against the door, my head pressed into it. That was not a smart thing to do, not quite as bad as yelling cooee or going for rides in the wheelchairs, but not far off it. Lee put his arm around me and I turned and buried my head in his chest. I didn't cry, but I was grateful for his strong hold and his silent understanding. Deep inside Lee there seemed to be a place that I didn't think I had. Maybe it was the place his music came from. Whatever it was, I connected with it then for a few seconds and gained a little strength. It was like a blood transfusion.

'Would you go first?' I asked, lifting my head out of his nice warm chest.

He did, letting me go, twisting the handle of the door and opening it. He went in and held the door open for me. I slipped in there, into the darkness. A frightened voice gasped 'Who's there?' For a moment I thought it was Corrie and I too gasped. I thought it was a ghost, or a miracle, that Corrie had suddenly recovered consciousness and was talking to us. Then I remembered Mrs Slater.

'It's me, Mrs Slater. Ellie. And Lee's here too.'

'Ellie! Oh! Lee!' She jumped up, knocking something over.

We knew Mrs Slater pretty well. She was one of

those people who packed about thirty-two hours into every twenty-four. Her husband had died in a tractor accident years ago, and since then she'd run the farm, raised the kids, written two gardening books, learnt calligraphy and quilting, and done half an Arts degree through the Open University. She even found time to do canteen duty at school: her last kid, Jason, was in Year 10.

She'd said to me once, 'There are two kinds of people in the world, Ellie. The ones who watch TV and the ones who get things done.'

Now she gave me the biggest hug of my career, and finally I cried. It had been a long time since the last tear. But she was the first adult I'd seen who I knew, the first one to hug me, the first link with my old, loved, happy world. The first link with my parents, because she was such a good friend of Mum's.

'Oh Ellie,' she said. 'You poor kid. And you smell terrible.'

'Oh Mrs Slater!' She made me laugh, and I thumped her in the chest in protest. Then she hugged Lee.

I guess we'd been living together so long we didn't notice how bad we smelt. We took regular baths in the creek, but with the water getting so cold we hadn't been doing it a lot lately.

'Don't worry,' she said. 'They all smell worse at the Showground. A lot worse. But we patients get a shower every second day, so we forget.'

But I wasn't listening any more. I'd turned to the bed, where Corrie lay so silently. The only light in the room came from the car park, through the windows. You could see where condensation had misted the glass. The room itself was very dim, like a church in the late afternoon before the lights come on. The things that stood out were the things that were very dark and the things that were very light. A cupboard door was like a dark scar on the wall. The bedside locker was a white shape crouching watchfully beside Corrie's bed. It seemed quite bright. The sheet that covered Corrie glowed with a quiet luminosity. Her head on the pillow was a little black patch, an unmoving round stone. I could not make out her features. I tried to see her eyes, her nose, her mouth. Not seeing them I was suddenly frightened of the black patch, as though it was not human, was not Corrie at all. I peered and peered, fighting to keep the fear in my stomach, to stop it coming up my throat and into my mouth. Was that her mouth, or just a shadow? Were those her eyes, or just black marks, tricks of the light? I wasn't aware of Lee or Mrs Slater. Not only were they not in the room; they had ceased to exist. There was just me and the shape in the bed. I slowly took three short steps towards it. And suddenly, with the different angle and the light falling differently across the bed, I found Corrie again. There she was; her soft skin, her plump face, her closed eyes. My own mouth was slightly open, in wonder, because she looked so different to the Corrie of my past friendship, and the Corrie of my fearful imaginings. She did not look gaunt and battered and bruised, but neither did she look happy and lively and talkative. She looked like a wax doll, a fully formed impression of Corrie. I could see her lips move slightly with each breath in and breath out but there was no other movement. She was alive, yet somehow not with us any more.

I was not scared of her, but I was scared to touch

her. I had meant to ask Mrs Slater if I could touch, if it was safe, but now that thought had fled my mind. So after a while I leant forward with a shivering finger and ran the tip of it down the side of her right cheek. This was not the Corrie who I hugged and used as a pillow and beat up on, the Corrie who'd sat on my lap so often on the crowded school bus. That Corrie had slipped quietly away, leaving behind this peacefully breathing, pale replacement. I leant further forward and kissed her on the forehead, then lay my head on the pillow beside her. I didn't say anything. I didn't really think anything either. Her skin was cool, but I didn't notice that at the time, just thought about it afterwards. Through her cheek, next to mine, I could feel her breathing. I stayed like that for some time, a long time.

Finally I got up again and whispered in her ear, 'Take care out there Corrie. Look after yourself,' and I slipped out into the corridor and waited for Lee. I didn't even say goodbye to Mrs Slater, which was a bit rude.

Lee was quite a while, so I hid behind a laundry basket, but eventually he came out. I popped up and went ahead of him back to B8 to say goodbye to Nell.

'Are you OK, love?' she asked. 'Did it upset you?' But I didn't answer that. Instead I asked her a question that had been bugging me.

'You know how you said before that Kevin was all right "now"?' I asked.

'Oh, did I?'

'Yes, you did. What did you mean "now"?'

She tried to think of a reassuring lie, but she couldn't. After a minute of silence she gave in and told me.

43

'They beat him up pretty bad Ellie.'

We snuck along the corridor, towards the exit. We knew from Nell where the soldiers would be – at the nurses' station near the exit door. Hiding in the little kitchen about twenty metres away, I grabbed Lee's head and pulled it down so I could whisper in his ear.

'I want to find a knife.'

'Why?'

'So I can kill the soldiers.'

I felt his body give a little jerk, like he'd touched the terminals of a battery. But he didn't say anything for a minute, just stood up straight, while I continued to crouch beside him like the animal I'd become. Then he bent down again and put his mouth to my ear.

'You can't do that Ellie.'

'Why not?'

'There'd be reprisals against the patients.'

We didn't speak again, just waited. We were waiting for a break in the soldiers' routine, a chance to slip past their defences. We could hear them talking occasionally, in their guttural language. There was a kind of wailing music in their voices that was almost attractive. Occasionally, too, we could hear a girl's voice, low and husky, usually laughing, sometimes making a comment that sounded like English, but pitched too low for us to make out the words. After what Nell had said I had the worst suspicions of what the girl was doing, and I raged against her, there in the darkness.

One soldier walked past our little hidey-hole to go to the toilet, but we couldn't tell where the other one was, so we dared not move. That was at 3.45 am. He returned a few minutes later, and there was no other

44

movement till 4.20, when the other one made the same trip to the toilet. Seconds later, a tall girl maybe about nineteen appeared at our kitchen door and whispered into the darkness, facing towards us, 'Quick, the other one's asleep. But don't make any noise.' We were startled, wondering for a moment if she could possibly be talking to us. Then we realised that she must be. We rose and slipped around the food trolleys towards the door. The girl had already gone. Who was she? How did she know we were there? I still don't know the answers to those questions, but whoever she was, and whatever else she might have been doing, I know we owe her something special.

Chapter Four

Homer was quite impressed to hear that we were so well-known, so notorious. 'Let's show them we're still in business,' he said, smiling his slowest, most dangerous smile.

I shivered slightly. Despite my murderous impulse in the Hospital I still couldn't get used to exposing myself to danger, to standing up and waving at death the way Homer seemed to enjoy. Did he enjoy it? I remembered how he'd said courage was a state of mind; you had to think brave, so I tried to do that. It actually worked, a bit. I found myself joining in the conversation like I was talking about a game of Netball or a Chem test. We talked about targets, tactics, risks, ideas. It took us a day and a half, but it was quite strange. In all that time we didn't have a single argument. No one shouted or even raised their voices. But there weren't many jokes either. It was something to do with the description Lee and I had given them of Corrie, and the news we'd had of Kevin; something to do with the news of the way people held at the Showground were starting to crumble; and especially to do with a new feeling in us: that as some of the few people free we should have done more already. We had a responsibility to do more now.

So we'd become deadly serious. And I mean deadly.

We decided that Wirrawee should not be our main target. Much as we loved Wirrawee, much as it was the centre of our lives, we had to recognise that the fate of the country wasn't going to depend on our little town. To hit the enemy hard we had to find a more important part of their operations, and that meant going back to the highway from Cobbler's Bay. The last time we'd been there it had been lousy with convoys; Cobbler's Bay was obviously a major landing place for them, and trucks were flowing from there to the major battlefields. Blowing up the bridge must have complicated their lives, as it would have caused them a big detour. But it wasn't going to lose them the war.

So we took another long walk out into the countryside. We left Wirrawee at 2.30 am, when we were at our coldest and most tired, and trudged along, going through the routines that we now followed for self-protection: travelling in pairs, checking each intersection, keeping silent through the streets of the town. We went via the bridge, which none of us had seen since the big night of the petrol party. I walked with Fi this time, as I needed a break from Lee, and although I was still very depressed after seeing how ill Corrie was, I did cheer up a bit when I got to the bridge and saw the damage we'd done. Basically it had burnt to the ground. Or to the river, to be more accurate. It had been an old wooden thing, and after the explosion it must have burnt so fiercely that no one was able to do much about it. There were just a few blackened pillars sticking out of the water and the mud, and no other evidence that there'd been a bridge there. On the bank though, on the town side, were long rows of concrete slabs. It looked like Wirra-wee was going to get the new bridge people had wanted for so long, and it looked like being more solid than the one it replaced.

Fi and I stood there a while, giving each other big grins, mainly of disbelief, but with a bit of pride. We felt a bit shocked, I think, to see what we'd done – at least I did. I can't speak for Fi. So many times we'd driven over that bridge. I'd never thought that one day I'd destroy it. It seemed strange that we'd go down in local history as the people who'd blown it up. I wanted to be remembered as someone who built things, not someone who wrecked them. But we'd done it in a good cause. So many things had changed as a result of this war, and one of the smallest changes was that teenagers could now wander round the countryside blowing up anything they wanted, and being praised for doing it. When the Careers teacher at school, Mrs Goh, had given us all those forms to fill out, I sure hadn't put 'terrorist' or 'guerilla' down.

We crossed the river about a kilometre down-stream, where a narrow timber structure carried a large pipe across. Probably for sewerage or some-thing; I don't know, but I felt nervous and exposed crossing it. We went one at a time, but we still would have been completely helpless if soldiers had appeared and started firing.

When we got out to the highway, we found a few changes. There was traffic, even at that hour of the morning. In ninety minutes we saw two small con-voys going from Cobbler's Bay and one going to it.

But they were leaving the highway at Jigamory and going down Buttercup Lane, past the Jacobs' place. That was one change, but it was one we'd expected. We'd figured that was the most likely route for a detour, though it took them through some rough country. There was a bridge about eight kilometres down the road that could take heavy traffic. 'I'll bet they've got it heavily guarded,' Robyn said, with a little smile.

The other important change was that the patrols were much smaller. We saw two, both on foot, one with three soldiers, one with four. We couldn't figure out any reason for this. Maybe they were confident that they now had this part of the country under control, although it hadn't been that long since we'd blown up the Heron Bridge. Maybe they needed soldiers so desperately in other areas that they'd been forced to cut numbers around Wirrawee. And although it sounds like small patrols would be better for us, it actually made things more difficult. The bigger patrols had been easy to spot, because they made so much noise. These two patrols both came close to catching us, because they moved so stealthily. Maybe that was why they'd cut down their numbers.

Before we knew it, dawn was starting to nibble away at the edges of the sky, and we'd almost left it too late to get back to our hideout in Wirrawee. We had to go like stink to make it before peak hour. Peak hour in Wirrawee was never going to cause major traffic jams, invasion or no invasion, but good boys and girls were home in bed by daybreak, and we were good boys and girls. The last half-hour, going through the streets in the first grey daylight, did scare me. We heard a truck in Maldon Street and we saw two cars speed through an intersection. But we got back to the house and we had the information we needed.

After we'd slept we continued our planning, but this time we planned details: times and places and equipment.

Part of our planning was to give ourselves a decent night's sleep before we made our attempt. We were rather pleased with ourselves for being so well-prepared. We didn't know of course that you can't prepare for luck and coincidence. Watching the street from an upstairs bedroom, as I did my afternoon sentry duty, seeing work parties from the Showground being driven past in old trucks and buses, wondering if my parents were among them, I felt strangely peaceful and confident. It was the sense of rightness that we were doing things again, instead of hanging sourly about in Hell. Action is its own kind of thinking. We had to fight now: these people were a cancer who had crept into our stomachs and infected us all. We had to be surgeons, bold and clever, not thinkers and talkers.

Nevertheless the next day crept so slowly. It was like watching an eggtimer filled with clay. Late in the morning I ordered myself not to look at the clock for at least half an hour, but ten minutes later my eyes were creeping round to it again.

When my sentry duty ended I went looking for company, for distractions, and found Chris in the upstairs sitting room, gazing at the grey television screen again.

'Good?' I asked, dumping myself on the sofa beside him.

'Mmm. Not bad. There's not much on, but.'

'So, what are you watching?'

'Um, MTV.'

'New band?'

'Yeah, it's a whole new style of music. Blank rock. It's very subtle.'

'Sure looks it. It's strange, isn't it? I've hardly thought about TV. I never used to watch it much anyway, so I s'pose that's why.'

'I watched it heaps. TV addict. But I don't miss it that much.' He turned to me suddenly, laughing, to say something. But a moment later, before his words began, his breath reached me, and I recognised the sweet sickly smell of alcohol. I was so shocked I didn't even hear what he was saying, something about setting up a radio link so he could hear the TV in his bedroom. It was only 11.30 in the morning and he'd been drinking already! I struggled to control my face. Now that I'd smelt his breath, I noticed other little signs too: he was having trouble saying long words, his eyes weren't quite focusing, and his smile was a bit lopsided, as though he couldn't quite make it fit his mouth. I muttered something about having to go to the bathroom, and walked out, my face burning. I couldn't get a grip on this at all. In fourteen hours we were going to attack a whole convoy, and we'd be relying on a drunk to help us.

For want of a better place I did go to the bathroom, closed the door, and sat on the dunny seat. I leaned forward and hugged myself. I was starting to get really scared for us all. Corrie in hospital, Kevin a prisoner, and now Chris drinking on the sly. We were in big trouble. We were cracking up. One or two or six of us could get shot tonight. By tomorrow, who would be left? Five bodies and Chris with a hangover? They

51

said God looked after babies and drunks. I wished I was a baby again. I was hugging my stomach now, because that's where things seemed to hurt most. I wondered what would happen if I got appendicitis. Would Homer cut me open with a Swiss Army knife? I started biting the side of my left hand, still holding my stomach with the right. I sat there for a long time. Before, I'd been overconscious of time; now I had no awareness of it at all. In the end I got so cold I thought I'd frozen there; that I wouldn't be able to move again, that if I straightened or stood up my bones would crack and break.

After a long while someone knocked on the door, then Robyn called, 'Ellie, are you in there? Are you OK?' I didn't answer but she opened the door anyway and came in.

'Ellie! What's wrong?'

'I think I've got appendicitis,' I mumbled.

She laughed, but only a little bit, and quietly, which I was grateful for. 'Oh Ellie, you've got the panics. Boy, do I know the feeling. You start imagining every disaster possible, and before you know it you've convinced yourself that every one of them is totally and absolutely inevitable. In fact, you think they're already happening.'

She sat on the edge of the bath. I wanted to tell her about Chris but didn't know how. Instead I asked her, 'Robyn, do you think we're falling apart?'

She didn't give a flip answer, like a lot of people would. That wasn't Robyn's style. She thought for a while, and then said, 'No, I don't think so. We're doing OK. It's not a normal situation, is it? So there's not much to compare us with. But I think we're doing OK.'

'It's all so hard. I don't know how we'll survive.

Maybe we'll all go mad. Maybe we're mad now, and don't know it.'

'You know what it reminds me of?'

'What?'

'Shadrach, Meshach and Abednego.'

'What the hell are they?'

'They're from my favourite story. They're my heroes, I guess.'

'They sound like a Russian rock band.'

She laughed. 'Nuh uh. Not quite.'

'So tell me the story.' I guessed it'd be from the Bible. When it came to religion Robyn was rock solid, not that I minded that. Anyway I've always liked stories. The three names sounded vaguely familiar to me, but I couldn't think from where.

'Well Shadrach, Meshach and Abednego lived in Babylon, way back, way way back. They wouldn't worship a golden idol and so the King had them thrown into the furnace. The furnace was so hot that even the guys who chucked them in got burned to death. No one could get close; but from where he was watching, the King got glimpses of the three men, through the flames and smoke. And the funny thing was that it looked like there were four people, not three. And even stranger was that no matter how hard the flames burned, the men walked around as though they were untouched by the fire. So after a while the King ordered the furnace door to be opened. And out came the three men, Shadrach, Meshach and Abednego. And the King realised that it had been an angel in there with them. And he also realised that the god who'd looked after them in his furnace had to be stronger than any golden idol, so he was converted.'

'Mmm, that's a good story,' I said.

I liked the way Robyn didn't preach at me, and never had. After a while I said, 'So what's the connection with us?'

'Well, we're in the furnace.'

'With an angel?'

'Sometimes I feel that there's someone with us, that we're supported.'

'But not all the time?'

'I guess all the time. I just can't explain how certain things happen, like Corrie being shot. It seems sometimes that nothing can stop the man with the scythe, not even God. Death comes walking across the countryside swinging that scythe, and he might get you or he might not. Or to put it another way, sometimes God saves you and sometimes he doesn't. I don't know why he makes those choices; I just have to trust him and have faith that he's doing it for his own good reasons.'

'Hmm.'

There was more knocking on the door: Homer.

'Come in,' we both called, and he did.

'Honestly,' he said. 'Girls in bathrooms. Someone could write a TV series about girls in bathrooms.'

He wanted to go through his checklist for the night. There were a few things we needed, that we had to pick up from farmhouses, things more likely to be found in farmhouses. We went down to the dining room, spread his sheet of paper out on the table, and went to work. Not for the first time I was amazed at the knowledge of odd things Homer had picked up from all over the place. He'd had some help from Chris, who also knew a lot of weird facts, and I had the suspicion that he'd been listening in Chem more than

I'd realised. I'd always known he was a smart guy, but I'd never thought of him as having much interest in Science.

The list wasn't that long – there weren't many things we needed – but it was obvious we'd have to leave town early, as soon as it was dark. That was increasing our risks a little, but it was the only way we could do everything we wanted.

So at about nine o'clock we went, moving with maximum caution. We had a lot of walking ahead of us. I knew we'd be tired by morning. I was just tired of walking anyway. I longed for those motorbikes that we'd used to escape from the bridge, and that were still hidden on our property. But safety first. We hardly took a step without looking around.

We got most of what we wanted at the Fleets' place, which we'd used before as a hideout. The hardest thing to find was nails that were big enough, long enough, strong enough. After a bit of scrounging and a bit of carpentry and a bit of improvisation, we left there at one-thirty, running late, but not too bad. And an hour and a half after that we were where we wanted to be: approaching a steep cutting on Buttercup Lane. It was thick bush up there. We'd already dived into it once when we heard a convoy coming; and just before we reached the cutting, Fi, who was leading, gave the signal to hide again. It had to be a patrol, so I crouched, and scuttled into the scrub as fast as I could. Behind me a dark shadow that was Lee dived off the embankment and landed about two metres away. I couldn't see the others. Chris and Homer were behind me, and Robyn ahead somewhere, with Fi. Almost as soon as I was in hiding I heard the scrunch of the boots: three soldiers in single file walking quite casually along the road above my head. I crouched even lower and hoped that the others were well hidden. The soldiers' footsteps seemed to be slowing, and then they stopped completely. I risked a glance and saw just the back of one of them moving slowly away from me. It was a woman, I thought, and an instant later she was out of my sight.

I didn't know what to do. I couldn't imagine why they'd stopped, unless they'd seen one of us, but there were none of the urgent sounds I'd expect if they had. Desperate thoughts rushed through my head. What should I do? What could I possibly do? I lifted myself and crept forward a metre, frightened that if I went any further I might crawl straight into a trap. Then suddenly I flattened myself: a shotgun fired to my right, so close that my ears rang with the noise. I lay there unable to breathe. I could hear several cries, then a scream, hoarse and horrible. The shotgun fired again, a little more muffled this time. I could smell its spicy burnt smell now. I hoped that it was a double-barrelled one and that no one else had a weapon, and with only that thought in my head I launched myself up the bank and onto the road.

The first thing I noticed was the sound of footsteps; someone running in panic down the road. I couldn't see much, just a dark shape, but it was one of the soldiers, not one of us. Then there was a crashing sound from the bushes. I spun round, wondering if this was my death, the last movement I would ever make, the last sight I would see. But it was Homer, stumbling towards me, and Chris just behind him, a little to his left, making awful retching noises. I realised as Homer reached me that he had blood all down the front of his shirt, thick and sticky. The others were now emerging from their hiding places and rushing at us. I ripped Homer's shirt open and felt around his chest and shoulders but couldn't find any wound.

'No, no,' he said, pushing me away. 'I'm not hurt.'

'What happened?' I shouted at him. I was completely bewildered. 'Did you grab their guns?'

He shook his head and waved his arms around. He didn't seem able to answer. But Chris, who was trembling but becoming suddenly and amazingly calm, answered for him. 'Homer had a shotgun in his pack,' he said. 'Sawn-off.'

Fi gasped. We all looked at Homer in shock. We'd talked about our meagre little stock of weapons a few times and agreed that with such limited firepower we were better off with nothing. We knew if we were caught with weapons on us we were gone, one hundred per cent certain.

A willy-willy of feelings stormed up inside me – anger, confusion, disbelief. But I had to postpone them, and I did. I was still holding Homer by the tail of his shirt but now I let him go and shouted at Chris, 'What happened? What happened?'

'It was just the worst worst bad luck. There were three of them, two men and a woman. The men decided to take a leak, right where we were. They dropped their rifles and came down into the scrub. They were about three steps from us and still coming, unbuttoning their daks. They would have walked right over the top of us. Homer had his pack beside him and his hand inside it, holding the shotgun I guess. He just suddenly pulled it out and lifted it up and fired.' Chris was talking fast, reconstructing it in his mind as he went, trying to recall it all, then describing it to us as he ran the movie in his head.

'The guy fell backwards. The other guy gave a shout then dived at Homer. Homer seemed to swing the gun around. He was still lying down. The guy landed half on top of him, then there was another shot and all this blood was coming out and Homer got out from under him and came up here. The woman ran off down the road, but we couldn't do anything about her. It's a double-barrel gun but I don't know if he's got any more shells, and there wouldn't have been time to reload anyway. She was running flat out.'

'Let's get off the road,' Robyn said. 'In fact, let's get out of here.' Even as she spoke I caught a glimpse of lights in the distance: the dimmed headlights of a convoy beginning the long climb up the road towards the cutting. The thoughts were queueing up in my mind so fast that they were crashing into the back of each other. The convoy was coming from the opposite direction to the way the soldier had fled. How long would it take her to get help? Would she be able to communicate with the convoy? I grabbed Chris.

'Check the road. Where did they drop their guns?'

'Just back here.'

'Grab them. And anything else. Everyone else up to the cutting. Fi, you take Homer. Put the nails out and be ready.'

I ran back with Chris. We picked up two guns, one an old .303; the other a more modern automatic weapon that I didn't recognise. With them was a small pack. I tore it open and pulled out what I'd hoped to find: a small two-way radio. Chances were they wouldn't have more than one radio in each patrol.

'Where's your stuff? Yours and Homer's?'

'Still in there.' Chris pointed to the bush behind us. I grabbed my torch and looked at Chris.

'What if they're still alive?' he asked.

I paused, then shrugged, and led the way into the scrub. We only had to go a few metres of course. In the torchlight I could see blood on the grass, then some scratched up earth. That led me to a body: a soldier on his back, eyes open, but dead. His chest looked like two giant hands had taken it and ripped it open. I swung the torch around and saw the two packs, and the bloodied sawn-off shotgun near them. Chris picked up the packs as I got the shotgun, trying not to shudder as my hands touched the sticky butt. I straightened up and at that moment heard the worst sound in the world, a sob and a squeal. I swung the torch around. I could see his boots, about ten metres away, sticking out from under a little acacia. I walked over there, as Chris backed away. I despised him for that, but wished I could have done the same. I parted the branches of the bush and shone the torch down on the man. It was amazing that he'd been able to crawl even those few yards. He was lying twisted to one side, with his right hand stretched out to the trunk of the wattle, holding it lightly. His other hand was holding his stomach. He was whimpering occasionally but I don't think he was conscious. There was blood all around him, some of it smeared across the ground but fresh red blood pumping out from under his stomach. It looked thick and treacly. His hand was trying to hold bits of his stomach in but I could see all kinds of things, disgusting things, entrails and stuff. I walked over to Chris. I knew how my face must have looked to him: cold and hard, no expression. 'Which is

59

Homer's pack?' I asked him. He gave it to me and I searched inside. There were at least a dozen shells rolling around loose. I only took one, loaded the shotgun, and went straight back to the soldier and held it to his temple; then, Jesus help me, without thinking about it, deliberately not letting myself think, I pulled the trigger.

After that everything was a wild rush. I figured we had about two minutes. My ears were ringing with the noise of the shotgun. I ignored that and ignored what I'd just done. We ran like hell up the road to the cutting. The others had put out the nails. I almost trod on one. They were fifteen centimetres long, each hammered through a piece of wood which served as a base and kept them upright. Fi was waiting for us. She was so white I thought she'd gone albino.

'What was the shot?' she asked, trembling all over.

'Nothing Fi. Be brave.' I touched her arm and ran up to the other three. 'Are we ready?'

'Yes, but… what about the one who escaped? Won't she…?'

'I don't think so. I found a two-way. I can't believe they'd have more than one radio.'

'Hope you're right,' said Robyn.

'She's right,' said Lee, grimly.

In one of those strange crazy flashes of intuition I realised how much Lee wanted us to make this attack; if tanks had been rolling straight at us I don't think he would have moved. He was very into honour, and revenge.

Homer looked calmer but he hadn't spoken. He had a bottle in each hand.

I could hear the trucks now; the leading ones were dropping a gear, so were probably close to the cutting.

I grabbed my bottles, and fished out the cigarette lighter. The dull headlights of the first truck were starting to show through the trees. The convoys always had their headlights covered by some stuff that kept the light down to a soft glow. I guess they were scared of air attacks, but we didn't see too many of our planes these days, so I'd say these drivers felt pretty safe.

We were hoping to change that.

Now the straining engines relaxed; there were several quick gear changes and the trucks started to roll, gathering speed through the cutting. We had placed ourselves on a bank so that as they came out of the cutting we'd be above them, on a curve. We reckoned they would be travelling fast, easing across the road towards us as they entered the bend. And we were right. They sure did accelerate. They seemed to be there in an instant. The roar of the engines was suddenly coming straight at us, unobstructed by any more trees or banks. I had a good view of the first three, all of them trucks, dark green in colour, tray-tops, with gates and tarps. Then everything went wild. The first truck seemed to blow both its front tyres at the same moment. It was like a bomb going off. There was an almighty explosion. I couldn't believe how loud it was, nor how much smoke. Bits of rubber, strips of rubber, went shredding across the road. The truck slid straight across the road at high speed, back tyres screaming, and slammed against a tree. The second truck must have missed all the nails, because it kept its tyres intact; but in trying to miss the other vehicle it wobbled wildly across the road as the driver fought to keep control. It finally straightened up again fifty metres past us and accelerated away. I was disgusted. I couldn't believe that the driver would desert his mates like that. But I was more interested in the next few in the convoy. The third one blew out a front tyre with another huge bang, and so much more white smoke poured out that it became hard to see anything. But I saw enough to satisfy me, as this truck followed the same route as the first. It slewed wildly across the road and slammed heavily and hard into the back of the other one. The fourth one blew a rear tyre and did a 360, ending up fifty metres away and in the middle of the road. The fifth one stopped so hard that it sat there shuddering for a moment before the one behind it slammed into its rear. I heard a couple more crashes back in the cutting, but it was now impossible to tell what was happening. There was so much smoke, and the noise was like the end of the world.

I saw a flaming torch fly through the air towards the fifth truck, and realised Lee had gone into action. I needed that to spur me back into life. I lit my first cocktail, waited a second, and threw it in the same direction as Lee's, then followed fast with my second one. The others had joined in. For a minute the air was full of hot shooting stars. I could see plenty of flame through the smoke, so something was burning, but there were no explosions. A gun opened up; an automatic weapon of some kind, firing wildly at first, through the trees above us, but gradually lowering its aim until it was just above our heads.

We all got out fast, crouching low and snaking through the tearing, wild, brambly scrub. Homer was just ahead of me; I realised he was still carrying his Molotov cocktails. He hadn't thrown them. I called out 'Drop the bottles Homer', which he did, and for a moment I thought I'd caused a disaster, because at the exact moment the bottles hit the ground there was an explosion so vast that the ground heaved under my feet. It took me a second to realise that the explosion was behind us, and hadn't come from Homer's bottles at all. Then a shock wave hit me, almost knocking me over, followed by a blast of heat, a dry airless heat. It felt like someone had opened the door of a steel furnace. I steadied myself, got my balance again, and started to run. The others – the ones I could see – were doing the same. I heard trees screeching as they split and fell behind me. We sure as hell weren't going to win any conservation awards. I ran on. I wasn't too frightened though. I knew that they could never and would never follow us through the bush. This was our natural environment. I felt as much at home here as the possums and wombats and galahs. Let no stranger intrude here, no invader trespass. This was ours, and this we would defend.

Chapter Five

I was feeling pretty unusual, walking back across the paddocks. I imagined a huge shadow of me was moving across the sky, attached to me, and keeping pace with my little body on the earth. It scared me, really scared me, but I couldn't escape it. It loomed over me, a silent dark creature growing out of my feet. I knew that if I reached out to feel it I would feel nothing. That's the way shadows are. But all the same, the air around me seemed colder and darker, as the shadow clung to me. I wondered if this was the way my life would always be from now on, and if for every person I killed the shadow would grow larger, darker, more monstrous.

I looked across at the others. I tried to focus my gaze on them, and gradually, by doing that, my shadow faded away. Then, as though I'd had a rush of blood to the eyes, I suddenly started seeing them very strongly. I became very aware of everyone, of the way they all looked. Maybe it was the light or something. Suddenly they were on a huge movie screen, with the clouds and the darkening sky behind. It wasn't like I was seeing them for the first time; it was like I was seeing them as others would have. I was seeing them the way strangers, outsiders would.

We were all wearing clothing that camouflaged well. We did that as a matter of course, these days. I sometimes had a terrible longing to wear bright and colourful clothes again, but there was no chance of that yet. And this day I wanted only my khaki and grey; I wanted it to cling to my body, to be my mourning suit.

We were spread out across two paddocks in quite open country. It was dangerous but probably not too bad. The only real risk was from the air, but we thought we'd hear planes or helicopters in enough time to take cover. There were plenty of trees around.

It had been a long walk. God I was tired. We all were. Chris had his head down and was trailing a bit. With my new vision I saw how small and lightly built he was: a fair-haired serious boy who looked a bit younger than the rest of us. Across from him, and fifty metres in front, was Fi, who even now in her exhaustion walked gracefully, as though her feet needed only to brush the ground on each step to keep propelling her forward. She was looking around as she walked, like a wild swan searching for water. Not for the first time I wished I had a quarter of her style. When you looked at her you forgot that her clothes were as grubby as yours, her body as smelly and dirty. She had class without being conscious that she had it; that was her secret, and because I knew that, I would never have it.

Well, that was one reason I would never have it.

A hundred metres to my left was Homer, almost out of sight among a line of thin poplars that had been planted as a windbreak. He was big and burly, looking more like a bear than ever as he walked with his shoulders hunched up, his face closed against the cold wind. It was hard to tell what he was going through. He'd been in trouble so many times in his life that he should have been used to it. But this was just a bit different. I still didn't know whether to be angry at him or not. He'd broken one of our agreements, but my anger at that was overlaid with my pity and horror at what he'd done, and my confusion because he'd probably been right and we'd been wrong. There'd been no time to check how he was feeling, to see if he was OK. That would have to wait till we were back in the peace and safety of Hell. Meanwhile, thinking about how he might be feeling helped me avoid thinking about how I was feeling.

On the other flank was Robyn. Looking at her I thought of those old-time heroes. Those old kings for instance, who'd all had titles to go with their names: Edward the Confessor, Ethelred the Unready, William the Conqueror. Robyn was Robyn the Dauntless. When things were going quietly and normally she kept a low profile. But when the going got tough, Robyn grabbed the axe, swung it round her head, and charged. In the most frightening times, the most horrifying moments, she was at her best. Nothing seemed to deter her. Maybe she felt nothing could touch her. I don't know. Even now she was walking along quite casually, head up. I had the impression that she was singing something even, by the way she was tapping her left hand on her thigh.

The other one who was pretty up was Lee. The night we wrecked the bridge he was happy, but he hadn't been able to do much because of his wounded leg. This time we'd done a lot of damage – we knew that – and Lee had been in the thick of it. Lee always moved like a thoroughbred racehorse when we were out in the open or walking a big distance, and now he moved along eagerly, head pointing forward, long legs covering k after k. Occasionally he looked across and smiled at me, or winked. I didn't know whether to be pleased that he was feeling so proud, or worried that he was enjoying killing people and wrecking things. At least it made life less complicated for him.

As for me, my mind was so crowded that thoughts were being squeezed out of my ears. I wouldn't have been surprised to find them dripping from my nostrils. There was just too much to cope with. Instead I shoved it all away and started going through French irregular verbs. Je vis, tu vis, il vit, nous vivons, vous vivez, ils vivent. Je meurs, tu meurs, il meurt, nous mourons, vous mourez, ils meurent. It seemed safer doing that than thinking about our ambush, and it seemed to keep my huge dark shadow from haunting me for a little bit longer.

We got back to my place in the last moments of daylight. I didn't go in the house this time. Already it was starting to look unfamiliar, as though it were just an old building we'd lived in once, a long time ago. You could tell it was unoccupied. The lawn had grown wildly, all straggly and confused. One of the bow windows in the dining room had cracked right across, I don't know how. Maybe a bird had flown into it. Half the grape vine had fallen off the trellis and was now dragging across the path and garden. That was my fault. Dad had told me a dozen times to tie it on better.

The faithful Land Rover was waiting patiently in the bushes, hidden from prying eyes. I drove it to the shed and filled it with petrol. We were lucky we had our petrol in an overhead tank, so I could gravity-feed it to the car. Eventually though, we'd run out of petrol. I didn't know what we'd do then. I sighed, twisted the hose to cut off the flow, and climbed back up onto the tank to shut down the valve. Running out of fuel was only one of so many problems.

Our work for the evening was just beginning. We drove out to a property right up in the hills. It was a small place that I'd forgotten about, owned by people called King, whom I'd only met once, at the Post Office. He was a part-time social worker at the Hospital and she taught music at the Primary School two days a week. But their real interest was in becoming self-sufficient. They'd built this little mud-brick place on some land they'd bought from Mr Rowntree – poor land too, and they'd paid a premium price. Dad thought they'd been ripped off. Anyway, they were out there at the end of a dirt road with no electricity and no phone, running a mixture of cattle and pigs and chooks and geese and coloured sheep, with a couple of very grubby, very shy kids.

The scene there was the usual depressing sight. Decaying buildings and fences, too many carcasses, a paddock full of hungry sheep who'd eaten all the feed in it and were very thin and wonky. At least we saved them by opening their gates. I hoped the work parties were allowed to feed and move stock: a lot of animals would need hand-feeding to get them through winter, and some places should have started already, if they wanted the stock kept in prime condition.

I'd half thought the Kings might have still been there, hiding, but there was no sign of them. I think Mrs King had some of her violin students performing at the Show, so they'd probably gone into town that day and been caught. But in the house, and in the shiny new galvanised-iron shed behind it, we struck a jackpot. Bags of spuds and flour, jars of preserves, a carton of canned peaches that they'd got cheap because the cans were dented. Chook food, tea and coffee, and a dozen bottles of homebrew, which Chris eagerly carried to the car. Rice, sugar, rolled oats, cooking oil, home-made jam, chutney. Tragically, no chocolate.

When we'd finished, we grabbed all the bags we could find and headed off to the fruit trees. The trees were young but, despite the possums and parrots, were bearing well. I'll never forget the first crunchy juicy bite of the first crisp hard Jonathan I picked. I've never seen anything so white and pure, never tasted anything so fruity. We'd eaten the apples at Corrie's a few days earlier, but these seemed different. It wasn't really that the apples were different of course; it must be that I was different. I was looking for absolution and in some strange way the fruit gave it to me. I know that once you lose your innocence you never can get it back, but the immaculate whiteness of the apple made me feel that not everything in the world was rotten and corrupt; that some things could still be pure. The sweet flavour filled my mouth, a few drops running down my chin.

We stripped the trees. Johnnies, Grannies, Fujis, pears and quinces. I ate five apples and got a bit poohy again, but I felt a little better, a little more alive, after picking that beautiful fruit, that cool sharp evening.

Our last pick-up was an impulse. We were back in the Landie, bumping slowly down the road, all very quiet. I had the parking lights on, because we were under a canopy of trees, so it seemed safe. Driving at night without lights is nightmarishly frightening. Of all the things we'd done since the invasion, that was almost the scariest. It was like driving in nothing, in a dark limbo. It was weird, and no matter how much I did it I never seemed to get used to it.

Anyway, in the little light we had, I saw a couple of pairs of eyes peeping curiously towards us. Most of the stock we passed these days was already getting quite wild and running away, but these little critters didn't. Bad luck for them that they didn't. They were two lambs, about six months old, black wool, and probably twins. I'd guess their mother had died, but not till they were old enough to wean themselves. They were in good nick.

'Roast lamb!' I said, and braked. It was just an impulse, but then I thought, Why not? I stopped the car completely, and looked around at the others. 'Do we want roast lamb?' I asked. They seemed too tired to think, let alone answer, but Homer reacted. He showed more enthusiasm than I'd seen from him in twenty-four hours. He got out one side and I got out the other. The lambs stood there sheepishly. Yes they did, sheepishly, and I'm not going to change it. Now Robyn and Lee started to get excited as they contemplated the thought of a good meal. None of us are vegetarians – being a vegetarian is a capital offence in our part of the world. We grabbed the lambs and up-ended them, found some cord and tied their legs, then somehow cleared space for them in the back of the car.

'They won't eat the potatoes, will they?' Fi asked anxiously, trying to move the heavy sack of spuds from near the head of one of the lambs.

'No Fi, and not the sugar either.'

Callously I went and picked some mint when we got back to my house. That short walk to the mint was almost the end of me though. As I bent down to cut it I felt my great black shadow return, hovering above me like an eagle, a predator. I was scared to look up. The night was dark enough anyway, but I knew that however dark the sky may have been, my tagging shadow was darker.

The mistake I'd made was to go to the mint patch on my own. It was the first time I'd been alone since shooting the soldier in Buttercup Lane. It was as though as soon as I strayed away from my friends the sky filled with this terrible thing.

I crouched there for a couple of minutes. The hair on the back of my neck was prickling and I could no longer smell the mint, although my face was buried in it. After a while I heard Homer calling for me, and then I heard his heavy footsteps and his body brushing through the overgrown wallflowers. It took him some time to find me, as I didn't seem able to answer his calls, but I could hear his voice getting more and more concerned. When he did find me, he was surprisingly gentle, rubbing the back of my neck and mumbling words that I didn't exactly understand.

I went back to the Landie with him. Without a word to the others, and without looking up, I turned the key in the ignition. We at last began the slow ascent to the place I now thought of as home: Hell. We hid the Landie in the usual spot, tethered the sheep and gave them a bucket of water, then picked up a few supplies and began the walk in. I should call it a stumble rather than a walk. We'd gone to our limits, physically, mentally and emotionally, and I was glad we didn't have to dig any deeper to find more energy. I don't think anyone had much left. I got into a groove, putting one foot ahead of the other, and did it so successfully that I think I could have gone on forever, except for the steep downhill bits, which strained my thigh muscles too much. When we got to the camp-site Homer had to prod me in the back to stop me, like he was searching for my off button. We stumbled into our tents and mumbled goodnights to each other, before crashing into our private hells of sleep.

I did sleep, though I hadn't expected to. All night I dreamt of someone very large, very angry, hovering very close to me, and speaking to me in a voice so loud that it reverberated through my body. I woke early and huddled in close to Fi. I don't know what was going on in my head: I seemed haunted by the idea that I had to hide, that I daren't be on my own. There was a sense that doom was overshadowing me, and like a rat threatened by an owl I wanted to burrow under something. Only, unlike the rat, I wanted to get under a human being, not a thing.

Seems like since that night I've done less of every-thing: less sleeping, less eating, less talking. I feel I'm less of a person because I killed a dying soldier and that now I do less living.

I got up eventually, and washed my face.

The day went grinding by, hour by hour. No one did anything much. Certainly no one talked about anything important.

We'd left most of the supplies at the Land Rover. It was tempting to leave them there forever. But late afternoon, after I'd had a nap – one of those daytime sleeps that leave you feeling worse than you did before – I forced myself to round up a posse. I was thinking of the sheep, mainly, and I wanted to prove to the others that I was still useful, that I wasn't a bad person, even if I did kill people.

But it was hard work persuading them to come. Chris just whined, 'It can wait till tomorrow, can't it?' Without looking me in the eye, he slunk back to his tent. Homer was so deeply asleep I didn't like to wake him. Lee didn't look too keen but he had too much pride to say no so he put down his book and came without a word. Robyn gave me about twenty reasons why we didn't need to go till the next day, then at the last moment, just as we were leaving, she changed her mind and came. Fi was the best: she crawled out of her sleeping bag saying, 'Exercise! That's what I want, more exercise.'

I forgave her the sarcasm because she was cheerful, just when I needed some cheerfulness.

We set off at about four. The physical movement was good for me now; it seemed to restore some health and energy to my mind. We all knew the track so well that we could talk easily as we walked, not having to concentrate on where we put our feet. We trudged up the path as it wound around the cliffs and through the bush, across the beautifully crafted hand-made bridge left there by the only other human to have lived in this wild rocky basin. If that old hermit had popped out as we crossed his bridge, like the troll and the billy goats gruff, he would have swallowed his beard in surprise. How could anyone have predicted what had happened, and the use to which Hell had been put? If we couldn't have predicted that, maybe we would be equally amazed by the next event, and maybe that event would be the ending of the war. That was one nice rational thought

73

with which I consoled myself as we slogged up to Wombegonoo.

We didn't talk about anything much. I realised after a while that the others were trying to be bright and cheerful, to make me feel better. Fi got us playing 'I remember' for quite a while, which had become one of our favourite games. It was a good way to pass the time, and simple enough: just say a sentence starting with 'I remember', and make sure it's true. I think we liked it because it helped bring back our normal lives, before the invasion. I was hardly in the mood for it this time but I tried to force myself to join in.

Fi started.

'I remember when Sally Geddes' parents took me to your restaurant, Lee, and I ordered lamb cutlets, because all those Chinese names looked too strange to me.'

'Not Chinese. Thai and Vietnamese,' Lee muttered, then, more loudly: 'I remember when my fingers ached from hours of violin practice, and my teacher told me to do another hour.'

'I remember when I thought Mr Oates said there'd be fire crackers after church and I was very excited and rushed outside, and then I found out he'd actually said choir practice.'

'I remember the first time I saw traffic lights.'

'Oh Ellie! You're such a rural!'

'I remember making jelly, following the instructions carefully, and step three was "Stand in fridge", and I thought "Why should I have to go and stand in the fridge?"'

'Fi! You made that up!'

'It's true, I swear.'

'I remember thinking that all teachers liked me,

and then one day in Year 2 I heard the teacher say I was the kind of kid she'd left the city to avoid.'

That was Lee again.

'I remember how in Year 7 Ellie always saved a seat for me and then one day you didn't, Ellie, and I felt like it was the end of the world. I went home and cried.'

I remembered that too, and felt guilty. I'd just been a bit sick of Robyn's company and wanted to make some new friends.

'I remember when I was little I was walking past a heifer that was in a crush, and she lifted her tail and pooed on my head.'

'I remember in Year 1 I told the teacher our cat had been shovelled, and it took ages for her to work out what I meant.'

'What did you mean?'

'It had been spayed of course.' Fi gave her little light laugh, like wind chimes.

'I remember going into the girls' changing room at the pool by mistake.'

'A mistake. Sure Lee, sure.'

'I remember when I was in love with Jason and I used to ring him up all the time and talk to him for hours, and one day after I'd talked for a while I stopped and there was nothing, just a long silence, until finally I hung up, and next day at school I asked him what had happened and he admitted he'd gone to sleep while I'd been talking.'

'I remember being so excited about my first day at school that I wore my uniform to bed, underneath my pyjamas.' I sure had changed my mind about school since those days.

'I remember my parents wanted to send me to

boarding school and I went and hid under the house for four hours, until they changed their minds.'

'I remember swapping my violin for a Mars Bar when I was in Year 2, and when my parents found out they chucked the biggest mental and got on the phone to the kid's parents to cancel the deal. I can't even remember who the kid was now.'

'I remember,' Fi said. 'It was Steve.'

'That'd be right,' I said. Steve, my Steve, my ex, had always been a smooth talker.

'Your turn Robyn,' Fi said.

'OK, I'm still thinking. OK, I remember Grandpops picking me up to give me a hug, and he forgot he had a cigarette in his mouth, and it burnt me on the cheek.'

'I remember when we were little I watched Homer take a leak and I decided I wanted to do it standing too, so I pulled down my pants and tried. It didn't work very well,' I added, probably unnecessarily.

'I remember the last time I saw my parents,' Fi said. 'Mum told me that just because I was going bush didn't mean I shouldn't brush my teeth after every meal.'

'I remember my father saying we were the most disorganised bunch he'd ever seen in his life and if we were jackaroos he'd sack every one of us,' I said, going out of turn. I was starting to feel dismal again. 'Then he charged off on the motorbike without even saying goodbye.'

'I remember Dad being so anxious as I was going,' Lee said, 'and telling me to be very careful, not to take any risks.'

'And you've been so obedient,' Robyn said. 'Well seeing we've got onto this depressing subject, I'll tell you how I last saw my parents. I opened their bedroom door to say goodbye and caught them both in the nick making passionate love on top of the doona. Luckily they hadn't heard me, so I shut the door quietly, waited about a minute, then banged on the door and yelled goodbye as loud as I could and raced out to the car.'

Robyn had achieved the impossible with her story: made me laugh.

'I wondered why you were grinning so much as you got in the car,' Fi said, after we'd stopped laughing. 'I thought it was just the sheer pleasure of seeing me.'

'Well that too of course,' Robyn said, as we arrived at the top of Wombegonoo.

It was cold on the exposed summit, out of the protection of Hell. The sky was clear but the wind was blowing sharp and hard. A few wisps of cloud, as light as fairyfloss, and almost close enough to touch, were shilly-shallying around. We'd had a long run of dry weather but the cruel cold of the wind suggested it might be bringing something wild in. Beyond the furthest mountains we could see the tops of some thick white cloud. It seemed to be lying in wait. I stood and tried to see as far as Cobbler's Bay, anxious to count the ships, if there were any, but it was too dark to see.

We sat there for five minutes to get our breath back, and spent the time admiring the ferocious beauty of our home, in the last of the light. I could see why it had looked so frightening to me for so many years. Even now, when we knew it so well, it had the same look of potential violence that some animals in zoos manage to keep. Or maybe it was me, that everything now seemed threatening. Hell was a vivid mess of trees and rocks, dark green and reddish-brown, grey and black. It looked like a dumping ground for the gods, a great smashed mess of living things that grew without help or guidance, according to their own wild rules. It was the right place for us.

We'd brought Corrie's radio, which we could use only sparingly, as our few batteries were fading fast. But we'd learnt where and when to find the news bulletins, and we tuned in now to an American one. We had to keep it on for a few minutes, as we were no longer the top story, and hadn't been for a fortnight. This night we were down to number four. The world was quickly forgetting us. And there was little new to report. Economic sanctions were in place and supposed to be having some effect. We'd lost control of all but the most desolate outback and a few of the bigger cities. An American Air Force jet had kindly taken our leading politicians to the States, where they were torn between making inspiring speeches about courage, and passionate denials that their policies had weakened us in the first place. It was hard to restrain Lee from crushing the radio at that point.

Guerilla activity was continuing in some areas but large portions of the country were now so firmly held that the first colonists were already settling in with their families. Only New Zealand was giving direct military help, sending troops and supplies. There was unofficial and private support from elsewhere, especially New Guinea, but the PNG government was torn between the fear of attracting an attack and the fear that they would be next anyway. The balance of power in Asia and the Pacific had changed so much that people still couldn't come to terms with it. A woman from India, a politician, was trying to broker a peace deal on behalf of the UN, but all her proposals so far had been firmly rejected.

The next item on the news was a broken leg suffered by a famous basketball player in Chicago.

The news depressed us. We walked to the Landie in silence. Robyn and I each shouldered a lamb and the others loaded up with all they could carry. There was still plenty left for at least one more trip. We'd been lucky to think of the Kings' little hobby farm. It had guaranteed our survival through winter and beyond. The time might come when we'd have to steal food from farmhouses colonised by our enemies, but like the future of our fuel supplies and the fates of our families and friends, we'd have to worry about that later.

Chapter Six

Lee and I were sitting outside the door of the Hermit's hut. In this tiny shelter a man who'd fled from a dark and horrifying world had found some kind of peace. Maybe. We didn't know that. We had fled an ugly world too, but we were not able to cut off from it the way he had. We'd brought some of it in here with us, and we had to keep going out into the rest of it.

Nevertheless, I felt some peace when I was at the old cabin. There was no place more remote for us to escape the human race. Sometimes I'd crawled here along the creek bed, like a sick dog crawls into the dark bushes to wait until it dies or gets better. Sometimes I'd come here to reassure myself that other human beings had ever existed. Sometimes it was because of an obscure idea that I might find answers I wouldn't find elsewhere. After all, the Hermit had spent a long time here alone. Free from the distracting noises of the world he must have had a lot of time to think, and his thinking would have had some special quality, surely? Or was I just being naive?

I'd started cleaning the hut, slowly, and occasionally with Lee's help. It'd never gleam like a suburban home in a television ad, but the left-hand side was looking quite neat, and it stood out more distinctly from the bush that had almost engulfed it. I'd never been a fan of housework during the peace but I was quite proud of what we'd done here.

This day though, so soon after the attack on the convoy, I hadn't felt like continuing the cleaning. I just sat, leaning back into Lee's warm chest, letting his long arms come around me and his fine musician's fingers do what they wanted. I hoped if he held me hard enough and touched me hotly enough he would prove to me that we were still alive, and maybe even chase my shadow away. The day was cold and grey; I felt cold and grey inside and out.

We'd never really discussed the attack on the convoy; none of us I mean, not just Lee and me. That was unusual; we normally talked passionately about everything that happened. But maybe this had been too big. Not so much blowing up the trucks; that was big all right, but it was like the bridge – dramatic, scary, exciting. The hard things were the close-up personal things. Homer not telling us about his gun, Homer shooting the soldiers, me killing the wounded soldier. They were so intimate that I couldn't talk about them. It would have been like talking about my own blood.

Still, at least that day Lee and I did talk about real things; things that mattered.

'Are you OK since the big shooting match?' he asked.

'I don't know. I don't know how I feel any more.'

'But you still have feelings?' His hand was under my T-shirt, stroking my stomach.

I smiled. 'Oh yes. Just one or two. But they mostly seem bad ones nowadays.'

81

There was a pause of a minute or so before he asked, 'Such as?'

'Fear. Anger. Depression. How's that for a start?'

'No good ones at all?'

'Not a lot.'

'None?'

'Oh I know what you want me to say. Love for you and all that stuff, I suppose.'

'No, I didn't want you to say that.' He sounded hurt. 'I wasn't even thinking of that. I was just worried about you.'

'Sorry. Sorry. I don't seem able to think like a normal person any more. Everything's distorted. Can you believe those other countries won't do anything for us?'

'Well, seems to me there were a few countries overseas who were invaded and we didn't do anything about them.'

'I thought we were different. I thought everyone loved us.'

'I guess they only liked us. There's a major difference between like and love.'

'Mmm, tell me about it. What is it with you then, like or love? Do you like me or love me?' I asked it lightly but I was nervous, waiting for his answer.

'That's a big question.' He made circles around my belly button with his middle finger, then went a bit higher. My skin felt alive at each point where he touched me, though the rest of me was still cold. Then he said, very slowly, 'I like you with all your faults Ellie, and I think that's love.'

I was a bit angry at first, thinking of all Lee's faults – his brooding silences, his flashes of temper, his hunger for revenge. But I knew I had faults too – my bossiness, my tactlessness, and the way I was over-critical sometimes. And then I began to realise what a big compliment he had paid me, what a big statement he'd made. He was right, there's a difference between the way you feel before you know a person and the way you feel after. I'd had those rushes of heat that I'd thought were love, when you see someone so beautiful you want to follow them for the rest of your life, just so you can keep staring at them. That kind of love didn't mean much. It was like some of my friends at school saying they 'loved' a film star or a pop singer. That wasn't love. Lee was talking about feelings as big as these mountains. For a moment a new world opened in my mind, where I was an adult, working hard, holding a group of people together, being a leader. With a shock I realised I was thinking about parenthood. Forget it! That was not on my agenda. I sat up and peeled Lee's hand from my breast.

'What's wrong?' he asked.

'I don't want this to get too serious.'

'Yes you do.'

'Lee! Don't tell me what my feelings are.'

He just laughed. 'Well you don't know what they are, so I might as well tell you.'

'Oh! Excuse me!'

'So you do know what they are?'

'Yes! Yes, of course.'

'OK, fire away.'

'What do you mean?'

'Well, you're so sure you know how you feel, go ahead and tell me. I can't wait to find out.'

'Oh! You're so annoying. All right, how do I feel? Um. OK. Um, um, um. OK, got it. I feel confused.'

'See! I was right! You don't know how you feel.'

'Yes I do! I feel confused. I just told you that.'

'But confusion's not a feeling!'

'Yes it is!'

He wrestled me down again. 'Ellie, you're up to your old tricks. Too much thinking, not enough feeling.' He kissed me hard, for a long time, till I was kissing him back just as hard. Then the kisses became slow and soft, kind of messy, but nice. But I was still bothered by a few things. So when we paused for breath and Lee was nuzzling my shoulder I started again.

'Lee, I know you're trying to kiss me into silence, but seriously, I am worried about us, about you and me. I don't know what's going to happen, how we're going to end up. And don't say something dumb like "no one can predict the future". Tell me something I don't already know.'

'Well what else can I say? The future is... I don't know, what's the future? It's a blank sheet of paper and we draw lines on it, but sometimes our hand is held and the lines we draw aren't the lines we wanted.'

Lee said this in a dreamy way, gazing up at the canopy of branches above us, but I was deeply impressed.

'Far out, did you just think of that?'

'More or less. I mean, I've thought of it before but that's the way it came out this time. Anyway it's true, and that's all that matters.'

'Mmm, I suppose it is. But here in Hell we get to draw the lines how we want most of the time – or much more than we ever could before. There's no adults around holding our hands.'

'No, but we've got our own thoughts, which do the

84

same job. The way we've kept our heads together proves that. I bet a lot of people would have expected us to be into an orgy of sex, drugs and chocolate, but we've been pretty straight. So far.'

'Oh yes? What does that mean?'

'You know.'

'Are you referring to sex, drugs or chocolate?'

'Well, I know which one means the most to me, and it sure ain't chocolate.'

'You think we should do it, don't you?'

'"It",' he teased me. 'What's "it"?'

'You know.'

'OK, yeah, I think we should do it.'

'I knew you did,' I said, but I wasn't sure if he was serious or being funny.

'And you want to do it too.'

'Sometimes I do,' I admitted, going a bit red.

'That's what this conversation's really about, isn't it?'

'Maybe it is.' I sighed, and brushed my hair away from my face. 'Christ, Lee,' I said, turning to him suddenly and grabbing him by the top of his shirt, 'sometimes I want to do it so badly my skin's swollen with it.'

'Do you think Homer and Fi have done it?'

'Nuh. Fi would have told me.'

'Girls are funny, the way they tell each other all stuff like that.'

'And guys don't? Come on, give me a break.'

'Anyway, after she read what you wrote about them, she mightn't tell you so much.'

'After what I wrote about them they've hardly touched each other.'

'Yeah, they did go a bit funny. Hey, wait a minute, are you going to be writing down this conversation?'

'If I do I won't be showing anyone.'

'You better not. So.' He turned to me and picked up my hand and began to stroke the back of it. 'So, what's the story El? What's going down? Why are we having this conversation?'

'I don't know. I'm crazy with worry about so many things. For instance, sometimes I think maybe we're with each other just because there's no one else around. If we were back at school and we'd never been invaded, we might hardly be friends. So, is this meant to be, or isn't it? It might be like one of those summer romances they have in American movies, and somehow it doesn't seem real if that's all it is.'

Lee went to say something, but I stopped him. 'OK, I know what you're going to say, I think too much. I admit it. But I guess I'm dodging the big issue. And the big issue, well it's sort of what you said. We've been together a while now and we've been pretty good. But there's something in me wants to go further, and I don't mean only physical, although there's definitely that.' As I talked I began for the first time to get an inkling of what it might be. 'I think it's to do with all the things that have happened to us. The invasion and being here and going out and blowing things up and killing people. I'm sort of asking, is that all our life is going to become? Just sitting here, spinning our wheels? Every few weeks go out and kill a few more soldiers? If that's all life has to offer for the next fifty years, then forget it. I want to go forward, no matter what else is happening around us. We haven't gone forward one space since we got here. We haven't built anything, except a few crummy chook yards. We haven't learned anything. We haven't done anything positive.'

'We've learned a heap, I reckon.'

'Oh, about ourselves and stuff. But I don't mean that kind of learning. I mean stuff that's useless for its own sake and so it's beautiful, if you see what I mean. Like, the names of constellations and the shapes they form in the sky. Like the way Michelangelo painted the Sistine Chapel, on his back with paint dripping in his eyes. Like, oh, Fibonacci sequences or the Japanese tea ceremony or the French word for railway. They're the kind of things I'm talking about. Can't you understand?'

'I guess so. You mean, if we lose those things we'll be defeated, no matter what else happens, no matter what military victories we win.'

'Exactly. You do understand! We have to do things that say yes, not just things that say no. Planting all those seeds, that was a good thing to do. But we should have planted flowers too. The Hermit understood that. That's why he put in these roses, and when he made that bridge he didn't just shove a few logs across the creek. He made it beautifully, so it'll last hundreds of years. We have to create things, and think in the long term. Leave stuff behind us for others. Life rules! Yeah!'

And I leapt away and did a dance through the Hermit's dark little house, coming back with dozens of rose petals that I scattered generously on Lee's face. But that wasn't nearly enough. I'd suddenly built up so much energy that I could have planted a thousand trees, kissed a thousand guys, built a thousand houses. Instead I ploughed my way back down the creek at high speed, ran in zigzags through the clearing, then jogged on up the track to watch the sunset from Satan's Steps.

When it was dark and the flies had gone to bed for the night, Homer and I killed one of the lambs. I knelt on it while he cut its throat, then I jerked back its head to break the bone and let the blood run out, the life flow away. We skinned it between us, Homer using his big fist for the belly and brisket. I hadn't been looking forward to doing all this. I'd thought that I mightn't be able to; that it might bring back the terrible memories from the ambush. But it didn't. I don't know if the conversation with Lee had cleared the sky of my menacing shadow, but as soon as I grabbed the lamb I automatically started doing what I'd done in the old days. We'd always kept our own killers. You never get blase about slaughtering an animal; for instance taking out the warm heart, which feels like the life is still held in it, is a powerful experience, no matter how many times you do it. It is for me, anyway. So you don't do it like you're a robot, or like you're peeling spuds. But to my relief I found it went pretty much as it always had done – and that really was a relief.

We cut off its head and chucked it into the pit Fi had dug for the leftovers. I'm not into brains, and that particular night I couldn't bring myself to skin its face or cut out the tongue. Then we strung the carcass up over a branch to gut it. We were under so much pressure from the others to provide a barbecue that we went ahead and butchered it straightaway, even though it's better to wait and let it cool. But we hacked off the first chops, with some rough bush butchering, and onto the fire they went. It was midnight before our hungry mouths closed on the hot pink meat, but it had been worth the wait. We ate well, grinning at each other as our blackened greasy fingers tore at the food. The death of one thing can be the birth of something else. I felt new determination, new surety, new confidence.

Chapter Seven

What happened after that was my idea, I admit it. The buck stops with Ellie. It came out of being so restless, feeling that we weren't doing enough, weren't making a difference. I'd always thought that there must be a route out the other side of Hell, using the creek as a path. After all, it had to run somewhere, and it couldn't go uphill. In the next valley was the Holloway River, and Risdon. I had no idea if the route would be passable for humans but I thought it was worth a try. I longed for new fields, new scenes, new people maybe. It was like wanting a holiday. Despite what the radio and our own common sense told us, there was some vague feeling that things would be different there, that we'd walk out of the mountains into a new and green land, a peaceful land, leaving the ugliness and despair of Wirrawee behind. I didn't tell the others of my dream. I just said we needed to establish a line of retreat, and it might be important for us to find out what was happening in the Holloway. Knowledge is power, after all.

They were quite keen. They didn't need much persuading. Homer had suggested a few times that we needed to find more people, to meet up with other groups, and there was a chance we could do that in Risdon. Besides, I suppose we all were ready to try something new. It helped us feel that we were being constructive. Only Chris wanted to stay behind. It was useful to have someone stay back, to look after the chooks and the remaining lamb, but I wasn't sure if leaving Chris alone was a good idea. He was becoming increasingly solitary, writing in his notebook and sitting on his own, gazing at the cliffs. He drank all the beer we got from the Kings' I think, because when I looked for it I couldn't find it, and Lee said he didn't know where it had gone. But there was no more grog then, as far as I knew, and I thought maybe that had put him in a bad mood. Occasionally he had bursts of activity – for instance, he built us a good big woodshed for keeping our firewood dry. That took him three days and he wouldn't let anyone help him, but once he'd finished it he didn't do much more.

We knew we might be away for a few nights if we did get through to Risdon, so we packed proper backpacks, with sleeping bags and jumpers and japaras. Instead of tents we took a few flies and groundsheets, which were lighter, and good enough for what we wanted.

There was a big argument about how to walk the creek. Homer, who was gradually returning to his usual assertive self, said we should wear boots because we'd be less likely to slip on the rocks. I said we should use bare feet so our boots would be dry and warm when we finally got out of the creek. Walking through that cold water for a long distance, with autumn coming on fast, wasn't something that appealed to any of us.

But that argument at last led into the one we should have had ages ago: the one about Homer taking guns on the Buttercup Lane ambush.

It went like this. Homer said something typically domineering, like 'Well I'm wearing my boots, I don't care what the rest of you do.'

I said, 'Great. And when you get blisters we'll have to carry you I suppose. Homer, if we don't look after our feet we'll be good for nothing.'

'Yes mother,' he said, flashing his brown eyes at me.

I've always had this feeling with Homer that I must never back off or it'll be the end of me. He's so strong and he intimidates so many people, and then I think he despises them because they're too weak to stand up to him. So I always stand up to him, and I did it again this time.

'How come when I tell people what I think they should do, you make comments like "Yes mother", and when you tell people what to do you expect them to jump into action? You wouldn't be just a tiny bit sexist would you Homer?'

That was like asking a fish if it was a tiny bit wet.

'Ellie, I know you hate it when you don't get your own way on every little thing...'

'Oh yes? And when's the last time I got my own way on anything?'

'Oh oh! You're asking me? Try this morning at breakfast, when you stopped Chris lighting the fire. Try two hours ago, when you wouldn't let Lee open a can of peaches.'

'Yeah, and you notice something about both those times? I'm trying to do the right thing by us, by this group! I'm trying to keep us alive! If anyone sees

91

smoke out of here, we're dead. If we pig out on all the food we're in big trouble. I'm not just saying stuff for my own sake, because I like to hear my own voice, you know.'

'You ought to listen to others more Ellie. You keep wanting to be a one-man band.'

Now I was really mad.

'Thanks very much, I'd never want to be a one-*man* band; a one-woman one maybe. You're just proving what I said before. And by the way, this is pretty good coming from you. You're the moron who secretly cut down the shotguns and secretly took them with you after we'd all agreed we wouldn't have firearms. You put our lives at risk Homer, by being a one-man band, and you did it in cold blood. I've never done anything like that. You're so sure you're right on every little thing, you don't care what anyone else thinks.'

'And I was right, wasn't I? Chris and I'd be dead now if I hadn't had those guns. All of us might be dead. I saved your life Ellie. Hey, I'm a hero.'

'Trust you to cash in just because you got a lucky call. You were so bloody lucky Homer, you haven't even started to figure it out yet. If those blokes had taken their rifles with them when they went into the bush, there's no way you'd have had time to get your precious shotgun out.'

'I had it in my hand Ellie. I'm not that slow. I was ready.'

'And suppose a patrol had jumped us? Suppose we'd been caught with sawn-off shotguns? We'd have been put against a tree and shot and you'd have five people's blood on your hands.'

'But that didn't happen, did it? That proves I was right.'

'That doesn't prove anything! That was a fluke!'

'No, because the fact that it didn't happen proves that we'd covered ourselves properly. There's no such thing as a fluke. It's like that golfer said, good players always have the luck. As long as we keep being careful, and smart, we'll keep being lucky. I don't believe in flukes. I figured all this out before I decided to take the guns.'

'Homer! You're crazy! Anything could have happened out there! Don't believe in flukes? You don't understand life. It's all flukes. You're acting like you can control everything. You think you're God! Jeez, even in golf, the ball can hit a tree and bounce off into the hole. How do you explain that? Anyway, that's not the point,' I said quickly, in case he could explain it. 'The point is that you've got to go along with group decisions. You can't ignore us and do what you want. We're all in this together. Don't go calling me a one-man band. You're not only the band, you're the roadies as well.'

'Break it up, guys,' Chris said. The others had been reacting to us in their different ways. Robyn had been standing leaning on a mattock, watching and listening with great interest. Fi, who hated conflict, had gone off to our current dunny, fifty metres away in the bush. Lee was reading a book called *Red Shift* and had not even looked up. Chris had been whittling a piece of wood into the shape of a dragon. He'd been doing a lot of stuff like that lately, and was getting really good at it. But he looked upset and angry at the way we were fighting, and a few minutes after he interrupted us he went off to the creek, while the rest of us started getting organised for the expedition.

I was packing in a bit of a rage, throwing things

around, growling at everyone. It wasn't till Fi came back from the dunny that I calmed down a bit. Well, to be more accurate, she calmed me down. She picked up a stick that I'd knocked over, one that we used for drying clothes, and tried to put it back in its position. One end of it sat in the fork of a tree and she couldn't quite reach it, so I went to give her a quick lift. To my horror she flinched slightly as I grabbed at her. It was only the slightest movement, but for that second she looked like she thought I was going to hit her.

'Oh Fi!' I said. I was really upset.

'Oh, I'm sorry Ellie,' she said. 'You just took me by surprise, that's all.'

I sat down on the ground beside the tent and crossed my legs. 'Fi, have I turned into a monster?'

'No Ellie, of course you haven't. There's just so much happening, it's hard to get used to it all.'

'Have I changed a lot?'

'No, no. Ellie, you're a strong person and whenever you have strong people around, you have fireworks. I mean, Homer's strong and Robyn's strong and Lee's much stronger than people realise. So there's bound to be clashes.'

'Everyone's strong in different ways. I didn't think Kevin was strong until he drove off with Corrie to the Hospital. You were so tough when we blew up the bridge.'

'I'm not strong with people though.'

'Do you still hate me for what I wrote about you and Homer?'

'No! Of course not! It was just a shock when I read it, that's all. Your trouble is you're too honest, and that was the shock. You wrote down the things that most

94

people think but never say. Or else, people write them in their diaries and never show anyone.'

'But you and Homer still haven't got it back together.'

'No, but I don't know if that was because of what you wrote. He's so difficult. Some days he's so loving and beautiful and other days he treats me like I don't exist. It's very frustrating.'

Seemed like I had a lot of significant conversations that day. Maybe it was the fact that we were on the move that got everyone talking suddenly. The last one was with Chris and that was even tougher than the one with Homer. I went down to the creek deliberately to find him, because I felt guilty about neglecting him lately. The more morose he became the more I avoided him. Everyone did. And I suppose that just made him worse. So Saint Ellie decided to fix things, and away she went, determined to do something good for once.

I found him sitting on a rock looking at his left foot, which was bare. For a moment I couldn't see what he was looking at but then I saw this nasty black bulge on his skin, like a long ugly blood-blister. I looked at it, shuddered, looked again, and realised it was a leech. Chris was sitting there calmly, watching it grow fat on his blood.

'Er, yuk,' I said. 'What are you doing that for?'

He shrugged. 'Passes the time.' He didn't even look up.

'No, seriously, why?'

This time he didn't answer at all. For the whole time we were talking the leech stayed there, getting bigger and blacker. It made it hard to have a conversation. I couldn't take my eyes off it. But I tried.

'Can you make sure you check for eggs behind that flat rock? Blossom's been laying there occasionally.'

Blossom was a rather depressed looking red hen who wasn't popular with the other chooks.

'Sure.'

'So how are you going to spend the time while we're away?'

'I dunno. I'll find things.'

'Chris, are you OK? Like, you seem so cut off these days. Do you hate us all or something? Is anything getting you down?'

'No, no. I'm fine.'

'But we used to talk, we used to have these great conversations. How come we don't do that any more?'

'I dunno. Nothing to talk about.'

'So much is happening. We're in the middle of the biggest thing that we'll ever see in our whole lives. So much is happening.'

He shrugged again, not lifting his eyes from the foul slug on his leg.

'I'd love to see some more of your writing, your poetry.'

He gazed at the leech for a long time, but without answering. Finally he said, 'Yeah, I liked what you said about the other ones.' Then, as if he were talking to himself, he added, 'Maybe I should. Maybe yes, maybe no.'

He turned and stretched out past me to get something from his jacket, which was lying on a rock. Mechanically I picked it up and handed it to him. As I did so I smelt again the stale sweet smell of alcohol on his breath. So he still did have a secret collection of grog somewhere. He pulled out a box of matches. He seemed to be ignoring me. I felt flat and dispirited. I'd been in a better mood after talking to Fi but that was lost again. I could hear Robyn yelling for me; our expedition was ready to move out.

'Well, see you,' I said to Chris, 'in a couple of hours or a couple of days.'

He didn't even answer. I slouched off up the hill, grabbed my pack and headed for the point where the creek slid under the thick growth of bush, the route to the Hermit's cabin and beyond. Fi and Homer and Lee were already there; only Robyn had waited for me. I took off my boots and socks. We'd agreed on a compromise – to wear boots and keep our socks dry – so I put the boots back on and followed the others into the cold water. Was this trip a good idea? I couldn't decide but I didn't care all that much. It was something to do, and if we were careful we couldn't come to much harm. Except for frostbite, I thought, as I felt the water trickle in around my toes. And leeches. I kept glancing down nervously to make sure they weren't making sneak attacks on me.

We passed the little old cabin and kept going. We were in new territory now. It didn't take long to get quite uncomfortable. Bent over, slipping on rocks, getting pain up my legs from my freezing feet, I grunted and grumbled my way along. I kept trying to move the pack on my back into new positions, feeling more like a tortoise with every passing minute.

'This is a tough way to earn a living,' I said to Robyn's bum. She laughed. I think that's what she did, anyway.

Turning her head a little she said back to me, 'Hey El, do yabbies bite?'

'Yeah, count your toes every time we stop. They're hungry little critters.'

'And dragonflies?'

'Them too.'

'Bunyips?'

'They're the worst of the lot.'

We had to duck even lower then as undergrowth pulled at our hair. It was the end of conversation for a while.

We went on like that for a long time. Once I got into a routine it wasn't so bad. There's those first few minutes when you're sweating and in pain, then it becomes a kind of rhythm and you go with the flow. It's happening inside you and outside you, but the first intensity wears off, luckily. So I plodded along, following Robyn who was following Lee who was following Fi who was following Homer. Sometimes the creek widened and rippled over gravel, which was nice and easy; sometimes I slipped on smooth rocks or felt the pressure of sharp ones; sometimes we had to clamber around deep pools. In one place the creek flowed straight and dark for about eighty metres, with a sandy bottom, and we were able to walk along it with our heads up as though we were on a highway.

I'd always thought of Hell as being a basin, a bowl, but I had no real evidence of that. From Tailor's Stitch the far side of Hell looked to be a ridge of rock and trees, a lot lower than Tailor's. It certainly gave the impression of forming one side of a basin, with Mt Turner the only really high point. But beyond that was the Holloway Valley, and the creek had to reach there somehow.

We slogged away for two hours, losing height most of the time. I was wondering if I'd be able to stand straight again or if I'd be locked into this position forever, a hunchbacked monster from the bush. Suddenly I realised that Robyn's bum had swung around and was going away from me; in fact it was rising, leaving the creek. I glanced up from under my pack. Robyn was clambering out of the water to join the others, who were sprawled along the bank pulling off their boots, groaning as they tried to rub their legs back into life. We were in a clear length of bush for the first time since leaving our campsite. There were only a few metres of flat, but it was enough. There was even some warm sunlight to lie in; the thick canopy of trees was broken and we could see a clear pale blue sky.

'Mmm, this is nice,' Robyn said.

'Thank God it was here,' I said. 'I couldn't have gone much further. That was one mother of a paddle. Whose idea was this anyway?'

'Yours,' came the four voices, on cue.

I pulled off my saturated boots and looked around as I rubbed my feet and legs. The creek flowed on without us but it changed its tune a little further down. I could hear a wilder, louder, lonelier sound. And through the trees was more sunlight, a light blue background instead of a thick green and brown one. Walking like a hospital patient on her first day out of bed I hobbled along to the end of the clearing, followed by Homer. We went a few metres into the belt of trees, and stood, looking. There was the Holloway Valley.

To a lot of people I suppose it wouldn't have been beautiful. It had been a dry summer and although the river flats were a soft green, the paddocks beyond Risdon had burnt off into the ochre sameness that

99

seemed part of my life, part of me. The lush green of our springs and early summers never lasted long. I was more used to that dry monotonous yellow; so used to it that at some stage it had soaked into me, till I wasn't sure if there were boundaries between me and the landscape any more. I remember Mr Kassar at school saying that he'd come home after living a year in England and his heart had ached with love when he saw the sunburnt plains again. I knew what he meant; boy did I know what he meant.

Even the yellow wasn't all yellow of course. There were dark green dots of trees and lines of wind-breaks, the flashing of galvanised-iron roofs like little square pools of water, the tanks and sheds and stock-yards and dams, the endless boring fences. It was my country, even more than the bush and the mountains, and definitely more than the cities and towns. I felt at home in those hot, rustling paddocks.

But between us and the valley were a line of cliffs and a lot of bush. We'd skirted around Mt Turner without even realising it, and it was now quite a way over to my left. Homer and I were standing at the brink of one of the lowest cliffs, where the creek trickled over the edge in a long thin stream, falling to rocks fifty metres below and then gurgling away into undergrowth again. The bush down there looked as thick as the stuff we had come through in Hell.

'Lucky Kevin isn't here,' Homer said, gazing down at it.

'Eh? How do you work that out?'

'Didn't you know? He's terrified of heights.'

'God! Is there anything that guy isn't afraid of? And he always acted so tough.'

'Mmm. Guess he came through in the end, but.'

'Guess he did.'

We went back to the others and told them what we'd seen. We left our packs and went for a walk along the cliffs, looking for a way down.

'Short of bungy jumping...' Lee said, after ten minutes.

'We've got to be able to get back up again,' said Robyn, always practical.

The cliffs were fast becoming impassable in this direction, crowded by trees, breaking away in a few places, and with some dangerously slippery sheets of rock. We gave up and tried the other way, passing the creek again and striking out across some more bare patches of shale. We found only one possibility: a tree which had fallen head-first down the cliff and died there. Its bare white skeleton now leaned against the wall of rock; branches like bones stuck out on all sides, a kind of natural stepladder.

'Golly,' said Fi in her grandmotherly voice as we stood there and gazed down at it.

'No way,' said Lee.

'I don't see why not,' Robyn said.

'I don't have medical insurance,' Lee said.

'We should have brought some rope,' Homer said.

'We should have brought an escalator.'

'I think it's possible,' I said. 'If someone does it without their pack first, and if that works we can think about getting the packs down.'

They all looked at me as I said that, and they kept looking at me after I'd finished. I started to feel uncomfortable. 'Whose idea was it we come on this trip?' Homer asked again. They kept looking at me. I sighed, and began to take my pack off. Was it my imagination, or did they press closely around me as

101

they escorted me to the edge of the cliff? Seemed like I had the proverbial two chances of getting out of this: Buckley's and none. I got down on all fours and began sliding backwards over the edge.

'Hang onto my hands,' Homer said.

'There's no point. If we can only get down here by holding onto people, then what does the last person do?'

The top of the tree was about three metres below, but I thought I could reach it. The edge of the cliff was rounded, not sheer, and my biggest problems were the loose gravel and the need to connect my feet with the top of the tree. With a few instructions from Robyn, I lined myself up, then hung at full stretch for a few seconds. I needed to take a leap of faith. A slide of faith, anyway. I took a breath, swallowed, and let go. The slide only took a second but there was that horrible long thought that I might miss the tree and slide forever. I pressed myself into the gravel harder and scrabbled at the rockface with my fingers. Then my feet hit the broken trunk and almost immediately my legs were wrapping round it. I let myself slip a little further and hugged the old white wood with my arms as well, closing my eyes and resting my face against it.

'Are you OK?' Robyn called.

'Sure.' I opened my eyes. 'I'm just not thinking about getting back up again.'

I looked down, searching for a place to rest my feet. The spikes of wood were arranged neatly below me, all the way to the bottom. It seemed pretty straightforward. I put my left foot down to the first spike and rested my weight on it, straightening a little in relief. The branch immediately snapped. I hugged the tree again, as advice started pouring down on top of my head. 'Keep your feet close to the trunk.' 'Don't put all your weight on one branch.' 'Test the branches first.' They were sensible enough suggestions, but I could have figured them out for myself. I could feel the sweat starting to make my shirt sticky and my forehead hot; I gritted my teeth and searched for the next branch.

By keeping my feet so close to the trunk that the soles of my boots were twisted against it, I made progress. Boots weren't ideal for this kind of work, but they were all I had. It took me five minutes, it felt like fifteen, but at last I was standing, wild with relief, at the base of the trunk, my back to the bush.

'Come on,' I yelled.

'What about the packs?'

'Put the fragile things in your pockets, and chuck the packs down.'

And that's what they did. We didn't have many fragile items, torches, radio, a pair of binoculars. Then I had to dodge the falling packs. I'm sure they weren't aiming them at me. I'm quite sure they weren't. And I resisted the temptation to set fire to the trunk as they gingerly worked their way down it, one by one.

'We'll have to pick up a bit of rope somewhere,' Homer said, when we were all standing, a bit breathless, at the bottom. 'From Risdon maybe. It'll help us get back up.'

There was no path through the bush, and the trees were packed tightly. It was going to be a grunt. We went over a ridge, found a bit of a gap along a line of rock, and followed that until it ran out. After that we just had to struggle on. It took us about an hour to travel a kilometre. 'I'd rather be back in the creek,' I said to Fi.

And that's when we heard the voices.

Chapter Eight

Our first view of Harvey's Heroes was from a ridge of rock overlooking the camp. We'd snuck up on them so carefully that we could hear their voices clearly. It was such a relief that they were speaking in English. We lay there wide-eyed, watching them and gazing at each other in amazement. A month earlier we would have gone in yelling and screaming and waving our arms, but now we were so cautious we would have looked a gift horse in the mouth, nose, ears and throat before we'd accept it. And then we'd ask for references.

Still, there was no doubt that these people were fair dinkum. Some of them were in military uniform, there were rifles leaning against a large gum tree in the centre of the clearing, and the tents were camouflaged by fresh-cut branches. I could see at least twenty tents and in the few minutes that we watched we saw twenty different people, all adults, mostly men. They moved quietly around the camp. They had a relaxed air that I found attractive. My only worry was that their sentry system was so poor that we were able to spy on them without being caught.

'Well,' said Homer, 'are we going in?'

Lee started to rise but I pulled him back.

'Wait,' I said. 'What are we going to tell them?'

'What about?'

'Well…' I hesitated. I wasn't sure what I meant, what impulse had caused me to ask that question. Finally I said the only thing I could think of. 'Are we going to tell them about Hell?'

'I don't know. Why not?'

'I don't know. I just don't want to, for some reason. I want to keep it as our secret place.'

Homer paused. 'I guess it wouldn't hurt to keep quiet about it. Till we find out more about these people, anyway.'

I had to be content with that. Homer stood, and we followed him. We walked forward about ten metres before anyone noticed us. A man in jungle greens, carrying a shovel, came out of a tent, saw us, gaped in disbelief, then straightened up and gave a bird call. It was meant to be an imitation of a kookaburra but it wasn't very good. Nevertheless, it worked. Within seconds we were surrounded by men and women who came from every part of the camp. There were thirty or forty of them. Some of the women, to my astonishment, wore make-up. The unnerving thing though was that they were so subdued. A few of them patted us on the back, but most said nothing at all. They crowded us quite closely, close enough for us to smell their sweat and hair and breath. They didn't seem unfriendly, just wary, watchful. They seemed to be waiting for something.

I spoke up. 'Hello. We sure are glad to see you. We've been on our own a long time.'

A short tubby man came pushing through the

105

crowd. He was about thirty-five, black-haired, puffy-faced, with his head held at a rather strange angle, slightly to one side, and leaning back a little. He had a large, sharp nose that gave his face a strong look. He was dressed in a dingy yellowish-green military uniform with tunic and tie but no hat. His tie was khaki, as was his shirt. The others shuffled back, making room for him. The man gazed at us for a moment, then focused on Homer.

'Hello youngsters,' he said. 'Welcome to Harvey's Heroes. I'm Major Harvey.'

'Thanks,' Homer said awkwardly. 'It's fantastic to find you. We had no idea anyone would be here.'

'Well, come with me, and we'll have a chat.'

We still had our packs on our backs as we followed him through the camp. It was a clearing that wasn't a clearing, as there were so many gum trees that at times it was difficult to squeeze between them. Tents were placed in all kinds of odd corners. But compared to the thick bush around us it was a clearing.

Major Harvey's tent was so big by our standards that it was like a drawing room. The five of us could have slept in it, no worries. But all it contained was a camp stretcher covered by a mosquito net, a table and three chairs, and a few boxes and trunks. We dropped off our packs at the entrance. Major Harvey walked briskly to the chair behind the table and sat there, leaving us to sort out where we'd sit. In the end Homer and I took the chairs and the other three sat on the ground.

The major caught my eye as I glanced at the mosquito net and gave a rather nervous laugh. 'Bit of a luxury that,' he said. 'Fact is, I've got rather sensitive skin.' I smiled a stupid lopsided sort of grin and said nothing. The major turned back to Homer.

'Now,' he said, 'firstly, congratulations on still being free of the enemy's clutches. You've obviously done very well for yourselves. You'll have to tell me what you've been up to.'

I leaned back in the chair. I felt tremendously tired. Suddenly I could hardly stay awake. Adults! At last we had adults around us, people who could make the decisions, accept the responsibility, tell us what to do. I closed my eyes.

'Well,' Homer began nervously. I was surprised by how nervous he sounded. His confidence seemed to have left him, in the face of this man who made it so clear that he was in charge. 'Well,' he said again, 'we were camping in the bush when the invasion started. So we missed the whole thing. When we came out we found everybody had disappeared. It took us quite a while to work out what had happened. When we did realise, we shot back into the bush in a hurry, and we've been there ever since. Except for a few raids. We've done a bit of damage. We blew up the Wirra-wee bridge and we attacked a convoy, and we've been in a few other fights. We lost one of our friends, who got a bullet in the back, and another of our friends who drove her to hospital, and Lee here got shot in the leg, but apart from that we've done OK.'

I opened my eyes and looked at Major Harvey. He was gazing thoughtfully at Homer. His face was expressionless but his eyes were alive, brown and sharp. After a few seconds, when it was obvious that he wasn't going to say anything, Homer stumbled on. 'We're rapt to find you. We just came into the Hollo-way Valley to have a look around. We had no idea there'd be anything like this. You look like you've got a small army.'

There was silence again. I couldn't work out why he wouldn't speak, but my brain was too heavy and slow to work properly. Was there something obvious that I'd missed? After all, now that we were back with adults, we expected a bit of praise, a bit of recognition. Wasn't that what adults were for? We weren't looking for medals but we felt we'd come through some hard times and done the best we could. I'd expected the major to get a bit excited when he heard what we'd achieved. Maybe he thought we hadn't done enough?

When he did speak I really did get a shock.

He said: 'Who gave you permission to blow up the bridge and attack convoys?'

Homer gaped at him, mouth open like Jonathan Jo. He gaped at him for so long that I finally took over as spokesperson. 'What do you mean, permission?' I asked. 'We didn't have anyone we could ask about anything. We've hardly seen an adult since this whole thing started. We've just been doing what we thought was best.'

'This bridge. How do you know so much about explosives?'

'We don't,' Homer answered. 'We don't know anything about them. We used petrol.'

Major Harvey gave a tight little smile. 'All right,' he said. 'I'm sure you feel you have done your best. It's been a difficult time for everybody. But you can hand things over to us from now on. No doubt that'll be a relief to you. Although none of us here are regular soldiers, I have had Army experience and this is a military camp, run to military standards. From now on you'll come under my command. There'll be no more independent action. Is that understood? By all of you?'

We nodded, rather dumbly. He seemed to relax a bit when he realised that we weren't going to put up a fight. Everyone was mentally exhausted, not just me. We sat there and listened as he explained the set-up of Harvey's Heroes.

'The enemy are currently in control of this valley,' he said. 'But the troop concentrations here are much less than in the Wirrawee area. Wirrawee is vital to them because as long as they control Wirrawee they control the road to Cobbler's Bay. And we believe Cobbler's Bay to be one of their main landing points.

'Our job is to harass the enemy as much as possible, causing maximum inconvenience to him and disrupting his activities at every possible point. We are severely outnumbered in terms of manpower and severely disadvantaged in terms of firepower. Nevertheless, we have made a difference in our own small way. We have sabotaged a number of enemy vehicles, destroyed two power stations and inflicted significant casualties.' He gave a tight little smile. 'I think I can say that the enemy is more than aware of our contribution.'

We smiled back and muttered polite comments as he continued.

'In a few moments I will introduce you to my two ic, Captain Killen.' I let out a giggle at this name, but the major looked at me blankly.

'Sorry,' I said.

He continued to talk, without looking at me, and it took me a moment to realise that I'd seriously offended him. 'We are a combat unit on active service,' he said.

'And you have just had a perfect demonstration of why you will not see many members of the fairer sex among our numbers. A tendency towards levity at inappropriate moments is not something we encourage.'

My little giggle was replaced by cold violent anger, mixed with disbelief. Only Homer's quick hand on my knee stopped me saying something. The fairer sex? Levity at inappropriate moments? Jeez, all I'd done was laugh.

I didn't notice the rest of the speech, just sat there smouldering until the two ic, Captain Killen, came in and was introduced. Only then did it strike me that the major hadn't even asked us our names.

At least the captain seemed harmless enough; a tall thin man with a soft voice. He had a prominent Adam's apple which bobbed up and down as he talked, and he kept blinking all the time. He was a man of few words though. He spent a minute with us outside Major Harvey's tent, pointing out the layout of the camp, then said he'd show us our sleeping quarters. He led us through the camp again, to the western edge, and stopped outside another big tent.

'The two boys,' he said, pointing at the opening. Homer and Lee hesitated, and looked at us. Homer raised his eyebrows, rolled his eyes and disappeared into the tent. Lee, his normal impassive self, followed. Captain Killen was already walking away and we three quickly caught up with him. We threaded our way along a row of tents, stepping across fly-ropes. Beyond that row was a brush fence, a rough bush job, about a metre high, and beyond the fence more tents, all green coloured.

The captain stopped and called out 'Mrs Hauff!' It sounded like a cough, the way he said it. From the front tent Mrs Hauff emerged. She was a big woman, about fifty, and heavily made up. She wore a black sweater and blue jeans. She looked at us a bit like a shop assistant looks when you're trying to exchange a top you don't like.

'So you're the girls I've got to find room for?' she said. 'All right, just come with me. Thank you Brian,' she said to Captain Killen, who nodded and turned on his heel. Nervously we followed Mrs Hauff. She allocated us to separate tents, me to one next to Fi, but with a sleeping bag in it already. Robyn was eighty metres away.

'Now we haven't got any girls your age,' Mrs Hauff said to us as she pointed out the tents. 'And we don't want any nonsense. I've raised three girls myself and I know what goes on. You'll pull your weight the same as everyone else. Don't waste your time expecting it any other way.'

I was too subdued by all these adults to say anything. I crawled into the tent, pushing my pack ahead of me, and unzipped it. All I wanted to do was sleep. I moved the sleeping bag that was already there, before pulling out my own one and laying it down the right-hand side. Stuffing a few clothes into a shirt to make a pillow, I lay down slowly, like a tired old lady with arthritis. For a few minutes I was too weary to think about anything. I watched the light glowing green through the sides of the tent. The day was ending, and as I lay there the light changed quickly, to a darker, dimmer shade. A shadow, large and distorted, passed across the fabric as someone went past outside. I shrank away from it, remembering the shadow that had clung to me after I'd shot the soldier. As my mind began to settle I asked myself what I was thinking, what I was feeling. Slowly I realised it was relief. I didn't care how stupid these people were, how unreasonable, how prejudiced. They were adults, they could do all the worrying and make all the decisions. I could leave it to them. I didn't have to fight with these awful choices any more. I'd just do what they told me: be a good girl, shut up, veg out.

My eyes were closed by then and I welcomed the slow drift into sleep.

I was woken by someone bumping around in the tent beside me. I opened my eyes abruptly, but unwillingly. It was too dark to see anything except for occasional glimpses of a figure struggling with the bits and pieces scattered around the tent: the boots, the toilet bags, my pack.

'Sorry,' I said, reaching out sleepily to move my jeans.

The girl didn't look around, just said, 'You'll have to be a lot neater than this if you want to stay in this tent.'

'Sorry,' I said again. She sounded older than me, and irritated, but it must have been a drag for her to find a stranger suddenly sharing the little tent.

I lay there watching, as my eyes adjusted to the light. She was arranging everything in neat lines. She pulled off her jeans, folded them, and placed them so they were square to the base of the sleeping bag. 'Jeez,' I thought, 'I'll have to lift my game.' All these weeks without Mum had left me pretty slack about stuff like that.

I slept again and woke at daylight. It was shivery cold outside but I got up anyway and dressed quickly, hoping to trap as much heat in my clothes as possible.

As I dressed I kept glancing at the girl in the other sleeping bag. In the dim dawn light it was hard to pick out the details of her face. She had red hair, which immediately reminded me of Corrie, but they didn't have any other features in common. This girl looked about twenty-five and had a small, thin mouth, with her lips pressed together even in sleep. She had mascara on, or the remains of mascara – it could have been just the dark circles of tiredness, but I didn't think so. The idea of make-up still seemed amazing to me. First Mrs Hauff, now my tent-mate. It had been a long time since I'd seen anyone with it, or even thought of it. This place was a beauty parlour.

I left her to her sleep and hopped outside to a cold damp log, to finish putting on my boots. It was always such a struggle to get them on but once they were on, they were comfortable. The morning wrestle was worth it. I did them up and went for a walk around the campsite, past the brush fence and along the tent lines. I could see Major Harvey's tent and as I caught further glimpses of it through the trees I saw him sitting at his desk in full uniform, head over a pile of papers, writing steadily. He didn't see me. I headed on down through the trees, where there seemed to be more light. I was curious to see what lay beyond this bush, to get another glimpse of the Holloway Valley perhaps. I went a hundred metres but although the bright light gave the impression that at any moment I would burst through into the open, that didn't happen. The trees continued, as thick as ever. After ten minutes I stopped and gazed around. Sometimes the bush seemed like an ocean, the same in every direction. Perhaps if I had a better sense of smell I could have noticed more differences. The earthy

113

smell of soil rich with moisture and growth; the musty smell of mist; the faint eucalyptus tang from the gum leaves: I knew these varied from tree to tree, from place to place, but I never seemed to have the time or patience to explore them properly. Suddenly curious, I got down on all fours and snuffled at a heap of damp leaves. I felt like a wombat, and started wondering if I might turn into one. I scuttled across the slope for a few metres, trying to imitate the rhythmic trot of a wombat on a mission. I dug my snout into another pile of brown and black wet leaves.

There was a cough behind me, unmistakably human.

It was Lee.

OK, I felt really stupid, but I'm sure people do stuff like that all the time when they're on their own. But maybe not pretending to be wombats. Maybe not sniffing at leaf litter either. OK, maybe they don't do anything like that.

We sat on a log and he put his strong lean arm around me.

'What were you looking for?' he asked, trying hard not to laugh.

'Oh, the usual. Roots, shoots and leaves. Were you looking for me?'

'No, you're a bonus. I wanted to get away for a few minutes, to think. It's good early in the morning, isn't it?'

'Mmm, if you can talk yourself into getting up.'

We watched the light getting stronger and harder as the day got drier.

'What do you make of this mob?' I asked.

'Huh! Some of them are weird! They entertained me for two hours last night, telling me what heroes

114

they are. Seems like their biggest thrill was setting fire to a truck that had broken down. They'd seen the soldiers leave it there and drive off in a ute, so the danger level was about two on a scale of nought to a hundred.'

'Did you tell them what we've done?'

'Nuh, they just wanted to talk about themselves, so I sat there and listened. Homer was the smart one; he'd gone to bed. I don't know why I didn't. Didn't have the energy, I guess.'

'The women wear make-up.'

'Yeah, I noticed.'

'I guess living on this side of the mountains, it's not the same as Wirrawee, where everything's so tightly held. It's like Major Harvey said, this is not an important area, militarily. So Harvey's Heroes probably haven't had to be too heroic.'

'"Harvey's Heroes"! It's such a sterile name.'

'I reckon.'

'What does it make us? Homer's Heroes?'

An hour later we wandered back to the camp, and found ourselves in trouble. We were greeted by my tent-mate, who came marching towards us as soon as we appeared out of the trees. She didn't look at Lee, just at me.

'Where have you been?' she asked me. 'And what are you doing with him?'

'Him? You mean Lee?'

'Look, you'd better get a few things straight. You don't go outside the boundaries without permission. You don't go into the men's camp. The only place you can mix with the men is at the campfire and in the cooking and eating area. There are jobs to be done here, and you're meant to be helping.'

'Sorry,' I said stiffly. 'Nobody told me any of that.'

I knew I was being a wimp, but I didn't have the strength to stand up to her. The fight had gone out of me. It had fled, the moment we found ourselves surrounded by adults. I'd gone back to being eight years old. It's not so surprising. For some time now we'd been running at higher revs than we were built for. At last I could turn my engine off. I just wanted to get into a hidey-hole and stay there. So I didn't mind making a few compromises to stay with these people, and I certainly didn't want to get on their bad side. I winked at Lee and followed the girl to the cooking area, where she thrust a tea towel at me. Seemed like I'd missed breakfast, and the sight of bits of food floating in the greasy grey washing-up water made me feel nauseous. But I did the drying-up without complaint, and hung the tea towels out on a line behind the tent. Then I went looking for the others.

Chapter Nine

Two days later we were at a meeting called by Major Harvey. I was sitting towards the back, separated from Fi by my tent-mate, Sharyn, and Fi's tent-mate, Davina. Robyn was two rows ahead of me and the boys were right up the front. All the males sat in the front section of the meeting area and the females at the back. Major Harvey stood on a stump, with Captain Killen at his right hand and Mrs Hauff at his left.

For those two days my only conversations with the other four had been brief and unnatural. We were made to feel that we were doing something wrong by talking to each other. Sharyn seemed to hover around me all through every day. I felt like I was a skydiver and she was my parachute. In one way I hated it, but in another way it was addictive. I was starting to depend on her for every little decision. 'Sharyn, do you think I should sleep with my head up this end of the tent?' 'Do these jeans need washing?' 'Sharyn, will I put the potatoes in the blue dish?'

She was a big girl, Sharyn, and always wore black jeans which were too tight for her. Like many of the women, she wore a lot of make-up. Although she tried to get me to put some on I couldn't bring myself to do it. It seemed too unnatural, wrong for our environment.

The only decision Homer and I made, after a quick conversation with the other three on our second evening, was that the two of us would go back the next morning to get Chris. Only an hour after we'd made the decision I happened to see Major Harvey slipping through the trees towards his tent. I thought it would be a good idea to tell him what we were going to do, so I intercepted him.

'Excuse me Major Harvey, could I see you please?'

'I was under the impression that you already were.'

'I'm sorry?'

'You're looking right at me, so I assume you're seeing me. Or perhaps it's darker here than I realised.'

I ground my teeth. His sharp eyes glanced at me, then looked away again.

'Well could I speak to you for a minute please?'

'Go ahead.'

'Well it's just that we've got one other friend, Chris, who we left back at our campsite, and so tomorrow morning Homer and I thought we'd go and get him. It shouldn't take long. We'll be back by tea time.'

There was a long silence. Suddenly it seemed like it had got much darker. I could hardly make out the Major's features any more: his eyes had become just little black sockets.

At last he said something, but it wasn't much. All he said was 'Follow me', as he turned on his heel and walked quickly away. I followed, all the way to his tent, then stood in front of his desk and waited as he seated himself and lit a candle. He didn't ask me to sit. The flickering light of the candle made shadows dance on his face. Occasionally, as he moved his head slightly, there'd be a glint from his eyes, but most of the time he didn't move at all.

Only when the candle was burning steadily did he speak.

'What was it I said to you and your friends in this very spot, just twenty-four hours ago?'

'Um, well, you said that things weren't as bad here as in Wirrawee, and, um, that you'd blown up some power stations, and all about how this was, um, a military,' I suddenly realised why the Major was so mad, 'a military operation.'

'Exactly. A military operation. And what does that mean, in practical terms?'

'Well, that we have to obey orders and stuff.'

'Exactly.' His voice strengthened. 'Do you know what's wrong with this country? Do you know why we've been invaded?'

Now he moved. His head came forward like a snake that's heard a dangerous noise. 'I'll tell you what's wrong with this country. We've become slack, we've become soft, we've lost our way. If you ask me, these people have done us a favour by invading. We can learn a lot from them. They're a disciplined organised force of well-led soldiers. You won't hear any talk of consensus from them. You won't hear any talk of "individual rights", or "personal freedom". They know what's what. If we can stiffen the spine of this country we might end up with a nation to be proud of, instead of a self-indulgent bunch of whingers.' The candle flared, and showed for a moment the dark anger in his face. 'I'll tell you what we want here. I'll tell you what people need.' He was starting to shout now. I just stood there numbly. 'They need strong leadership, leaders they can respect. They need leaders they can look up to. This country took a wrong turn years ago, and it's time to put things right again!'

Uh yeah, whatever you say, I was thinking, backing away a little.

The major sat back in his chair and picked up a file of notes. 'Now,' he said, talking in a calm reasonable voice again, 'I am prepared to consider your request. Your young friend, I assume he has adequate food and shelter?'

'Oh yes.'

'Then there is no great urgency?'

'Well, we didn't want to leave him there on his own for too long, that's all.'

'You should have thought of that before you set out. You people who just make things up as you go along have a lot to learn. You may make a written request to me for permission to go back to your camp to collect him. Include a detailed map, estimates of the time required, and the supplies and personnel you will need. That is all. You may dismiss.'

I left, feeling a little shaky. I didn't have the energy to cope with this. But the other thing, almost more disturbing, was the relief I'd felt when he turned down our plans. I knew we had to go back and get Chris, but that was the only reason I was doing it, because I knew we had to. Secretly, I had no enthusiasm for the gruelling trek, and no enthusiasm for Chris either at the moment. I felt really guilty about that, because I knew how I'd feel if I were back there on my own, and I also knew how important it was for us to hang together, the six of us. A lot depended on that.

Then, the next morning, the morning of the meeting, I'd had another ugly session with the major. Sharyn had given me a bucket of cleaning materials and told me to go clean his tent. Looking back now I can see it was a set-up, but I didn't realise that at the time. Instead I trudged off to his tent feeling resentful. I was thinking about Harvey's Heroes, and thinking that their problem was that they were trying to pretend there was no war. Underneath all the military disguises was just a group of ordinary middle-aged townspeople who were trying to live out here in the bush the way they had always lived in their nice brick-veneer houses in Risdon. They gossiped; they swapped gardening tips and talked about their children; they cleaned or cooked or pottered around doing odd jobs. One of them had asked me the day before if I played bridge. Only Major Harvey was different. He was driven by some lust that the others didn't have. I think he enjoyed his power over them but at the same time was frustrated by the fact that they weren't combat-hardened troops whom he could throw into the front line of some huge battle.

Thinking all this, I began my cleaning job in a mood of resentment, hostility. It just seemed too ridiculous to be dusting and sweeping. And I felt humiliated that I, Ellie, who blew up bridges, should be at the beck and call of this little imitation Hitler. Aggressively, I swept out the leaves that had blown in, pulled down a cobweb in the back left-hand corner of the tent, and polished the two visitors' chairs. I didn't even look at the bed; there was no way I was going to touch that.

I moved around to his side of the desk to start work there. I saw a pile of papers; the top one a manila folder with *Confidential* written on it. I didn't hesitate. With no real fascination, just a casual thought of, This should be good for a laugh, I opened it. The top page was an A4 sheet headed *Report of Power Station Attack*, and filled with small writing. I bent over so I could read it properly, but as I began the first line I became aware of a presence in the tent. I looked up quickly. There was the major, standing in the doorway, head tilted to the right, fierce dark eyes staring at me.

There was nothing I could do of course. I was completely in the wrong, or at least that's what I thought at the time. And I knew already that he had no sense of humour, so it was no good trying to make a joke of it.

'Sorry,' I said apologetically. 'Just looking.'

He folded his arms but said nothing. That was an annoying habit he had. I knew my face was red but there was nothing I could do about that. Finally I shrugged and turned back to the table, and began polishing it. That's when he spoke.

'It seems that you've remembered nothing from our conversation last night.'

I didn't answer, just kept scrubbing.

'You have a lot to learn about discipline, young lady.'

Scrub scrub.

'Forget the cleaning. Go back to Mrs Hauff. I don't want you in this tent again.'

My skin was burning. I picked up my gear and walked towards him. There was a problem when I got there though; Major Harvey was blocking the doorway and didn't look like he was going to move. And there was no way known that I was going to shove past him. So I stood and waited. After a minute he turned to one side and stood there, still with arms folded. That was obviously the only concession he was going to make, so I squeezed through the gap and out into the fresh air, without looking at him again.

It was a relief to get back to Sharyn. She could be rough and bossy and bad-tempered, but I wasn't scared of her. She wasn't sinister.

I didn't have time during the afternoon to write the application to go and retrieve Chris, and when I told Homer he said to leave it till the next day, when Harvey might have calmed down. So I went to the meeting instead.

Major Harvey's meeting wasn't much like our meetings back in Hell. It consisted of Major Harvey making a long speech. The first part was about the threat to our country and the need for courage.

'These are terrible times,' he said. 'Like many brave people before us, we find ourselves having to defend our shores, to protect what is rightfully ours, to safeguard our women and children.'

When he said that I felt my face going red again, from the chin up, like it only does when I'm really angry. It was the last straw. Obviously all the brave people he had in mind were male. I swallowed, then breathed out hard through my nose. Maybe it was another lesson in discipline for me. Major Harvey added a few words about patriotism, then went back into history a little.

'Men like Winston Churchill changed the course of history. Of course I would not put myself in the same class as Winston Churchill. But I will do my best to lead you. You can be sure I will not let you down.'

He moved on to the second part of his speech, about military action. This was more the stuff I wanted to hear. I'd had enough housework.

'We will shortly be striking another blow against the enemy,' he announced. 'I will be speaking to some of you later about the details. Captain Killen and I have identified a number of important strategic targets. As you know, we are very low on numbers and weapons and we are up against an enemy who is highly trained and well equipped. So we must proceed with the greatest care. Despite our manifold disadvantages, we have done a lot of damage to enemy forces and made a contribution that is well out of proportion to the size of our gallant little band of Harvey's Heroes. We can indeed be proud of ourselves. As you know, two power stations and a number of vehicles have already fallen victim to our forces.'

Most of this, and a lot more of the same stuff, twenty minutes more in fact, was like the comments Major Harvey had made when we first arrived. It was hard for me to concentrate. I was getting hot flushes of déjà vu that went even further back than our interview with the major, so I concentrated on trying to identify them. It took me five minutes, but at last I worked it out: I felt like I was back in a school assembly.

Major Harvey moved on to the third and last part of his speech.

'Once again I find myself paying tribute to Mrs Hauff and her band of helpers. The campsite continues to be maintained in immaculate condition and meals are served on time and beautifully presented. As Napoleon said, "An army marches on its stomach", and the present good morale of Harvey's Heroes is in no small measure due to Mrs Hauff's girls.'

Mrs Hauff's expression didn't change but I felt as though a wave of approval was slowly rippling through her large body. I continued to prickle. I hadn't seen any males doing housework. For two days I'd done little else, scrubbing pots and pans, washing sheets – no joke in cold water – and darning socks. The guys were occupied doing guy things – digging drains, collecting firewood, and making a small wooden cabin which was meant for Major Harvey's headquarters. The thing that puzzled me most was that everyone seemed so happy with these arrangements. Everyone except us five, anyway, and I wasn't at all sure about Homer. If we hadn't constantly bullied him back in Hell, he'd have had his slippers on every night and sat in front of the fire waiting to be served.

'Finally,' said Major Harvey, 'we welcome our five new recruits. It's a pleasure to have some young people join us, and I'm sure they will soon get used to the discipline of a military operation. As I have said on a number of occasions to the longer established members of Harvey's Heroes, "When told to jump, your only question should be 'How high?'"'

He beamed straight at me as he said this, as though it was a line he'd thought of himself. He seemed to be in a better mood, so I smiled weakly back.

The meeting broke up and I walked off with a lady of about thirty, a plain-looking brown-haired woman, who always seemed tired and exasperated, no matter what she was doing. Her name was Olive. Sharyn watched us go, but didn't try to follow. I think she thought I was safe with Olive, but I decided to take a risk and say something irreverent.

'I was trying to think what that meeting reminded me of,' I said. 'And I worked it out. It was like being back in a school assembly.'

She laughed, then looked around guiltily.

'Do you know what Major Harvey did before the invasion?' she asked. 'Is that why you said that?'

'No. Isn't he a soldier?'

She laughed again. 'You must be joking. He was the Deputy at Risdon High School.'

'Oh!' I felt cheated. All this time I'd thought he was an Army superstar.

'So where'd he get his military knowledge?' I asked.

'What military knowledge? This outfit's as military as a bowling club. Harvey was in the Army Reserve for eighteen months. That's about it.'

'But all that talk about blowing up power stations and enemy vehicles?'

'Talk, yeah, there's a lot of it going around.'

'So is that all it is? Talk?'

She shrugged. 'Well, they blew up two power stations, sure. One was the power grid for South Risdon and the other was the telephone exchange for Duckling Flat. There wouldn't have been an enemy soldier within ten kilometres at the time. They're neither of them nuclear reactors. One was the size of an outdoor dunny, and the other wasn't much bigger.'

'And the vehicles? What about the vehicles?'

'The first one was a troop carrier that had broken down and been abandoned. They set fire to it. Gold medals all round. Their other vehicle attacks have

126

been the same. They just look for disabled trucks, and cars that have been deserted, then they set fire to them.'

'I can't believe it.' I really was shocked, and angry. All the risks we'd taken, all the damage we'd done, all the terrible things we'd been through, and all that time these fat little men, and the women in their lipstick and make-up, had sat around telling each other how good they were and getting fatter still on their self-congratulations. And the way Major Harvey spoke to me, as though I were a bit of dog-dropping on a new carpet. I'd done ten times more than he had! How dare they?

I went off to find Robyn and Fi and tell them but they were with their minders. Then Sharyn saw me and dragged me into the cooking area to peel potatoes. Peeling potatoes when you're angry is not a good idea. As I started my third spud I cut deep into my left thumb and bled heaps, which made me angrier still. Olive came and bandaged me: she'd told me that she was a nurse and she bandaged me as if she was. It was a neat job.

Before I could talk to any of the others there was a sudden change in the atmosphere of the camp. Groups of men came past the washing-up area where I was teaching Sharyn to make a rack for draining dishes. Without a word she put down the pole she was holding and followed the men. I dropped my bits of wood and tagged along behind. No one was saying anything but there was an air of excitement, everyone leaning forward as they walked, as though that would get them there faster. I noticed that quite a few of the men were armed, carrying automatic rifles. They had much better weapons than we did.

We assembled again in the area where we'd had our meeting earlier. Captain Killen got on the stump this time, to address us. I wondered what he'd been before the invasion: an accountant? There was no sign of Major Harvey.

'Operation Phantom is ready to begin,' he announced in his thin dry voice. I could hardly hear him, though I was only twenty-five metres away. 'Although just a small number of men will be required for active service, others who wish to watch the operation may do so from a vantage point on the firebreak above the Cunnamulla road.'

Spectators!

'How much will we have to pay for our tickets?' I wanted to ask. But I still had enough smarts to stay silent. I looked at Homer, trying to catch his eye, but he was gazing expressionlessly at Captain Killen, and refused to look around.

'Operation Phantom will hit the enemy at his soft underbelly,' Captain Killen continued. 'We will wallop him where it hurts most. This will be the biggest operation ever undertaken by Harvey's Heroes, with the most important military target yet attacked. The following men have been selected to take part: Olsen, Allison, Babbage...'

There were a dozen names altogether. Apparently that was Captain Killen's definition of a small group. Neither Homer nor Lee was among them, I was glad to hear. And there was no chance of Robyn or Fi or me being chosen. Girls didn't rate with Harvey's Heroes, except for cooking and cleaning. But I didn't hesitate when Sharyn asked me if I wanted to go and watch. It seemed quite comical to me, but Sharyn and the others weren't laughing: there was a serious and silent air through the camp as people made their preparations. Of course it was serious, I reminded myself angrily – any contact with the enemy was serious – but I just wished they'd stop acting like characters in an American war movie. Everything seemed so different to the way we'd done things. Our violent fights with the enemy were starting to seem like bad and impossible dreams; so much so that I was having trouble believing they had happened at all.

There seemed to be no reason for spectators, except to make Captain Killen and the other heroes feel big and important. But that didn't bother me. I figured I could go and watch without having to accept these guys as legends. So I joined the gang, hoping that Major Harvey wouldn't notice me there and stop me from going. There were about fifteen of us, including Fi and Robyn and Homer and Lee, but of course before we could leave we had to be given the Big Talking To by Captain Killen.

'Now,' he said, looking at us severely, as though we were going on a school excursion to a museum full of fine porcelain. 'I want it clearly understood that we are on active service. Those of you allowed to accompany us must understand that you are to obey orders instantly. You must stay quiet, not get in the way, and keep all conversation to a minimum. Remain under cover at all times. And you kids,' meaning us, I realised with an angry flush, 'you kids in particular, I don't want to hear a word out of you. Stay out of the way, and behave yourselves.'

I don't know what he expected, that we'd start playing hide and seek, or singing Girl Guide hiking songs. I didn't dare look at Homer this time. He must have been seconds away from meltdown.

I was waiting for Major Harvey to appear but then the others started moving off, and I had to hurry to catch them. Only then did I realise that the Major wasn't coming. I was so angry I started grinding my teeth. I didn't trust myself to speak. Some leader! I despised him. All he could do was talk.

The dozen guerillas were led by Captain Killen; they soon branched off and went down a dry creek bed that took them straight downhill.

Our leader was a serious looking older man with glasses. His name was Terry. He didn't say a word, but he seemed to know his way around. He took us along a ridge through the trees. I hoped he knew the way well because it would be dark by the time we got back. I walked with Fi and her minder, Davina. Olive was just ahead of us, and Robyn at the rear with her tent-mate. Sharyn hadn't come. Physical exertion wasn't her scene. Homer and Lee were up the front, behind Terry.

We walked for about an hour. I enjoyed it, once I got over my anger. I like the bush and I like being fit, and I was sick of hanging round the camp all day, with Sharyn as my main buddy. I had no sense of danger, so my mood wasn't spoilt by fear. Captain Killen had told us we'd be a long way from the action and after my conversation with Olive I was sure there'd be a minimum of contact with the enemy.

Gradually the bush thinned out and we started to get glimpses of the valley. Far below I saw yellow pieces of a dirt road, like one of those tracks for battery-operated racecars when you break it up to put back in the box. Soon we could see quite long stretches of road, as the valley spread out into wider and flatter country. Now we had to avoid open ground and hug the line of trees for cover. I spent most of the time walking with my head tipped back. It was nice to see lots of clear sky again. There'd been a bit of conversation as we walked through the thicker scrub, but out here people were quieter, so I didn't have to listen to anyone any more. That was fine by me.

The firebreak was a long ugly stripe down through the bush: a bulldozed trail of clay and weeds and some regrowth, beside an old post-and-rail fence. Terry made us cross the firebreak in pairs, running with heads down, which was sensible. Then, with everyone over the other side, we climbed the hill. The sun was starting to drop; the air was getting colder quickly and the shadows of the trees were so long that they were lost in the bush on the other side of the trail. But the hard exercise kept us warm. The hill was steep and by the time we got to the top we were all red-faced and panting. It was worth it though. We found ourselves looking at one of the great views. There was some good land around Wirrawee, but these river flats were as fertile as you get in our part of the world. They picked up more rainfall than we did – because of the shape of the mountains or something – and a lot of people irrigated as well. You could see a long row of pipes on one place, looking like science fiction machinery. Further across was an orchard with white screening over the trees, a kind of outdoor sculpture. Even at this time of year a lot of the nearer paddocks were green, though they probably hadn't been irrigated since the invasion. It was only in the distance that the great dry yellow began. The setting sun was like a great watchful creature, guarding its kingdom. The land looked so tranquil, so

131

old, so calm and peaceful, as if these pathetic squabbles by humans for the right to live on its surface were of no interest. It reminded me of a line from one of Chris's poems: 'The ocean ignores the sailor, the desert ignores me.'

I was starting to worry about Chris now, and to feel guilty. The trip back to Hell was going to be such a grind. I made a resolution that I'd go and see Major Harvey early the next day and make him see how important it was we go back. I knew if it were Fi back in Hell, instead of Chris, I'd have gone back two days ago. Maybe I should get Fi to go and see the major in the morning.

Now, however, it was Homer who found his way over to me and drew me to the other side of the hill. Without a word, he pointed down to the road. And there was Captain Killen's target. It was a juicy one too, if easy. Slewed across the road with its gun barrel pointing into the bush was a large green tank.

'Unbelievable,' I muttered.

Even from our height you could see that the tank had met with some sort of disaster. It was tipped to one side and I thought I could see gouges in the road where it had gone out of control. The top was open and there was no sign of life around it.

'Just like their troop carrier,' I said.

'What do you mean?' Homer asked, only half listening. He was gazing down at the tank, probably with jealousy, I thought.

'Well, the first enemy vehicle Harvey's Heroes wiped out was a troop carrier, abandoned the same as this. And all the others since then, too.'

He started paying more attention then. 'How do you mean?' We were interrupted by a soft call from Robyn.

'There they are.'

We looked down. The guerillas were coming along the road about a k from the tank, walking in single file under the shadows of the trees, but not taking any great precautions. We recognised Captain Killen leading the way.

'They're pretty confident,' I said.

'I guess they've sussed it out,' Robyn said.

'I hope so,' Homer said. 'So what was that you said about the troop carrier?'

'Well, Olive told me. These guys are just pussies. They don't attack any target unless it's totally safe. They go for vehicles that have broken down or run off the road, like this one. They've knocked out a whole series of trucks like that.'

We were talking in whispers, though there was no need. Homer was getting a strange, worried look on his face.

'You mean they do this regularly?'

'I don't know how often. But Olive gave me the impression that all their attacks are the same.'

Homer started getting quite agitated. 'But you mean they… Do they think the enemy's going to let them keep walking up to vehicles and wiping them out?' He twisted round and stared down at Harvey's Heroes, anxiously, angrily. We could just see some of them through a canopy of trees as they started round the curve in the road.

'Do you think…?' I started asking.

'I think they're mad. If they've done this before…A tank's worth millions.' He led us forward a few metres so that we were quite exposed ourselves, but more directly above the tank. 'Use your eyes,' he muttered. 'Watch for anything.'

Terry was away to my left in thicker scrub, where he was talking to Olive. Now he called to us in an urgent whisper. 'Come in under the trees.'

I edged a few steps to the left but Homer and Robyn stayed where they were. Lee and Fi had been watching the tank from behind a patch of rock on the other side of the firebreak, but now they turned towards us.

'What's wrong?' Lee called.

'There!' Robyn said, at exactly the same moment.

A sharp ray from the setting sun had suddenly flashed on something in a tree way down near the road. It was a gun barrel. And all at once I saw everything. I was astonished that I hadn't seen it before. Maybe my eyes had needed all this time to get used to the light. Or maybe it was like one of those ambiguous pictures, where you're staring at it for ages and all you can see is the young woman's body and then your vision adjusts and all you see is the old woman's face.

Now, wherever I looked, I saw soldiers. They were hidden behind trees and among rocks, spread in a half moon above the road, waiting for Captain Killen and his men.

It was an ambush, a trap for fools.

'Time spent in reconnaissance is seldom wasted.'

Robyn was a second ahead of everyone else.

'COOOOOOOO-EEEEEEEEEEEEEEEE!' She was on her feet, hands to her mouth, and her call rolled around the hills like the cry of a giant bird. The effect was dramatic. It reminded me of times at home when I'd shaken a tree to send the bronzewings rattling out and beating away into the distance. But now there wasn't just movement from one tree. There was sudden scrambling movement everywhere. Soldiers started standing and I saw guns turning towards us. They obviously hadn't known they had anyone behind them. Terry came running out from the scrub like a demented sheep. He had no idea what was going on. He must have thought Robyn had gone mad. Or else that we were the stupid irresponsible kids that Captain Killen had thought. But I hardly noticed him or the soldiers. My eyes were on the guerillas. When they heard Robyn's call they were already around the bend and must have just come into the view of the soldiers. With every shred of my body I was begging them 'Run! Run! For God's sake, run.' But they seemed transfixed. They were staring up at us. I could see Captain Killen's face and could imagine the expression on it. He was probably already composing the speech that he would make back at camp. But that was a speech no one would ever hear. Not one of Harvey's Heroes had even unslung his rifle. They still hadn't seen the ambush. The three of us started screaming at them, pointing. A couple of them started to look around and one actually lifted his rifle. Then the shooting started. The men began to dance like mad puppets, just for a moment, turning in different directions, taking a few steps, then jerking and shaking as the bullets hit them. I didn't see any of them fall, because by then some of the soldiers had started firing in our direction. We had about a second, because they were still moving themselves. They hadn't got themselves into good positions, and they didn't have the range or the aim worked out.

We three went to our right, towards Lee and Fi. The distance from our positions to the edge of the firebreak was probably a bit greater than if we'd gone to the left, but our instincts attracted us to our friends. Also, the camp was to the right, and to have the firebreak between us and the camp was not a comfortable thought. I covered the last couple of metres in a dive, as bullets chopped branches from trees above me with savage ferocity. I think one bullet must have ricocheted from a rock, because it whined past me with a sound like a distant jet. I landed in gravel and some scratchy kind of dark green plant, crawled a few metres, then was up and running, just taking a moment to glance around at the others and check that they were all right. Fi was on my heels; she gasped 'They're OK', so I kept going.

We ran through the bush for twenty minutes. I could hear people blundering along on my left and my right, and Fi panting hard behind me. Then I heard Robyn's voice to my left calling dangerously loudly. 'Stop, everybody!' By then I needed to stop. I pulled up, wheezing, and grabbed Fi to steady myself. Robyn came running heavily up the hill towards us.

'Are you OK?' she asked.

'Yes,' I said, thinking, 'I hope I don't look as bad as you.' She had blood on the side of her head and more coming out of her nose. Fi went to touch her face but Robyn pushed her off.

'It's nothing,' she said. 'I hit my head on a branch.'

It was already quite dark. There was a snapping of undergrowth and rattling of gravel as someone came up the hill. I turned anxiously, trying to see through the gloom. It was Homer. 'Are you OK?' we all said simultaneously. He just nodded.

'Where's Lee?' I asked.

'Isn't he with you?' Fi asked Homer.

'No, he was with you.'

'No,' Fi said, 'he jumped straight down to where you were, just as you got into the trees.'

'I didn't see him,' Homer said.

There was a sudden silence.

'We can't yell out,' Homer said. 'Too dangerous.'

I turned on Fi, looking for someone to blame.

'You told me everyone was OK,' I said furiously.

'Well,' she snapped back, 'they were! He was. He was in the treeline and running and he hadn't been shot. How much more OK can you be? I wasn't going to stay and give him a medical.'

Fi was shaking, and I felt bad for having attacked her. But there wasn't time for apologies.

'Let's think this through,' Homer said. 'We've got to get back to the camp and warn them. And we've got to find Lee. If he's OK he'll be heading back to the camp. If he's not OK, well, we've got problems.'

'The others can warn the people at the camp,' I said. 'Terry and them.'

'But they might be on the other side of the fire-break,' Homer said. 'They might be trapped.'

'They might be dead,' Robyn said.

'We have to split up,' I said.

'Agreed.'

'I'll go looking for Lee,' I said.

'I'll come with you,' Homer said.

'OK,' Robyn said, 'we'll go to the camp. Then we'll come back and find you guys.'

'That's not going to work,' I said. 'We'll never find each other in the dark. Homer and I'll go back to the firebreak. If there's no sign of Lee there, and no trail we can follow, we won't be able to do a lot ourselves till dawn. If we can't find him we might as well go back to the camp too.'

137

And that's what we decided. We all thought we could find the camp again, even if it meant going right up to the base of the cliffs and looking for the ridge.

Homer and I hurried back the way we'd come. We weren't too worried about making some noise, because we weren't expecting to be chased through the bush now that it was nearly dark. But we had to try to calculate when we were getting close to the firebreak. As it turned out we overestimated and crawled along at the speed of an eroding rock for about half an hour.

The firebreak was like a pale highway in the moonlight, compared with the dark of the surrounding bush. We lay behind a bush for twenty minutes looking at it. Finally Homer whispered: 'Looks OK.'

'I'll go. You stay here.'

Before he could object I stood and started creeping down the side of the scar. Funny how with a group of people Homer nearly always took the lead, and with Homer I took the lead. I went almost the whole way down to the road. There was nothing worth looking at. No bodies, no soldiers, no guns. No tank either. Boy, had Harvey's Heroes been stupid to fall for that one. But, I had to remind myself, I'd fallen for it too. I'd thought we were going to see a free bonfire; instead I'd seen a free shooting gallery, a sickening useless massacre.

I edged along to the right, till I was nearly at the corner. I could see dark patches on the road and stared at them with a kind of gruesome fascination, not sure if they were patches of blood or shadows from the trees. Had everyone been killed? I started wondering what would have happened to survivors, and that began a chain of thoughts that sent me scrambling back up the hill to find Homer.

'Listen,' I panted, as I came round behind his bush.

'Supposing they weren't all killed? Suppose some were only wounded?'

'What? What are you talking about?'

'Well, what's the first question they'd ask anyone they caught?'

'What? Oh. Yes, I see what you mean. "Where's your camp?"'

'And if they had to torture them to find out...'

'They'd do it. Let's go.' He stood quickly, then paused again. 'What about Lee?'

'What about Robyn and Fi? If they've got Lee,' I said, and the skin across my forehead prickled as I said it, 'then they've got him. If he's hurt and lying in the bush we could search all night and not find him. If he's OK he would have headed back to the camp too. The three of them could be there and the place could be getting attacked right now, while we sit here having a talk about it.'

We were on our way as I finished that sentence. Yet another blundering, panicking run through the bush, getting scratched and hit. At one stage we had a good clear run for some minutes, with no blackberries or rabbit holes or fallen logs, then I suddenly slid on a mossy rock and fell heavily, jarring my knee. I nearly brought Homer down with me.

'Are you OK?' he asked.

'Why'd I know you were going to say that?'

'Well are you?'

'I don't know.' Then, trying for that mental toughness Homer talked about sometimes, I said, 'Yes, I am. Just give me a sec.'

I took about three, then said 'OK, help me up.' I stood but I was a bit wobbly. It wasn't so much the knee, just that I'd given myself a shock when I fell.

'Take it easy,' Homer said.

'How can I? Let's go.'

We ran and limped for twenty paces, then stopped again, abruptly. This time it was the sound of gunfire that brought us to a halt. It was some distance away, but there was the frightening yammering of machine guns, and in the background the dull thuds of shotguns. Homer and I stared at each other wildly. I wondered if he and I and Chris would end up living together in Hell for the rest of our lives. It seemed horrible, gruesome. What if none of us got back and Chris was left there on his own forever? Neither of us seemed able to think of anything to say. I could see Homer's mouth trembling as he tried to come up with some brilliant suggestion. I opened my own mouth, not sure what would come out.

'Let's go to the tree?'

'The tree? What tree?'

'The tree we came down the cliff on, from Hell. Our ladder.'

'Can you find it?'

'Yes, if we just go up to the cliffs and work our way around. That's where they'll go, surely.'

'OK.'

We knew there was nothing we could do at the campsite now that the soldiers were there. We had no weapons. Bare hands don't stop bullets.

We hurried on. I was still leading, travelling fairly well. I figured if I kept the knee hot it mightn't be too bad, and although it gave me the occasional sharp sudden pain, it was bearable. We kept going uphill, gaining ground all the time, to pass well above the campsite and strike the cliffs. There were still occasional bursts of gunfire, punctuated, now that we

140

were closer to the camp, by screams and hoarse shouts. I had no trouble keeping my knee hot; I was hot all over and sweating frantically. We were back in dense trees and running soon became impossible, but I ploughed on. The combination of dark, tiredness, panic, and thick bush made every metre a misery. I was hitting things, crying out in pain and frustration, banging my knee again and again. I got to a point where I came to another fallen tree and couldn't get over it – I had no energy left – and I just stood there making stupid little crying noises like a three-year-old.

'Come on,' Homer said, stumbling up behind me and giving me a prod in the back, not very sympathetically. I think he was too tired himself to be sympathetic.

I came on and climbed over the log, which wasn't even a big one, and kept going.

It was another half-hour before we hit the cliffs. I'd got to the point where I was convinced that we'd missed them, even though that was geographically impossible. But I hadn't realised how slowly we'd been travelling. I greeted the cliff like an old friend, leaning against it for a moment, feeling the cool stone on my cheek. Then I slowly, wearily, stood again, like an old lady, and pushed on. It was hard going still, as in a lot of places the trees grew right to the face of the cliff. But at least we knew we were on track for a definite target; the knowledge gave us some sense of purpose, even though there mightn't be anyone at the end of the journey.

At about 1 am we came to the old white tree, gleaming like a ghost in the thin moonlight. There was no one there. I sat on one side of it, leaning against it; Homer sat on the other side. We didn't say a word, just waited.

Chapter Ten

There was a hint of light in the eastern sky. Or was it my imagination? I'd looked for dawn so many times already, but with no satisfaction. Homer was asleep on my left, mouth open, snoring slightly. My eyes felt heavy and dull; as though they would look glazed and opaque to anyone staring into them. Luckily no one was staring into them. I looked around listlessly. A faint breeze tickled the leaves of the trees, made them move and whisper and play around. In the bush ahead of me a branch cracked and fell. It sounded surprisingly loud, though I didn't hear it hit the ground. A large bird, a white owl I think, flapped across the top of the cliff.

Then came the unmistakable sound of human footsteps. Only a cow sounds as heavy and purposeful as a human, and there wouldn't be cows in this dense bush. I felt sick with fear and hope. I grabbed Homer by the shoulder. As he stirred into life, I leant over further and clamped my hand on his mouth. He gurgled a bit, then, as I could tell by the sudden tenseness of his body, he woke.

We both sat there waiting, paralysed. We couldn't

move without making a lot of noise. And the footsteps kept coming. They were accelerating. I stood, crouching, to be ready. I could see a figure weaving through the trees. It was Fi. I held out my arms but she didn't even look at me. 'They're following me,' she said.

There was a horrible sick pause, then Homer asked quickly, 'How many?'

'I don't know. It might only be one. I'm sorry.'

We turned our ears back to the bush and immediately heard the footsteps, lighter than Fi's, less certain, less purposeful.

'I'm sorry,' said Fi again. 'I've been trying for ages.'

Her voice sounded thick and dead, with no emotion. She was all in. I squeezed her arm, quickly. Homer had picked up a hunk of wood. I wished now that he had his sawn-off shotgun. I looked around for a weapon. There weren't a lot of choices. I got a rock, about the size of a baseball, and gave it to Fi, but I don't think she registered what it was for. She just held it loosely, without lifting her arm. I got myself a rock too. None of us was sure what to do; we were just acting instinctively, but instinctively we looked for weapons. We could have scattered and run, but with the cliff behind us and thick bush in front, there weren't many options. And one look at Fi made it clear we'd have to stand and fight. She was leaning against the tree, the one we would be using as our ladder back up to Hell. Fi's head was down, but she kept holding the rock. As I glanced at her she suddenly retched and vomited. The sound attracted her pursuer: I heard the footsteps accelerate a little. Whoever it was came straight at us now, with more confidence. I looked for Homer but he had vanished, though I could guess which tree he was behind. I ducked behind another one. I saw the shadowy figure of a soldier slipping between the trees, just ten metres from me. Only one soldier; I couldn't see or hear any others. He had seen Fi and was going straight for her. His rifle was over his shoulder still. It must have been obvious that Fi wasn't going to give him a fight. And I think he had more on his mind than just capturing her. He moved in quickly, like a fox on a lambing ewe. He wasn't a big man; a boy really, probably about our age, and with Chris's slim build. He was hatless and dressed in light uniform, summer gear rather than autumn or winter. He didn't seem to have anything with him but his rifle. As he went eagerly towards Fi, I came out from my tree and followed him. I felt full of wild terror and still didn't know what I was going to do; couldn't believe what I was going to do. I was gripping my rock but I noticed that Fi's had fallen to the ground. The man was only ten steps from Fi. I was right behind him, but I couldn't bring myself to act. It was as though I was waiting for something to trigger me off, something to force me to do more than follow him helplessly.

Then he provided the trigger himself. He must have heard me because he suddenly started swinging round, raising his hand as he did so. I saw his eyes starting to widen with terror, and I felt my eyes reflect his. I raised my arm and, as though in a dream, began to bring it down on his head. I had a strange quick memory flash: a horror story I'd been told, about how a murder victim retains the image of his murderer on his retina. To look into a corpse's eyes was like looking at a photo of its killer. I was bringing my arm down, thinking about that, then realised I wasn't hitting with enough force and at the last moment struck harder.

The soldier got his arm up enough to deflect and soften the blow, but the rock still hit him pretty hard on the side of the head. My arm jarred badly, but luckily I didn't drop the rock. The man took a swing at me and I ducked, but got a stinging smack on the side of the head, which made me go a bit numb. I saw his dark sweaty face. His eyes looked half closed and I wasn't sure why, but I thought maybe I'd hurt him more than I'd realised. I poked at his face with the hand holding the rock, but he pushed my hand away. Then there was a rush of feet behind him. For the second or so that we'd been fighting I'd completely forgotten about Homer, amazingly. The man swung around fast and swerved his head away. Homer was taking an almighty swing at him with his branch but missed his head and got him on the shoulder instead. The man staggered at the knees and lost his balance. At that moment I lifted the rock with both hands and brought it down on his head, hard. There was a terrible dull thud, like hitting a tree with the back of an axe. The man's eyes rolled up in his head, and with a funny little snoring noise he dropped to the ground as though praying: kneeling, with his head bowed. Then he fell to the ground, sideways, and lay there.

I gazed at him, horrified, for a moment, before throwing the rock away as though it were contaminated. I ran to Fi and grabbed her by the shoulders. I don't know what I wanted from her, but I didn't get it. She just stared into my eyes like she couldn't remember who I was. Then I realised the man could wake up again at any moment. I shook my head hard, to try to get some sense back into it, and went back to him. Homer had his back turned and his face pressed into a tree, having his own private meeting with the devil. I bent over the soldier, not knowing whether to hope he was dead or hope he was alive. He was alive, breathing very slowly, with deep shuddering groans. There was a long pause between each breath. He sounded terrible. I realised then that it would have been better for us if he was dead, though I was shocked at myself for thinking that. I pulled his rifle off him and threw it a few metres away.

Almost immediately I heard another lot of footsteps coming through the trees, quite brisk and sure. I slid across the ground and grabbed the rifle again, trying to cock it, but it was an automatic one, too complicated to work out. I held it up desperately, as though pointing it at someone would magically protect me. But it was Robyn who was walking towards me, looking as calm as ever – until she saw the weapon.

'Ellie! Don't shoot me!'

I lowered it.

'Where'd you get that thing?'

'Over there,' I said, pointing, getting the shakes a bit, but putting the rifle down carefully. Robyn seemed so controlled, and I felt like I was on the brink of completely losing control.

Robyn lost her smile suddenly; she ran to the soldier and knelt beside him.

'What happened. Did you shoot him?'

'Hit him. With a rock. And a branch.'

'God, I think he's pretty bad.'

'He has to die, Robyn,' I said, trying to keep my voice steady. 'If he doesn't, he'll get his friends and they'll come looking for us. And the first thing they'll do is to climb that tree. They could track us right home, into Hell.'

She didn't answer, but left the soldier and went to Fi.

'Are you all right?' she asked.

Fi stared at her too for a moment, as she had at me. Then she nodded. I was relieved that she was at least functioning that much again.

'Has anyone seen Lee?'

'No,' Fi said.

I explained how Homer and I had gone back to the firebreak but hadn't spent time searching the bush for him.

'I'm rapt to find you,' Robyn said. 'It was just a sudden brainwave to come here. If you hadn't been here... I don't know what I would have done. I didn't have any other ideas.' She paused for a few seconds, as if thinking of something. Then she took charge.

'Come on guys,' she said. 'You can have your nervous breakdowns later. Like I'm going to have mine, for calling out at the men on the road. But you can't have them now. I'm not being funny about this. We simply have to keep ourselves together, if we're going to make it.'

'What happened back at the camp?' I asked.

As Robyn was talking we'd gradually moved in together, into a huddle around the unconscious young soldier, who was still lying on the ground, breathing his slow breaths.

'It was a disaster,' she said. 'Fi and I just didn't get there in time. We'd been lost for nearly an hour. Then we saw them at last, through the trees. We were so close to it. We could actually see the tents. I still can't believe how it happened. Then this firing suddenly started all around us. It was so loud, like standing in the middle of a whole lot of construction workers

147

with jackhammers. A soldier stood up right in front of us and started firing. We could have taken one step forward and touched him. It's a miracle he didn't hear us, hey Fi?' Fi just nodded, dumbly. Robyn was trying to humour her into talking again but I think she was too physically exhausted, if nothing else.

'Well,' Robyn went on, staring at her boots, 'what can I say? It was horrible, disgusting. Some of the bullets and shells they used were like fireworks; they glowed, they were so bright. And then they chucked in a flare or something. The people... they were running in different directions. They didn't know which way to go. It was a massacre. I was backing out fast so I didn't see much. At least it was so noisy that they couldn't hear me. Not just the gunfire, but the screams. I don't know how many people I've seen killed today.' She blinked furiously. Her face seemed to crumble for a moment. Her lips twisted and she put her knuckle to her mouth, struggling to keep control, until gradually she was able to speak again. But all she said was, 'Anyway, I tried to find Fi, and there was no sign of her.' She looked at Fi, inviting her to take over. I think she wanted the spotlight off her for a few minutes.

'I just ran,' Fi whispered. 'I'm sorry Robyn. I lost my head and ran. After a while I realised someone was following me. I hoped it was you but it didn't sound like you. I called out but there was no answer. They kept coming, so I kept running. I tried to lead them away from here and then lose them, but I couldn't. After a while I crawled under some blackberries and hid. I waited for hours, until finally I thought they must have gone. I hadn't heard them go but I thought no one could have just sat there waiting in the darkness for all that time. So I came crawling out again. And as soon as I did someone came running at me. I screamed and ran off. I just kept running around the bush. After a while I got so tired. Then I hit the cliffs again. I thought I'd better come here. I hoped there might be someone here. But I'm sorry. I made it so dangerous for you, doing that. I shouldn't have done that.'

We all made soothing noises: 'Of course you should', 'You did the right thing', 'That's exactly what I would have done', but I don't know if it had much effect.

In the middle of all my own mess of emotions I shuddered as I thought of the terrifying night Fi had spent, trying to shake off those footsteps in the dark bush, heading at last for the tree, but not knowing if she would find only the silence of the night there, knowing only that she was too tired to go any further, knowing that when she reached the tree she might have to turn and face her death. This had been a terrible night for all of us, but perhaps for Fi most of all.

That was assuming Lee was OK.

Robyn started speaking again.

'It's still pretty dark. What are we going to do? We've got Lee missing and this guy unconscious, right at the foot of our ladder back to Hell.'

Homer finally stirred into a little life again. It was an effort for all of us. We were trying to think normally, to talk normally, but the words seemed to come out slowly, like toothpaste slowly squeezed from its tube. 'We can wait a bit longer,' he said. 'Put yourselves in their minds. They're not going to be wandering round the bush at this hour looking for survivors, or even for one of their own people. Too dangerous for them. And they probably think they got everyone anyway. This guy chasing Fi, he was a one-off I think.'

'What happens...' I said. I had to clear my throat and start again. 'What happens if after another hour or two this guy is still alive?'

Homer didn't look at me. Hoarsely he said, 'What you did to that guy back in Buttercup Lane, the one I shot...'

'That was different,' I said. 'I did that because he was going to die anyway. It was euthanasia.'

'Look at this bloke,' Homer said. 'He's not going to live. Or if he does he'll be a vegetable.'

'You don't know that.' But I tried to explain the real difference. 'That was in hot blood,' I said at last. 'I don't think I could do it in cold blood.'

One of the things I find strangest and hardest is that we were having such conversations. We should have been talking about discos and electronic mail and exams and bands. How could this have been happening to us? How could we have been huddled in the dark bush, cold and hungry and terrified, talking about who we should kill? We had no preparation for this, no background, no knowledge. We didn't know if we were doing the right thing, ever. We didn't know anything. We were just ordinary teenagers, so ordinary we were boring. Overnight they'd pulled the roof off our lives. And after they'd pulled off the roof they'd come in and torn down the curtains, ripped up the furniture, burnt the house and thrown us into the night, where we'd been forced to run and hide and live like wild animals. We had no foundations, and we had no secure walls around our lives any more. We were living in a strange long nightmare, where we had to make our own rules, invent new values, stumble around blindly, hoping we weren't making too many mistakes. We clung to what we knew and what we thought was right, but all the time those things too were being stripped from us. I didn't know if we'd be left with nothing, or if we'd be left with a new set of rules and attitudes and behaviours, so that we weren't able to recognise ourselves any more. We could end up as new, distorted, deformed creatures, with only a few physical resemblances to the people we once were.

Of course, in among all this we had moments – days sometimes – when we acted in ways that were 'normal', vaguely like the old days. But it was never the same. Even those moments were warped by what had happened to us, by the horrible new world that we'd been forced into. There seemed no end to it, no clues as to what we would become, nothing. Just day-to-day survival.

Homer had leaned over the young soldier on the ground and was going through his pockets. He gradually accumulated a little pile of items as we watched in silence. It was hard to see details in the dark, but there was a wallet and a knife and a couple of keys. Then, from a breast pocket, he pulled out a little torch, no bigger than a pen, and switched it on. In its light I saw just how badly hurt the soldier was. There was blood coming out of his ears and nose, and his scalp was matted with blood, so that the hairs of his head were wet and stuck together. I also saw how young he was. He could have been younger than us. His smooth skin looked as if no razor had ever touched it. I had to remind myself urgently, harshly,

151

that he was a potential rapist, a potential killer. At the same time I knew I couldn't kill him.

'We could move him a long way off,' said Robyn doubtfully, 'so that they wouldn't connect him with the tree and the cliff.'

'And if he wakes up?' I asked. 'We're not doctors. We don't know what might happen.'

'He'd at least have concussion,' Robyn said, even more doubtfully. 'He probably wouldn't remember where he was or what happened.'

No one bothered to point out all the flaws in the plan.

We sat there quietly watching. After about an hour I began to realise that the young soldier was going to solve the problem for us. I realised that his life was slowly ebbing away. He was dying on the ground in front of us, as we looked on without a word being spoken. We made no move to save him, though I doubt if we could have done much anyway. I felt sad. In the short time we'd been gathered around him I'd come to feel that I knew him, in a strange sort of way. Death seemed so personal, so close, when it came slowly, almost gently, like this. In touching him it touched us all. Every quarter hour or so Homer switched the torch on, but although it was still dark under the trees, we didn't really need it. I could see each rise and fall of the uniformed chest, could feel each struggle to draw the next breath. I began to hold my own breath as he finished exhaling, willing him to find more air. But gradually each breath became lighter, and the pause between each one longer. A feather resting on his mouth might have fluttered a little as he reached for another moment of life, but the feather would not have lifted at all.

It had been a cold night, and it was a cold morning, but for once I didn't feel it. Fi was huddled against me, her face turned away from the soldier, and she helped keep me warm. Every so often she shook, with a spasm that might have been caused by the cold. Robyn sat beside the soldier's head, watching him calmly. There was something beautiful about her face as she gazed at his. Homer sat behind his head, also watching calmly, but there was a dark shadow on his face and an impatience in the way he sat bent forward, like a cocked rifle. It made me nervous to see him like that.

There was a distant crack through the trees, like the falling branch I'd heard earlier. There'd been noises all night of course, as there always are in the bush: the yowl of possums, the howl of a feral dog, the wing-beating of owls; a breeze through the trees and mysterious rustles in the undergrowth. I was used to all that and didn't respond; hardly noticed it. But this was different somehow, and I sat up a little and turned a little towards it. And then heard the shout.

'Ellie! Homer! Are you there?'

Wild relief ran through me.

'Lee! Over here!'

We heard his blundering footsteps then, running and crashing towards us. I stood and moved a few steps in his direction. He came clumsily through the tall trees, squeezing through a narrow gap right in front of me. I held out my arms and he grabbed me and hugged me, but all I could feel were the bones of his body. I didn't feel love or affection or warmth from him, just an ugly roughness, and relief perhaps. He pushed me away and looked around him. 'Anyone got any food? I'm starving.'

'No,' Robyn said, 'nothing.'

'We've got to get out of here,' Lee said. His eyes had passed over the soldier on the ground, but he hadn't shown any surprise. Now he focused on him. 'What's he doing here?'

'He followed Fi,' Homer said.

'He's still alive,' Lee said.

'Yes.'

'Well, what are you waiting for?'

I wasn't sure what he meant. 'We were waiting for you,' I said. 'And we didn't know what to do with him. But I think he's close to dying.'

'We've got to go,' Lee said again. His eyes scanned the ground. Suddenly he bent down and picked up the soldier's knife from the sad little pile of possessions. At first I thought he'd then overbalanced and fallen on the boy. I even gasped and started to say 'Look out!' But I realised at once that it was deliberate. Lee had landed clumsily with his knees on the boy's chest and at the same time had buried the knife in him, aiming at the heart. The boy gave a terrible gasp and both his arms lifted slightly, with the fingers flailing. Homer switched on the torch and in its sharp, focused light, like a scalpel, I saw the face go very white, and a rush of blood pour from the mouth as it slowly opened. It stayed open. Then something left the face, a spirit or something fled from it, and he was dead. His face became the colour of water, no colour at all.

Fi was screaming but then she took a big gulp and stopped herself, as though she'd swallowed the last scream. She put her hand to her mouth and gave a little hiccup. Her eyes were wide open and she was staring at Lee as though he were a monster, Jack the Ripper. I was scared of him myself, wondering if he'd changed forever, if he'd become a devil. Robyn was hyperventilating, with her hands to her throat. Homer backed away, eyes staring, his hands behind him as though looking for support. There was no support there. I just stood with my mouth open, looking at the young body on the ground. Homer had dropped the torch and I bent down and picked it up.

Lee stood and walked away a couple of steps, then came back. 'Let's get rid of him,' he said, but all the anger and harshness had gone out of his voice. He sounded almost normal, except that I didn't know if he'd ever be normal again.

'We can't bury him,' I said, my voice shaking, on the edge of hysteria. 'There's no time and we haven't got tools.'

'We'll move him down to the gully,' Lee said.

None of us moved, until Lee shouted at us, 'Come on, don't just stand there. Help me.'

I took his head, which was amazingly heavy, and Lee picked up his feet. None of the others was in any shape to help. We struggled along with the body, trying to pick a wide enough path through the bush. After we'd covered only ten metres I was sweating. I couldn't believe how heavy this light guy was. I was starting to drop him, but then Robyn arrived beside me and helped.

'We'd better not drag him,' I said, 'or they might see the tracks.' I was shocked at myself for saying something so cold-blooded, but neither of the others reacted. We limped on, each of us reluctant to be the one to say stop, until somehow we'd reached the head of the gully. We swung our arms as much as we could and rolled him heavily into it.

'He sure didn't help much,' I said, shocking myself

again, but I was trying to make everyone feel better, to drag us back from madness a little.

We stood there, looking at him. His body was all arms and legs now, a sprawling broken doll, with his head tipped back at an awful impossible angle. Without a word Lee turned away and went into the bush and came back towing a branch in each hand, which he then tossed over the soldier. Robyn began to help him, then I joined them. We spent ten minutes throwing rocks and branches on the body. It wouldn't stop the smell, and it wouldn't stop the feral dogs and other carnivores, but we had to hope that if there was a search it wouldn't last more than a day or two. That seemed a reasonable hope.

Soon we seemed to arrive at an agreement that we'd done enough. The grey among the trees was lightening quickly as the day spread into the bush. We stood there for a moment. I felt weird, like I didn't want to walk away without saying anything. I glanced at Robyn, and although her eyes were open and her lips weren't moving, I felt certain she was praying. 'Say it out loud,' I urged her. She looked at me in surprise. I said it again: 'Say something out loud.'

'I can't,' she said. She wrinkled her brow for a minute, then said, 'God, look after him.' Then after a pause she added in a strong voice, 'Amen.'

'Amen,' I said, and after a moment Lee said it too.

As we walked back to the others he said to Robyn, 'If you'd seen what I saw last night you wouldn't be praying for any of them. And you wouldn't be wondering if we've done the wrong thing. They're filth. They're vermin.'

I understood then why he'd pushed the knife into the soldier's chest, but I was still scared of him for having done it.

Chapter Eleven

So often it's the little things that are the hardest. We'd had a night of death and horror, of fear and panic; we'd seen many people die and we'd seen one die at the closest of quarters. We'd lost many of our possessions – anything we'd had in the tents at Harvey's Heroes campsite was gone forever. But trying to climb that tree to get back into Hell was the hardest thing of all.

Before that though I found I hadn't lost everything. We were standing waiting at the base of the tree for Robyn to return. She'd taken the odds and ends from the soldier's pocket and gone back to his bush grave to throw them in. She'd even picked up the knife, all sticky and red. It made me think of picking up Homer's bloody shotgun at the Buttercup Lane ambush, and I shuddered in memory when I saw Robyn reach for the knife.

The only thing we kept was the torch.

So there Lee and Fi and I were, waiting for Robyn, watching Homer, who was using a small branch to sweep the ground and conceal our tracks. We had to avoid drawing any attention to our stepladder. And as we watched, Lee felt for my hand and put a small object in it. It was warm and furry, and for a second I thought it might have been something horrible. I looked down with my mouth squirming. It was my little chocolate brown teddy bear, Alvin, only the size of a cigarette packet, one eye missing and both ears chewed, a big worn patch on his bum, but my Alvin, my bear.

'Oh Lee,' I said, my eyes filling with tears. 'I thought I'd lost him.'

I also meant: 'And I thought I'd lost you.'

He just shrugged, but I knew he was pleased.

'How'd you find him? Oh Lee, I was getting scared of you. You seemed like you'd changed so much.'

He ignored the last part of what I said, and answered my question instead.

'I got him from your tent.'

'What? How could you?'

'I was just sneaking in the back of it, to wait for you. You were the only person I felt like talking to, after what happened on the road. Then the shooting started. Alvin was on the ground, at my feet, so I grabbed him and got out of there.'

'Where'd you go?'

'Along the ground. Then I found some cover.'

'How? Where?'

'Behind some bodies.'

'Behind some bodies?'

'There were four people who'd been sitting together in the eating area. They'd fallen in a row when they were shot, each one leaning on the next one. I hid behind them.'

'Oh God.'

'I stayed there till the soldiers started coming

through the camp. They had a few prisoners. Every-one else was dead. I saw what they were doing to the bodies and I saw what they were doing to the prison-ers. So I ran.'

'Did they see you?'

Robyn had returned and although we should have been going up the tree we were all too hypnotised by Lee's story.

'Yes, but they couldn't shoot because they would have hit their own soldiers. They weren't very orga-nised. They fired a few dozen rounds in the bush after I was out of the camp area, but I was expecting that and I was dodging round and keeping flat, and using the trees. Last I saw of them they'd started burning tents. They didn't follow me.'

'They followed me,' Fi said in a small voice.

'Yes, but you're a girl,' Lee said grimly. 'I saw how they were treating the women they'd caught.'

Homer started climbing the tree.

'What happened next?' I asked urgently.

'I just ran and ran. By the time I'd calmed down a bit I didn't know where I was. Eventually I figured out that you might be here, if you'd survived, but then I had to figure out how to get here.'

Robyn began to follow Homer up the tree and Fi moved into position to do the same.

'What happened to you back at the firebreak?' I asked.

'Well, I ran like mad when they started shooting at us. When I realised I'd lost you guys I thought I might as well go straight to the camp.'

'Thank you for my bear,' I said. I gazed at the cliff for a few moments, thinking all kinds of thoughts, wondering how long this wall of rock would stand here and what else it would see and hear. I wished I could write its story, do something lasting, something good. I turned to Fi. 'Come on, Fi from Wirrawee. Make like a koala. Make like Alvin.'

I slung the dead soldier's rifle across my back and watched the three of them. Homer was now at the top, which was the thick base of the old white tree, because of course it had toppled from the top. Robyn was right behind him. Fi started slowly edging up towards them.

'I told you we should have got some rope,' Homer called down.

'Remember that Outward Bound stuff?' Robyn said. 'You've got to dig your toes in and use your fingertips.'

That was the extent of our knowledge about rockclimbing.

Homer abandoned the safety of the tree and began working his way up the last stretch of cliff. Even from the bottom I could see the tension in his arms and legs as he searched for holds. His head was sideways and he looked like a gigantic insect crawling up the vertical rockface. We watched nervously, knowing that we would soon have to follow him. It was only a few metres but the cost of failure was pretty high. But then he flung an arm over the top and with a last gigantic effort pulled himself up, rolling out of our sight for a moment before reappearing, standing, at the top, looking down and smiling.

'Piece of cake,' he said.

Robyn followed, doing it very quickly, going up in one continuous burst till she too rolled over the top. By then Fi was at the top of the tree and looking up anxiously.

160

'Come on Fi,' I called from the bottom.

Lee started up the tree as Fi began tentatively to reach out and feel for a handhold. Homer and Robyn were like stereo speakers, urging her on. She went very slowly, using the sides of her shoes instead of her toes, and halfway up she froze. I could see her legs shaking. 'Come on Fi,' we were all calling. 'I can't,' she cried. 'Come on Fi,' Robyn said urgently. 'The soldiers are coming.' They weren't, but it worked. Fi gained another metre with a little scrambling movement, then flung her arm up and grabbed at Robyn's. Luckily she caught it. I hate to think what would have happened if she hadn't. Even so Robyn had to haul and haul before Fi, hanging like a dead weight, was dragged over the top.

Fi had been brave so many times, shown such strength, but it seemed like she'd been wiped out by the last twelve hours.

Lee got up quite easily. It was a definite advantage being tall. I was at the last branch by then and watching him. I worked out my route, a bit further to the right than Lee's, and with a big gulp of pure fear I left the security of the tree and started out. The main thing was not to panic. Every time I started getting the wild feelings that I would fall, must certainly fall, I told myself to think brave, to get control of my mind, to be strong. But I found myself getting physically tired. I was hungry, my knee was hurting, and I was taking too long to make the climb, using up my energy. I accelerated a bit, glanced up, and saw Homer's hand outstretched towards me, just within reach.

'I don't need any help,' I said crossly.

At that moment I fell. It was so quick, without

warning. My fingers all lost their grip simultaneously. I knew I was too far across to catch the tree and I knew quite clearly that I had two choices: to use my hands to brake myself, and rip up my hands doing it, or to go into free fall and break my legs. I used my hands. I was so close to the cliff face that I could deliberately press into it, grabbing at it, scraping against it, using any point of contact possible, knees, toes, chest a few times, and hands, all the way down. I landed at the bottom without ever having reached out-of-control speeds, but I hit heavily, jarred my knee again, and rolled across the ground till I fetched up against a rock. I lay there grimly, hating everything. I didn't dare look at my fingers. I got up and shook the dirt off my clothes, then walked back to the tree. Angrily I started climbing it again, ignoring the stinging in my hands, the dull pain in my knee, the ache in my back. There were cries of distress above me, the other four leaning over and calling out, like lonely cockatoos. 'I'm OK,' I muttered, knowing that they couldn't hear me. I got to the top of the dead, white trunk again and paused there for a minute, hugging it, shaking a bit.

'Chuck up the rifle,' Homer called. I realised the automatic weapon I had slung across my back was still there. That was the ache in my back. I was lucky the rifle hadn't started firing. I clumsily slipped it off and held it balanced in my hands for a moment, then flung it hard and high up over the top. It only just got there, but Robyn grabbed its butt as it started to fall again, and hauled it up. A minute later she reappeared over to my left.

'Come this way Ellie,' she called.

There was an easy ledge over there but it didn't

lead anywhere, so none of us had used it. But I saw what they were trying to do. They'd formed a human chain. Lee was holding Robyn and she was dangling over the cliff holding the rifle. I couldn't see who was holding Lee. I edged my way over there and reached up. I could just grab the barrel of the gun.

'Oh Ellie, your poor hands,' Robyn said.

'I hope you've unloaded this thing,' I said.

'Yes, we have actually. Can you hold on?'

'Yes, go on.'

'You're sure?'

'Just do it.'

She began to shuffle back, as we both held on grimly. For a moment she had all my weight but then I was able to use my feet to help her, walking up the last wall of rock. Then Homer and Fi were grabbing me under the armpits, hauling me over the top. I landed on top of Robyn, then crawled off and collapsed by myself, utterly done.

Fi took my right hand and fussed over it. I lifted my head and looked curiously. The hand was shredded and bloody. The fingertips were red raw, all the pads gone, except on the thumb. The left hand looked almost as bad. The more I looked at them, the more they stung.

There was nothing any of us could do, except cry, and so we did that. 'Nothing like a good cry,' I remember my grandmother saying. We were cold, we were ravenously hungry, we all had aches and bruises and cuts, and above all we were shocked and desperately unhappy. It was probably only about seven-thirty and the sun was not yet strong enough to lighten or warm the terrible darkness that had filled us during the night. So we sat there, in under the trees

– we were still security-conscious – and bawled like little kids. My eyes ran, my nose ran, and when I tried to wipe all the drips away, my hands hurt too much to use them. Fi lay with her head in my lap and cried until my jeans got damp.

Eventually I dried up a bit. I lifted my head and looked around. We were a miserable sight. Robyn had dried blood all over her face, Lee had a swollen eye that was starting to darken. We smelt like we hadn't washed in months. Our clothes were torn and dirty. We'd all lost weight since the invasion, which made our clothes loose and shabby. I looked at Lee. He stood there with the bush behind him, gazing calmly back at me. Like a lot of tall people he usually stood with his head down a bit, so you could see the back of his neck, the way it arched. He wore a grey T-shirt with a lightning flash across it, and the words 'Born to Rule Tour'. I knew what was on the back, the name of his favourite band, Impunity. His jeans were gone at the knee and one boot had a lace which had been broken and retied so many times that it was hard to tell which was the bow. As always he wore the T-shirt out, not tucked in. It was torn off the right shoulder, torn again at the heart, and had a hole burnt in it under the world 'Rule'. The bottom of it was like ribbons, it was so wrecked.

Despite all that, he was so graceful, so dignified, that I fell in love with him completely at that moment, in a way I never had before. I gave him a little weak grin and lifted Fi off my lap.

'Come on guys,' I said. 'Let's get out of here.'

'Did you know that's the most commonly used line in movies?' Lee said. He had his head on one side as he looked at me. I had the uncanny feeling that he knew exactly what I was thinking.

164

But all I said was 'What?'

Lee just shrugged. 'That's the most commonly used line in movies. It's used in sixty per cent of movies, or something like that.'

He came over and lifted me as the others stirred into action. We limped over to the creek to start the trip I was dreading: the long uncomfortable struggle back upstream, hunched over, with the cold water constantly tugging at our legs. The only good thing – and bad thing – was that we no longer had packs to weigh us down. I spent quite a lot of the trip taking inventory of the things I'd lost. It was depressing. We'd had so much taken away already; it seemed unfair to keep losing more all the time. Maybe we'd lose everything eventually. Our happiness, our futures, our lives. Maybe we'd lost two out of three of those already. I cried a bit more as we battled our way up the creek into Hell.

The funny thing was that it was still only mid-morning when we straggled into the campsite. It felt like lunchtime at least. Before the invasion our days had hardly started at 9 am. We'd be sitting in a classroom, our hair rumpled, rubbing our eyes and yawning. Now we had been through more – had suffered more – before breakfast than we had a right to expect in a lifetime.

And that was another thing I had to learn, that expectations meant nothing any more. We didn't have a right to expectations. Even the things we took for granted – we couldn't take them for granted because those were expectations too. For one thing it had never crossed my mind that Chris wouldn't be there. That never crossed my mind. But he wasn't there.

165

At first we didn't get too excited, just tore at food held in both hands while we called out for him. At least, that's what the others did; I felt too sick and my hands hurt too much. I'd thought I was hungry but suddenly I couldn't eat. I sat on a log watching Robyn wolf down baked beans and cheese, Lee get into biscuits and jam, Fi eating an apple and dried fruit, and Homer attacking the muesli. With her mouth still full Robyn went and got the first-aid kit and brought it over to me.

'How are your hands?' she asked.

'All right. I think my knee hurts more.'

I'd let my hands trail in the water quite a few times as we'd laboured up the creek, so the gravel and dirt were washed out. Now the skin around my fingertips looked soft and tender, but the pads on the fingers were the dark strawberry red of blood, and little shreds of skin hung off them. Basically I'd sand-papered the pads off. I had gravel rash on both palms, which stung too but didn't look as bad as the finger-tips. Robyn smeared cream over all the bloodied bits, then carefully bound each fingertip in gauze and bandages. At the same time she fed me, like a mummy bird with her chick. Although I must have looked pretty silly by the time she finished, sitting there with my eight fingers sticking up in the air, each wrapped neatly in its own little white beanie, I did feel better, especially with some dates and sweet biscuits in me.

'Where do you think Chris might be?' I asked her as she finished wrapping my last finger.

'I haven't got a clue. We've been gone quite a while. I hope he's all right.'

'It must have been lonely here alone.'

'Yes, but I don't know whether that would worry Chris.'

166

'Mmm, he's a funny guy.'

After our meal we started looking for him in earnest. There wasn't far to look, in Hell. We knew he wasn't in the Hermit's Hut because we'd passed that on our way back to the clearing. Homer and Fi checked the path all the way back to Wombegonoo, while the rest of us started searching the bush, in case he'd had an accident. I walked around holding my hands in the air, feeling useless. But there was no sign of him in the bush. When Homer and Fi got back with the same report from Wombegonoo our fear and tension levels started rising again.

It seemed so cruel, after what we'd been through. But cruel didn't mean anything either; I'd learnt that ages ago.

We met again in the clearing.

'I don't think he's been here for a while,' Homer said. 'The fire looks like it hasn't been lit since we left.'

'Maybe he didn't bother to light it,' Fi said.

'It's been cold at nights.'

'All his stuff's still in the tent,' Robyn said. 'As far as I can tell. His sleeping bag's there, and his backpack.'

I went and had a look in the tent too. I was looking for Chris's notebooks. If for some extraordinary reason he had gone away from Hell, I was sure he would have taken them. But they were all there. He had four. I peeked into the one on top and it was only half full, so I assumed it was the current one. Surely he wouldn't have left that.

I came back to the group. Fi was looking scared and saying, 'You don't think anyone's been here do you?'

'No way,' I said. 'Nothing's been disturbed.'

Lee had checked the chooks and the lamb.

'They've got water and food,' he said. I went and had a look there too, not because I didn't trust Lee, but because I knew that as a townie there might be details he wouldn't notice. I came back to the others and reported, 'Their water's a bit stale. Hasn't been changed for a couple of days.'

What else could we do? Seemed like we'd already exhausted the immediate possibilities. We sat there looking at each other.

'I don't think we can do any more today,' Homer said. 'If he's left Hell he could be anywhere between here and Stratton. Or beyond.'

'He could have followed us into the Holloway Valley,' I said.

Fi gasped. 'Don't say that!'

'Look,' Robyn said, 'let's not freak ourselves out. There just isn't anything we can do right now. We need sleep desperately. Like Homer said, he could be anywhere. If there was one specific place we could walk to and have a chance of finding him, well, I guess we'd shake ourselves up and go there. But we're not in any shape to have an emu parade through the whole Wirrawee valley. Let's go to bed.'

'Easier said than done,' Lee said. 'We don't have any beds.'

He was right. Our sleeping bags had gone, prob-ably burnt by the soldiers by now, in the wreckage of Harvey's Heroes.

We started scrounging around. We had a couple of blankets, half a dozen towels, and quite a lot of warm clothing. We all got warmly dressed, wearing balaclavas and thick socks, and, for the other four, gloves as well. Fi had to dress me like I was a shop dummy. Then we dragged ourselves off towards the tents, carrying all the extra bits we'd found. 'No one's allowed to make any noise for the next four hours,' I called, as I waddled along on my jarred knee.

'Yes mother,' Homer called back.

Fi and I crawled in together. I lay down while Fi spread towels and a blanket over me. Then she did the best job she could of covering herself. When she'd finished we just lay and looked at each other. We were face to face and only about a metre apart. Neither of us spoke for a long time. Then I just said 'Oh Fi.'

'Yes,' she said. 'I know what you mean.'

'Lee doing that,' I said. 'It was horrible.'

'Do you know,' Fi said, 'with the soldier just lying there all that time, I sort of got to like him. I thought I knew him, sort of. I started forgetting how he'd been following me.'

'So did I.'

'How old do you think he was?'

'I don't know. No older than us.'

Fi shivered. 'What's this doing to us? What's going to become of us?'

'I don't know.'

'I'm scared,' Fi said. 'I don't know what'll happen.'

'I'm scared too.'

'But you never look scared.'

'Don't I? Don't I really? God, I sure feel it.'

'When you fell down the cliff…'

'I was scared then. But there's no time to get really scared when things like that happen.'

'Mmm.'

'Anyway, that was my own dumb fault. Homer offered me a lift up and I wouldn't take it.'

'Your fingers looked terrible, when you did get up.'

'You ought to have seen them from my eyes.'

'Do they hurt much?'

'A bit.'

'I wish I could be brave,' Fi said.

'You are, Fi. You don't realise. You've done so many things. You've never let us down, not once.'

'Those people on the road, Captain Killen and the others. We just saw about a dozen people killed, do you realise that? Dead, killed, dead bodies. And Sharyn and Davina and Olive, I bet they were killed too. I'd never seen a dead person before this started. The only dead things I'd seen were animals on the road. And our class guinea pig in Year 2 – GP he was called – he died, and I cried all afternoon. Now it seems like it's all death.'

'I wonder where Chris has gone.'

'It's weird.'

'Did you know he drank a lot?'

'What do you mean, drank a lot?'

'Well, any time he could bring grog in here he did, and then he drank it all himself, I think.'

'Well that wouldn't add up to much.'

'Mm, but the night we went out and attacked that convoy he was pretty pissed then I think. And the day we left, he was into it, at ten o'clock in the morning.'

'So what are you saying?'

'I don't know. Just that I didn't like it I suppose. The way he was doing it behind our backs.'

'Are you saying he's an alcoholic?'

'No, not that. But I think he's got some kind of problem with it maybe. And I think he's a strange guy and getting stranger, and we don't seem to be getting on with him like the rest of us do with each other. Don't you think he's getting harder to talk to?'

'Yes, but I've never been able to talk to him that easily. He was so out of it at school.'

'He's interesting though. He writes so well. I think he's a bit of a genius.'

'God yes. But I'll never understand him.'

'If you could choose one person to have here, who would you have?'

'My mum.'

'Not counting relatives.'

'Well, Corrie and Kevin of course.'

'Yes, but apart from them.'

'I think Alex Law.'

'Alex? She's so two-faced.'

'No she isn't. You just never made the effort to get to know her.'

'She hates me.'

'No she doesn't. You think everyone hates you.'

'No I don't. Just every girl in the school. And every boy. And every teacher. No one else.'

'So Mr Whitelaw likes you, huh?'

Mr Whitelaw was the school janitor and he really did hate me because I'd dobbed on him once for perving on the girls' changing room. He was lucky he hadn't got the sack, that time.

'Oh sorry, I forgot about him.'

'Who would you have?'

'Meriam.'

'Mmm. She's nice.'

I was enjoying this conversation. It seemed like the first normal conversation we'd had for ages. It was like we'd gone back to the old days for a while, before the invasion.

'What did you think of Harvey's Heroes?' I asked.

Fi thought for a bit.

'It was strange, wasn't it? Was Major Harvey really a Deputy Principal?'

'Apparently.'

'Where'd he get the uniform then?'

'Who knows. Probably out of the costumes cupboard. He'd been in the Army Reserve, Olive said, but not as a major.'

'I liked Olive.'

'Yeah, she seemed OK.'

'What about Sharyn?'

I considered for a moment. I remembered again that Sharyn was probably dead, and that made it hard for me to say what I really thought.

'She wasn't too bad. I mean, you wouldn't choose her out of the whole world to be your best friend, but I got to like her. I sort of depended on her.'

'Mmm,' Fi said. 'It was strange being round adults again. Good but strange.'

'It wasn't all good. They thought we were so immature. They didn't give us a chance. They were so annoying. I mean, we've done twice as much as them, and they treated us like we were barely capable of drying the dishes. Do you know, Mrs Hauff wouldn't let me heat water in a frying pan to clean it, because she said I might burn myself! And all that time Major Harvey's sitting around talking about how short of men and weapons they were! We've got six people and practically no weapons and we've done really big things, we've made a real difference.'

'Mmm. But adults. They're always like that.'

'Do you want to grow up?'

'Yes, of course! What do you mean?'

'Well, I've been thinking, adults often look so unhappy and depressed, as though life's so complicated and so much trouble. And they seem to have stuffed the world up for us. I know being our age isn't

172

always fun, and we have problems too, but I don't think they're as bad as adult ones.'

'We just have to do a better job, that's all.'

'Mmm, but that's probably what they said when they were our age.'

'You get so caught up in your own life.'

'We should have taken more interest in stuff. Remember when Kevin was asking about what treaties we had with other countries? None of us had a clue. We shouldn't have left everything to politicians.'

'Politicians!' Fi said. Suddenly she was angry. 'They're scum. They're slime.'

I giggled. 'Wow, Fi, that's pretty radical for you.'

'Those broadcasts. They make me sick to my stomach.' I knew what she meant. Listening to our political leaders broadcasting from Washington, their lies and excuses and promises, made all of us so angry that we'd agree to turn the radio off when they started talking.

'I thought you wanted four hours' silence,' Lee grumbled at us from the next tent.

'Sorry,' I said guiltily.

Fi was yawning, and shifting to a more comfortable position. 'I'm going to sleep,' she said.

'OK. Good night. Or morning.'

She seemed to go to sleep quite quickly after that. I didn't. I lay there all morning, drifting occasionally into a drowse, but waking up again almost straightaway. Sleep had been the last escape open to me, but even it was starting to close its doors. It'd been a problem to me ever since the Buttercup Lane ambush. For all I know it'll be a problem to me for the rest of my life. For all I know the rest of my life won't be long anyway.

Chapter Twelve

The next two weeks passed slowly; actually they didn't so much pass as crawl along in the gutter. There was not the slightest sign of Chris, not the slightest clue as to where he might have gone. The others went out of Hell three times searching for him; the first time just to my place; the second time to Kevin's and Homer's; and the third time a long bike ride at night to Chris's own house. They took a calculated risk and left a note there to say they'd been, because they thought that if he was anywhere that was the most likely place.

'If he was anywhere.' Of course he was some-where. Everybody's somewhere, aren't they?

I finally sat down and read his notebooks, turning the pages awkwardly with my mangled fingers. I didn't like doing it, but I'd asked the others what they thought, and they agreed it was OK, in the hope that it might give us an idea of where he'd gone. I thought it was quite ominous that he hadn't taken his note-books. They were so precious to him. But perhaps he had taken some; perhaps he'd had more than four.

Chris's notebooks were so different to mine. His

were more creative; all kinds of jottings and ideas and poems and stories and thoughts about life, like this: 'We kill all the caterpillars, then complain there are no butterflies.'

Some of the pages I'd seen already, but none of the later ones. There were a lot of references to Hell, but I couldn't always tell if that were our Hell, the one we lived in, or the other one, that we sometimes lived in too. Some of it was pretty depressing, but then I'd always known that Chris could get depressed easily.

A bad black horse
Steals into my head
And moves across the landscape
Of my mind, while I sleep.
He does what he likes in there.
Next day I feel
The damage.

In the quiet mist
I watch her go.
It feels like snow.
There's a feeling that I get.
I walk back home
Sad and slow.

But they weren't all depressing.

The foal burst into life:
A slither of wet limbs
And startled eyes among the straw,
And the rich wet smell of birth.
Then it was dawn; it was
The light of life.

This one I remembered from when he'd shown it to me in his first week with us. I'd liked it a lot. He often wrote things about horses; I guess because the Langs had quite a few on their place.

Mares and foals
Stumble
In the morning mist
Running from the dark
Where their shadows remain.

I live in the light,
But carry my dark with me.

This seemed to be the most recent one. I hadn't seen it before.

They will carry me to the field
Through the wreaths of mist
Moist on my face,
And the lamb will pause
For a thoughtful stare.
The soldiers, they will come.
They will lay me in the dark cold earth
And push the clods in upon my face.

'Life's harder, the deeper you feel things,' was all I could think as I put the books away. 'Feelings, who needs them? Sometimes they're like a gift, when you feel love or happiness. Sometimes they're a curse.'

Seemed like for Chris they were more a curse than a blessing.

I wondered again how Corrie was getting on, and Kevin. Poor Kevin. I could imagine him sitting

176

inside the Showground, looking through the wire and picturing us in Hell, still with our freedom. He probably envied us, wished he was here. But we weren't so well off. I'd always been taught that freedom was everything, but it wasn't. Better to be in chains with the people you love than lonely and free.

I was thinking, we should have an honour roll, a list of the people we'd lost – Corrie and Kev and now maybe Chris. Maybe there'd be more names on it soon. I suppose it was thinking about this that made me so wild with anger when I found Homer making a different type of list. He was standing by a big old gum tree, carefully carving vertical marks on it.

'What are you doing?' I asked.

'Keeping score,' he said.

'Keeping score? What of?'

'The casualties we've notched up.'

I could hardly believe my ears. 'Do you mean the people we've killed?'

'Yes,' he said, but the fury in my voice had alerted him, and he looked at me nervously as he said it.

'You must be bloody joking! You are bloody joking! You absolute stupid bloody idiot, do you think this is some kind of football match?'

'Calm down Ellie, it's no big deal.'

'Homer, you don't even like sport, you never have, and here you are turning the worst thing of our lives into some bloody game!'

'All right, all right, calm down. I won't do it if it gets you that worked up.' He was looking guilty as he started to realise that it hadn't been such a smart thing to do. I was so upset I couldn't trust myself to speak. I went storming off on my banged-up knee towards the track. Honestly, Homer could be so clever and such a leader, and then he'd go and do something like that. It was the story of his life, and even though he'd been great since the invasion, he was still capable of losing it completely, as he'd just proved. I was so upset about all the death and destruction we'd seen and taken part in that I couldn't imagine anyone else seeing it differently.

I don't know.

When someone intercepted me at the start of the track I was too upset to notice who it was. He grabbed my arm and said, 'Whoa, Ellie, calm it, calm it.' It was Lee. 'What's wrong?' he asked.

'Oh, just bloody Homer, being more annoying and juvenile than normal.'

He was still holding my arm and I turned a little more so I was pressed into his chest. I had a bit of a snuffle in there, then asked the question Fi had asked me. 'What's going to become of us, Lee?'

'I don't know.'

'Don't say that. That's what everyone says. I want you to be different to everyone else.'

'Well I am. I'm a murderer.'

I felt a tremble pass through his body as he said it. 'No you're not, Lee.'

'I wish I could believe you. But words don't change anything.'

'Do you think it was wrong?'

He waited so long I thought my voice must have been too muffled in his chest for him to have heard. I started to repeat the question, but he cut me off.

'No. But I'm scared at what there is in me that can make me like that.'

'So many things happened that night. They mightn't

ever happen again. Anyone would have gone a bit crazy, after what you saw.'

'But maybe when you've done it once, you do it more easily the next time.'

'I've done it too,' I said.

'Yes. I don't know why, but it seemed different when you did it. Chris told me how blown apart the guy was. And somehow, using a knife is different to a gun.' I didn't answer and he continued after a while. 'Do you think about it much?'

I really cried then, sobbed like my lungs were coming out of my mouth. I couldn't stop for ages. The amazing thing was, Lee just kept holding onto me, like he could wait forever. Finally I gulped out my day-time nightmare. 'I felt like there was this big shadow up in the sky, hovering over me. It made everything dark, and it followed me everywhere.'

When I'd calmed down a bit we went further down the track. I held on tightly to Lee, even though it made it difficult to walk along the narrow path. We sat on a rock for a while. A tiny spider was on my arm and I found the thin line of cobweb that connected him to me, so I could lower him to the ground.

'Spider bungy-jumping,' said Lee, watching. I smiled.

'Do you think what I did was wrong?' Lee asked, still watching the spider.

'I don't know. Ask Robyn. Ask Homer. Ask anyone, just don't ask me.'

'But you always seem to know what's right and wrong,' Lee said.

'What? What?' I held him at arm's length and looked at him in disbelief. 'You said what?'

'Well, don't you?'

'Lee, I have as much idea of what's right and wrong as that spider does.'

'Oh. Are you sure? You always seem so confident.'

'Good God, do I? And Fi said a while back that I never look scared. I thought you guys knew me pretty well. Seems like we might have to start again. The only thing I'm confident about is that I'm not confident about anything. I agonise about everything we do. Do you remember that time I slept with you and you never knew?'

He laughed. One night I'd got back to the camp late and there'd been no one there but us two. Lee was asleep and I'd crept into his tent and slept there beside him.

'Well, that night, on the way back into Hell, I stopped for a while on Tailor's Stitch and sat there looking at the sky and trying to figure a few things out.'

'Yes, I remember. You told me.'

'I only ever did figure one thing out, but it was pretty important to me. I realised that the only thing I had going for me was my lack of confidence, that it was a sort of gift.'

'How do you mean?'

'I mean that the more confident people are about their beliefs, the more likely they are to be wrong. It's the ones who are so certain, so black and white, the ones who never consider that they could be wrong or that anyone else could be right, they're the ones who scare me. When you're not confident at least you keep checking what you do and asking yourself if you're on the right track. So you gave me a huge insult just now.'

He laughed. 'Oh. Sorry. But you were certain back at the camp that Homer was doing the wrong thing.'

'Oh dear. Yes, but he was. Oh, sometimes I wish life was all black and white.'

'Racism'd get even worse.'

'Very funny.'

'What was he doing, anyway?'

'Don't worry about it. He just regressed to childhood for a few minutes.'

'Come on, let's go down to the flat rocks.'

The flat rocks were at a point where the creek emerged from the bush, its first glimpse of open air since its birth in a spring, up near Tailor's Stitch. To get to the rocks you had to leave the track and bush-bash a bit from the first of Satan's Steps to a little clearing in some scrub. Here the creek spread out and washed over a series of long flat stones, that were often nice and warm from absorbing the sun's heat. It took a bit of effort to get in there but it was worth it. I limped in on my sore knee, till we found ourselves a nice rock and stretched out side by side, listening to the soft shushing of the water, and the gurgling of a magpie. The two sounds echo each other, I thought.

'How're your hands?' Lee asked, holding me by the wrist.

'OK. They don't hurt as much. It's just a nuisance that they still need bandages.'

Lee moved a little closer and put his head next to mine, so that we were cheek to cheek. His skin felt as warm and comfortable as the rock underneath me. I realised he was in a romantic mood; I wasn't sure if I was or not, but decided to go with the flow, just like the creek. So when he kissed me I kissed him back, till his firm lips and his tongue did start to give me nice tingly feelings. I wanted to hold him more closely, but couldn't because of my bandaged fingers. It was a kind of crazy position to be in and I grinned as I pictured how it would look to anyone watching. But I kept the grin to myself, not wanting to upset Lee.

I realised Lee was pushing my T-shirt up, then trembled as his hand rippled across my stomach. These were fingers that were made for the violin, not for attacking and killing. He touched me so lightly, yet his fingers were firm, not soft or weak. By luck or experience he'd found one of my most ticklish and sensitive spots; I love being stroked across my tummy. He had my T-shirt up to my bra, which didn't worry me, but I wondered what he had in mind, how much further he hoped to get. He put his head down and blew raspberries on my skin, above my belly button, then used the tip of his tongue to make little circles in the same spot. I hadn't been feeling turned on at all, but he obviously was, and he was working pretty hard to get me going. It didn't take long. I started feeling better, then best. Little ripples of nice feelings were spreading under my skin, quite deeply, and they met other ripples that were spreading from further down. It was all nice and warm and slow and lazy, lying there on the warm rocks, with Lee so hot beside me.

He was on his side, leaning on one elbow now, using the other arm to touch me. With the flat of his hand he again made circles on my tummy, big, wide, slow ones.

'Oh that feels good,' I said, closing my eyes. The only uncomfortable feeling I had was that I needed to go to the bathroom, but I couldn't bear to get up, so I thought I'd wait a bit longer. Lee used the tips of his fingers, then rolled his hand over and used his knuckles. I felt so tired and lazy that I hoped he would just keep doing that forever, and although I knew it was selfish, I hoped I wouldn't have to do anything in return. But when he undid the top button of my jeans I figured I'd better not lie there for too long. I rolled over and embraced Lee with my elbows and fore-arms, clumsily working his T-shirt up at the back, holding him as closely as I could. His knee was between my legs and I kissed him hard and long. I did have in mind that holding him like that might stop him from getting too far with my buttons, but he got his hands inside my waistband anyway – at the back – and his warm hands rubbed slowly across my warm skin.

'Mmmm,' I sighed, long and slow, like a bee on tranquillisers. Lee wasn't saying anything. But the more pressure he put on the small of my back the more I needed to go to the loo. Gradually I started pushing him off.

'Don't,' he said. 'Don't stop.'

'Oh, I have to.'

I kept kissing him for several minutes, then peeled myself away. I was on my knees beside him, still holding my stupid bandaged fingers up in the air. I leant over and gave him a series of quick kisses right on his lips. But he turned his head to one side and said 'Where are you going?' He sounded quite cross.

I laughed.

'To the loo, if you really want to know.'

'Are you coming back?'

'I don't know if I can trust myself. And I know I can't trust you.'

He gave a reluctant smile. I stood up and lingered for a moment, looking down at him.

'I do like you,' I said. 'But I'm not sure... Living

down here, things could get a bit out of control. Out of my control, anyway.'

I wasn't certain if he knew what I meant. But he would have to be satisfied with that, for the moment. I limped off into the bush to find somewhere to squat. At least by the time I got my jeans unbuttoned and down, with no one to help me, he'd have had plenty of time to cool off.

Chapter Thirteen

Crackling static from our radio almost drowned out the voices. Reflecting the static was the rain, steadily beating away at the roof, dripping through the galvanised iron in a few places, running down the wall in others. It poured down the chimney in a steady shower, splashing from the fireplace out onto the bare wooden floor.

Dressed in all our woollies we huddled around the little black transistor. The batteries were tired and although for the first minute we'd heard the voices quite clearly, they were already getting distorted. Still, what we'd heard had been encouraging; the first encouraging news we'd had since forever. The American voice had promoted us to the third most important item.

'Much of the southern coastline has been recaptured. In fierce fighting around Newington, air and land forces from New Zealand are believed to have inflicted heavy casualties on a battalion of enemy troops. A successful landing by troops from New Guinea has been made in the north of the country, in the Cape Martindale area. And in Washington,

Senator Rosie Sims has called for an urgent review of US foreign policy, in the light of new power alignments in the Asia–Pacific area. Senator Sims is sponsoring a hundred-million-dollar military aid package to support the beleaguered country, and although the Senate is not expected to pass the Sims Bill, public sentiment in support of indirect intervention appears to be growing.'

Then we heard the voice of our Great Leader, the Prime Minister, who'd jetted out of the country in a wild hurry when he realised the war was being lost.

'We continue to fight to the full extent of our powers,' he said, 'but we cannot do…' There was a rush for the radio as three of us, encumbered by blankets, dived for the button. We got it off and then lay together on the four old mattresses that we'd pushed into a line along the wall, we watched the water dripping around the shed. We were at Kevin's, sleeping in the old shearers' quarters, which angled off at ninety degrees from the shearing shed. It was nice to sleep in a wooden building again, even one as leaky and draughty as this. Two weeks of relentless rain had got on our nerves so badly that we'd finally packed up and moved out of Hell. Everything we owned had become damp, then bedraggled, then soaked. Water had run out of our drains and into tents. It didn't seem worth getting up in the mornings, knowing that we couldn't go anywhere or do anything. So, we'd made feeders for the chooks, which meant we could leave them for longer periods of time, and at last, weighed down by the wet clothing in our swags, our improvised packs, we'd squelched out of Hell. We were thoroughly sick of each other's company and desperate for a touch of normality. It

186

had taken three nights of surreptitious fires to dry our things out, but at last I was starting to feel human again. There's something reassuring about having all your clothes and blankets clean and dry and organised, even if the five of us were sleeping on four old thin mattresses that were shedding more of their insides with every passing hour.

Actually, being dry and normal had put us in a silly mood. Homer and Robyn had been playing I-spy for half an hour before the news started, but the game had degenerated once Robyn began thinking of impossible words. Something beginning with I had turned out to be 'indefinable futures', and something beginning with E was 'erotic daydreams', which Robyn claimed we were all having. After the news we played hangman, then charades. I kept them guessing for ten minutes with my dramatic re-enactment of *The Effect of Gamma Rays on Man-in-the-Moon Marigolds*, which no one else had ever heard of. I'd seen it on video in Year 8 when I'd had a real Zindel craze, but the others nearly killed me when they at last gave in and I told them the answer.

The rain stopped and Lee went for a walk. He wanted me to come but I couldn't be bothered. I was halfway through a romance called *Send Me White Flowers*.

I was three-quarters of the way through it, with Fi watching from her mattress to see if I was going to cry or not, when Lee slipped quietly back in through the door. Shutting it softly behind him, he said, 'There are soldiers coming.'

I jumped up, dropping the book, and ran to the window. I stood behind it and tried to peer out, but it was too dangerous. So I did what the others were doing and found a crack in the wall, and stood with my eye pressed against it. We watched anxiously. There were two trucks grinding their way up the drive, one an Army one with a tarp over the back, the other a small traytop from Wirrawee Hardware. They pulled up to the west of the house, near the machinery shed, parking neatly side by side. Soldiers started to get out, two from the cab of each truck.

'Oh God,' Fi moaned. 'They must know we're here.'

I hadn't noticed Homer leave his position, but suddenly he was beside me, handing me a rifle, the one I'd taken from the dead soldier at the foot of the cliffs. He gave Fi the .410 shotgun, Robyn a sawn-off .22, and Lee the sawn-off 12 gauge. He kept the other automatic rifle for himself. Robyn accepted the .22 but I saw her look at it for a moment and then lay it carefully on the floor beside her. I didn't know what to think of that. Could we rely on her if it came to a shoot-out? If she did refuse to shoot, was she right or wrong? If she was right, that made me wrong. Sweat was prickling my skin, as though I'd rubbed against a stinging nettle. I wiped the moisture from my face and looked again through the long vertical crack.

People were getting out of the covered truck. The soldiers were lounging around, watching. Although they had rifles they hadn't bothered to unsling them. They were quite casual, quite confident. The people were obviously prisoners, ten of them, five men and five women. I couldn't recognise anyone, though I thought one looked a bit like Corrie's Mum.

The prisoners seemed to know what to do without being told. Some took bags from the back of the hardware truck and set off for the fruit trees. A few went into the house, and two to the machinery shed. A soldier accompanied each group; the fourth soldier stayed at the trucks and lit a cigarette.

I looked across at Homer. 'What do you think?'

'It's another work party.'

'Yes. Good chance to gather some info, maybe.'

'Let's just watch for a while.'

'Time spent in reconnaissance, huh? One of them looks like Corrie's Mum.'

'I don't think it is,' Fi said. 'It's just the silver hair. She's too thin. And too old.'

We returned to our holes and cracks, and kept watching. I saw glimpses of the people in the orchard, but there were no signs of the ones in the buildings. But after ten minutes the soldier who'd gone into the machinery shed came ambling out and joined his mate by the truck. He was obviously trying to bot a cigarette. It took him a few minutes but finally the first man pulled out the packet and handed one over.

Then they both got in the cab of the bigger truck and sat there to have their smokes.

'We'd better get out of here,' Robyn said. 'We've got these guns with us. We don't want any more trouble.'

'OK,' Homer said. 'Do a clean-up first. We can go out the end door and up through the trees.'

'You guys do that,' I said. 'I'm going down to the machinery shed.'

The others looked at me doubtfully.

'I don't think...' Robyn started.

'It's a really good chance,' I cut in swiftly. 'We haven't heard anything for weeks. I want to know how Corrie is. And our families. Robyn, can you take my stuff?'

She reluctantly nodded.

'I'll come too,' Lee said.

I was tempted, because I would have felt more confident with some company. But I knew it wouldn't work.

'Thanks anyway,' I said. 'Two'd be a crowd.'

Lee hesitated, but I wasn't in the mood. I wanted to do something, to prove to myself that I still had some courage, that the terrible night in the Holloway Valley hadn't turned me to junket. And all those weeks of rain had made me impatient. The last time I'd tried to be independent and strong I'd lost my fingertips. Now I was anxious to try again, to do better, to get back some self-respect. Maybe some respect from the others too.

The other four began packing, moving quickly and quietly. I went out of a window at the side and hurried deep into the gum trees, to get around the sheep yards. There was a belt of trees running all the way down the hill that gave good cover, and I stayed in its shadows till I had the machinery shed between me and the trucks. Then I started edging closer to the shed, using it as my shield. My problem was that there was no entrance to the shed except the eastern side, which was all entrance: it was completely open. I had to come out of the trees and creep along the side of the shed, aiming for the only cover left to me, a water tank at the corner.

Reaching the tank was nerve-racking. The hard thing was to calm myself, to stop my chest taking on its own life and breathing like a set of bagpipes. I had to clench my fists and yell at myself, silently, in my head, to get control and calm down, to get ready for the tough part. I went down on my hands and knees and wriggled under the tankstand. Then, with agonising slowness, a millimetre at a time, I put my head out and peeped around the corner. I don't mind saying it was one of the braver moments of my life. A soldier could have been standing a metre away. But there was no one there. Bare ground stretched away, brown and wet. I could see the trucks about fifty metres from me, looking huge and deadly from my position. I wriggled out a little further, twisting to the left as I did. From there I could see into the deep, dark machinery shed. There was a tractor and a header, and an old ute. Further back was a stack of wool bales. I couldn't see any people, but I heard a clink of tools and a murmur of voices away in the far corner.

I hesitated another few seconds, then took a breath. I steeled myself, like I was at the School Sports waiting for the gun, then took off, running silently for the wool bales, using the tractor as cover. If I'd had a bit of white fluff on my bum I would have passed for a rabbit. But I got there safely and waited, trembling, pressed against the smooth skin of a bale. The voices kept talking, rising and falling like a river. I couldn't make out the words, but it sounded like English. I started sidling along the bales, glancing at the entrance all the time so I could see if anyone came in. At the corner of the bales I stopped again. Now I could hear the voices clearly. I trembled and sweated, and tears smarted in my eyes as I recognised one of them. It was Mrs Mackenzie, Corrie's Mum. My first instinct was to sit down and bawl like a little kid. But I knew I couldn't give in to such weaknesses. They were for the old days, the innocent days, when we lived a soft life. Those days were lost, along with paper tissues and plastic supermarket bags and jars of moisturiser – all the useless luxuries that we took for granted before the war. Not only had we taken them for granted, we'd even thought they were important. Now they were as foreign and far away as the luxury of crying with relief at a familiar voice.

Corrie's Mum. Mrs Mackenzie. I'd had a thousand cups of tea and five thousand scones at her kitchen table. She'd taught me how to make toffee, how to giftwrap Chrissie pressies, how to send a fax. I'd told her about my cat dying, my crush on Mr Hawthorne, and my first kiss. When my parents got especially annoying or frustrating I'd pour it out to her and she'd soak it all up, like she understood exactly how I felt.

I peered around the side of the bales. I had a good view of the back corner of the shed. I was looking at the workbench, with the tools neatly arranged on the walls above it. With no power connected, the area was dark and gloomy but I could see the two people working at the bench. A man with his back to me was tinkering with something. I didn't recognise him from his back, and I wasn't so interested in him anyway. My enthusiasm was all for Mrs Macca. I looked at her hungrily, and felt at once the disbelief in my stomach. She was side-on to me, cleaning out a carburettor with a toothbrush. A shadow was on her face, but I could hardly believe she was Mrs Mackenzie. This person was old and thin, with silver hair, long and straggly. Mrs Mackenzie was middle-aged and nicely plump, red-headed like her daughter. I kept staring at her, my disappointment giving way to anger. I really thought it wasn't her after all. But gradually, as I looked, I began to see traces of Mrs Mackenzie in her face, in the way she stood, and in the way she moved.

Then she put down the toothbrush, wiped her hair away from her eyes, and picked up a screwdriver. And in the movement of her hand as she brushed her hair aside, I saw Corrie's Mum. In shock and love I cried out, 'Mrs Macca!'

She let go the screwdriver, which fell to the floor, bouncing and clattering. She spun round, her mouth and chin dropping, which made her face even longer and thinner. She went very white and clutched her throat.

'Oh. Ellie.'

I thought she was going to faint, but she leant quickly and heavily against the bench, putting her left hand to her forehead and covering her eyes. I wanted to go to her but knew I mustn't. The man, glancing out at the trucks, said to me, swiftly, 'Stay there.' I was annoyed, because I'd worked that out for myself, but I didn't say anything. I already knew I shouldn't have called out. Mrs Mackenzie bent down and picked up the screwdriver, but it took her three tries and she seemed like she wasn't seeing it properly. Then she looked across at me, yearningly. We were half a dozen metres apart but it may as well have been a hundred k's.

'Corrie, are you all right?' she asked. I was shocked that she'd called me Corrie and hadn't seemed to realise it. But I tried to act naturally.

'We're fine, Mrs Mac,' I whispered. 'How are you?'

'Oh, I'm just fine, we're all fine. I've lost a bit of weight, Ellie, that's all, but I've needed to do that for years.'

'How's Corrie?' I felt that awful dread in my heart again, but I had to ask, and now that Mrs Mackenzie had called me Ellie again I thought it was OK. But

193

she took a long time to answer. She looked half asleep, strangely. She was still leaning against the workbench.

'She's OK, Ellie. She's lost a lot of weight too. We're just waiting for her to wake up.'

'How are my parents? How's everybody?'

'They're all right. They're fine.'

'Your parents are in good shape,' the man said. I still didn't know who he was. 'We've had a bad few weeks, but your parents are fine.'

'A bad few weeks?' I asked. This conversation was taking place in urgent whispers, with many glances at the trucks.

'We've lost quite a few people.'

'How d'you mean "lost"?' I almost choked on the question.

'They've got a new bloke,' the man said.

'How d'you mean?'

'They brought in an Australian bloke from out of town. Some chalkie. He keeps picking people out for interrogation, and a lot of them get taken away after he's finished with them.'

'Where to?'

'How should we know? They won't tell us. We just hope to God it isn't a firing squad.'

'Who does he pick?'

'Oh, first it was all the people who'd been in the Army Reserve. He knew who they were. Then it was the cops, and Bert Heagney, and a couple of your teachers. Anyone who's a bit of a leader, you know what I mean? He doesn't know everyone, but he knows a lot of people. He does about five a day, and we're lucky if three of them come back in the evening.'

194

I said, 'I thought there were informers at the Showground already.'

'Not like this bloke. There's people who suck up to them, but they don't do this kind of thing. They don't help with interrogations. Not like this mongrel.'

There was so much anger in the man's voice at the end of his answer that his voice rose sharply in volume. I cowered down in the shadows for a moment, but no one came. I knew I'd have to go soon, but I wished Mrs Mackenzie would say more. She seemed so gaunt and tired and washed out. 'How's Lee's family?' I asked. 'And Fi's, and Homer's? How are Robyn's folks?'

Mrs Mackenzie just nodded.

'They're good,' the man said.

'What do you have to do here?' I asked.

'Get it ready. There'll be colonists moving here in the next few days. You kids'll have to be careful. There are work parties out everywhere now. We're expecting hundreds of colonists soon.'

I felt sick. We were getting hemmed in. Maybe one day I'd have to accept the unthinkable, the unfaceable, that we'd be slaves for the rest of our lives. A future that was no future, a life that was no life. But I had no time for thought. I had only time for doing.

'I've got to go, Mrs Macca,' I said.

To my horror she suddenly burst into wild sobs, turning away from me and falling forward onto the workbench, dropping the screwdriver again as she wept. She was sort of screaming and crying at the same time. My scalp felt like I'd had two-hundred and forty volts applied to it. It was like I'd been given an instant crewcut. Frightened, I backed away fast, scurrying to the far end of the wool bales and ducking behind them. I heard a truck door open and a soldier come walking into the shed.

'What's wrong?' he asked.

'I don't know,' the man said. He sounded quite convincing, like he didn't really care. 'She just started crying. It's those bloody Swedish carburettors, I reckon. They'd drive anyone to tears.'

I almost grinned as I crouched there in the darkness.

Nothing seemed to happen for a while. The only sound was Mrs Mackenzie's sobbing, which had now become quieter. I could hear her gulping, as she tried to get some air in her lungs, get some control back. 'Come on, love,' the man said. I heard more footsteps, which sounded like the soldier again. They went out of the shed and faded away towards the house.

'Go for your life Ellie,' the man said in a normal conversational tone, as though he were talking to Mrs Mackenzie.

I had to rely on his judgement, so I took off, without saying anything, slipping around the corner of the shed, past the water tank, and into the bush. I greeted the trees like they were my friends, my family. I hid behind one for a while, embracing it while I got my breath back. Then I toiled on up the hill, to find my friends.

Chapter Fourteen

We saw our first colonists only two days later. More rain had blown in and we'd retreated to the shearers' quarters for protection, huddling there as the timber creaked and whined and muttered. The rain came in squalls, rattling on the galvanised iron as though we were being roof-rocked. We took it in turns on sentry duty, keeping a twenty-four hour watch, but the weather was so bad that the work parties didn't return. We went and inspected what they'd done: the house was clean and tidy and the beds made. It was all ready for strangers, aliens, to move in and take over. It scared and upset me, trying to imagine these people sleeping in the Holmes' beds, eating in their kitchen, walking their paddocks and sowing their seeds in the Holmes' earth. I supposed that our farm would go the same way soon.

After two days the rain had stopped, though the sky was still grey, the air cold, and the ground wet and muddy. We'd decided to walk to Chris's place again when we got a chance, in case he'd turned up there. So at dusk, and despite the cold rotten weather, we took our gear and marched off across the paddocks.

Roads were too dangerous, so early in the evening, but we knew we could bypass Wirrawee and strike Meldon Marsh Road without much trouble, and that would put us close to the Langs.

It was a silent walk for a while. Being cooped up for two more days hadn't improved our tempers. But the open spaces were good: it was nice to be able to breathe again. I felt myself relaxing after the first couple of k's. I held Lee's hand for a while, but it was too hard to walk along in the dark like that; we needed both our hands for balance, after our frequent stumbles. I dropped back and left Lee on his own, and talked to Robyn about movies we'd seen: which ones we liked and which ones we didn't. I had a great longing to see a movie again; to be able to look up at a vast screen in the darkness and watch beautiful people, beautifully dressed, saying clever and romantic things to each other. I supposed that in other parts of the world people were still making these films and other people were still watching them, but it was a hard thing to comprehend.

We skirted around Wirrawee and got onto Meldon Marsh Road. It was now well after ten o'clock and we thought we were safe on the road. It was a relief to be able to walk on it, and we made much better time. But about two k's from Chris's we saw a house with lights on. It was a shock to us; it was the first we knew that power was being reconnected to rural houses. We stopped and looked in silence. It wasn't a welcome sight at all. In one way it should have been comforting: to see something that was so like old times. But life was different now. We were used to being feral animals, used to roaming the dark country at nights, used to running wild in the wild. If the colonists spread through the farmlands, reclaiming them with their lights and electricity and their own form of civilisation, we would be forced further and further out to the edges, having to skulk in caves and burrows, among the rocks.

Still without a word being said, we moved towards the house. We'd become human moths. The house wasn't one I knew, but it was a comfortable looking place, solid brick, with big wide windows and at least three chimneys. Shade trees grew around it, and a neat garden with brick borders made a geometric pattern at the front. The borders nearly proved my downfall; I trod on one of the bricks and felt a spasm in my knee, which had been free of pain for several days now. But I recovered my balance, and when I tested my knee it felt OK. I caught up with the others, who had bunched behind a tree and were looking towards one of the lit windows. Bad strategy, I thought. A soldier with a gun could wipe them all out in less than a second. I whispered that to them when I got to the tree; they looked startled, but quickly spread out to the cover of other trees.

I went around the eastern side of the house and found a peppercorn tree with wooden slats nailed to it, leading up to a kids' cubby, a treehouse. I scaled the ladder and sat in the first fork. It gave me a dress circle view of the kitchen. I watched grimly. There were three women working in there. They looked quite at home. They were reorganising everything. They had all the jars and plates and saucepans and cans out of the cupboards and spread across the tables and benches. They were wiping things down and putting them away, stopping every now and then to take a closer look at something, or to draw the attention of the others to it. There was a gadget with orange plastic handles made for getting the lids off jars, and that seemed to fascinate them. I guess they couldn't work out what it was for. They were putting their fingers through the hole in the middle and waving them around, then trying to screw each other's noses off with it. They were laughing a lot. I could just hear their voices through the wall, sounding thin and high-pitched, almost a little nasal. But they looked like they were having a lot of fun; they seemed happy and excited.

I felt such a mixture of feelings, watching them: jealousy, anger, fear, depression. I couldn't bear to see any more: I slipped down from the tree and went and found the others. Then we stole away through the garden and back to the road.

Comparing notes as we walked along, we worked out that there were at least eight adults in the house. I'd been assuming that they'd put one family on each farm, but perhaps they thought we were extravagant, having so much land between so few people. Perhaps they'd build houses all across the Wirrawee valley, till there was one family in each paddock, farming the land intensively. I didn't know how the earth would cope with that. But then, maybe we hadn't been making enough use of it.

We trudged on, each quiet with private thoughts and theories and dreams. It was after midnight when we got to Chris's place. There were no lights on, but we were being terribly careful, in case there were colonists asleep inside. But by then I was sick of tiptoeing. 'Let's rock the roof,' I suggested, thinking of the rain on the galvanised iron of the shearers' quarters back at Kevin's. The others looked at me pityingly, but I was in a dangerous mood, fed up with hiding and running and skulking around. 'No, let's,' I insisted. 'What's going to happen? If anyone's in there, they're not going to rush out into the darkness with guns blazing. They wouldn't be that stupid. There's plenty of cover around, so we can get away fast if we have to.'

My powers of persuasion were better than I'd realised, because within thirty seconds I'd talked them into it. I wasn't sure that I'd wanted to talk them into it – I'd been half joking – but to turn back now was to lose too much face, I reflected ruefully, picking up all the stones I could carry. We agreed on a place to meet if we got chased, then surrounded the house. At the signal – a long, frighteningly loud 'Coooeee' from Homer – I let fly. It was quite exciting. A squadron of possums wearing football boots and wheeling defective supermarket trolleys at high speed might have made as much noise, but they'd have had to work at it. I backed away fast, biting my bottom lip in amazement, and almost biting through it when I tripped over a garden seat. My shins and ankles certainly took a lot of punishment on these night-time excursions. One lone rock, an unexpected afterthought from someone, suddenly clattered across the roof, a full minute after all the others. There was still not a murmur from inside the house. It was impossible that there could be anyone there after that.

We gathered again near the front door and sent Homer to go and look through the kitchen window, after he admitted to throwing the extra rock. 'It's too dark to see much,' he grumbled; then, after looking a bit longer, he said 'I think it's the same as when we left that message for Chris. I don't think anyone's been here.'

And that's the way it was. It was a disheartening discovery. We checked the old piggery where Chris had hidden immediately after the invasion, but there was no sign of life there either. So we gathered around the dusty table in the musty kitchen, feeling tired and unhappy. The rush of excitement from the roof-rocking had quickly gone. We were so upset about Chris, yet so helpless. The only guesses we could make about his whereabouts were depressing ones. I was annoyed with myself that I hadn't thought to ask Mrs Mackenzie and the man in the machinery shed if they knew anything about him. But I'd been too confused and nervous. My only consolation was Robyn's comment that if Chris had been caught and taken to the Showground, the two adults would have mentioned it.

'Well, no news is good news,' Fi sighed.

'Honestly, Fi,' I snapped, 'that's a great help. That must be one of the most stupid expressions ever invented.'

Fi looked hurt. It was after one o'clock and we were all tired. Getting cold too.

'There's just nothing more we can do,' Homer said. 'To tell you the truth, the most likely thing is that he's... I hate to say this – that he's dead.'

We all squawked at Homer in outraged voices. We'd all thought of the possibility, of course, but to talk about it was to commit an obscenity. It was too frightening and horrifying to hear anyone say it out loud. Perhaps we were scared that our saying it might make it real, might make it happen. I'd already learnt a lot about the power of words.

'Well, what are we going to do?' Lee asked. 'We can't stay here.'

'Yes we can,' Fi said.

'I don't think it's too safe round here,' Homer said. 'Those colonists are just up the road. We don't know how far they've spread, this side of town. They could be at the Langs' tomorrow.'

'But it's so late,' Fi said. 'And I'm so tired. And cold. I'm so sick of everything.' She put her head down on her arms as she sat at the table.

Lee patted her hair sympathetically, but the rest of us were too tired to do anything.

'We could stay here for a few hours,' Homer offered. 'But we'd have to go again before dawn. I'd rather have a good sleep later than have a lousy sleep now.'

There was a silence as we all sat looking at Fi, hoping she'd give in gracefully.

'Oh all right,' she said at last, crossly, shaking Lee's hand off and getting up. 'Where are we going then?'

'Let's go into Wirrawee,' Homer said quickly. 'We haven't been there for ages, and we ought to have a look and see what's going on, see if there's anything we can do. If we leave now we'll make it by dawn.'

We were too tired to argue. No one had any other ideas anyway. I was quite pleased to go to Wirrawee. I wanted to be as close to civilisation as possible. I didn't want to see Hell for quite a bit longer.

It started raining again ten minutes after we left Chris's. The smart thing to do would have been to turn around and go back and find a dry shed, but no one even suggested it. I think that having started, we couldn't contemplate making another decision. So we plodded on in silence, getting wetter and wetter. It was very dark but we could stay on the road with no fears of getting caught, so we followed it easily enough. I don't think anyone spoke a word between our departure from Chris's and our arrival in Wirrawee.

We got to the music teacher's house at daybreak. But the grey wet light in the eastern sky was little different to the darkness of the night. Four of us stood shivering in the garden, hiding behind trees, wet and dripping, while Homer searched the house to make sure it was empty. I wondered where he got his energy. He seemed to have more than me, more than anyone. But at last he signalled us in. We squelched inside miserably, found towels and blankets and stripped off in the upstairs bathroom. Homer offered to do guard duty and no one gave him an argument. Robyn and Fi shared one bed and I took another, in the next bedroom. Lee disappeared down the corridor to the end room. I just hoped the house wouldn't get raided while we were all undressed, but there was no sign of anyone having been here since our last visit.

I lay there and as so often happened, having waited all night to get to a bed and get some sleep, now that I was in bed my eyes wouldn't close. I had never felt more awake. The coarse woollen blanket prickled my skin, but in a nice way. It felt rough and primitive. For a long time I couldn't get warm, and I pressed my legs together and huddled further under the blankets, trying to hot up. Eventually the blankets covered me completely. I crossed my arms and put my hands into my armpits. My skin tingled as the blood started to circulate again, until only my feet were still cold. I put the right one on top of the left, willing them to thaw out. At last the warmth, the snugness, the cosiness that I'd been needing for so long, spread through me, till I could relax all over. I lay there, feeling luxurious. Then I heard a whisper.

'Are you awake?'

I popped my head out in shock. I felt like a possum coming out of a tree trunk, and I know my eyes were staring and my hair was all mussed up from the blanket, so I probably looked like a possum too.

It was Lee.

'You look like a caterpillar again.'

'Not a possum?'

'Yes, that too. Can I get in with you?'

He was standing there wrapped in a blanket, shivering with cold. His brown eyes looked at me pleadingly. I felt a slow warm burn of excitement, but tried not to show it.

'No!' I said. 'I'm only wearing blankets.'

'That's what I was hoping. It's all I'm wearing too.'

'Lee!'

'Please?'

'No. Well, you can lie on the bed I suppose, but that's all. And don't think,' I added as he started quickly hopping over to me, 'that you're going to sweet-talk me into anything else.'

'But my charm and personality...'

'Yeah, yeah, I know all about that.'

He lay beside me with his head resting on his right arm, looking at me thoughtfully. He had the trace of a smile.

'What are you thinking?' he asked presently.

'Oh.' He'd caught me by surprise. It was too exciting having him this close. I was getting hot under the blankets. 'I don't think I want to answer that.'

'Go on.'

'I'll answer part of it. I was wondering why you were smiling.'

To my surprise he didn't say anything for quite a

while. But the smile had left his face. He looked very serious, like he was in church or something.

'Couldn't you sleep?' I asked him.

'No. I don't sleep so well these days. Not since that night by the cliff.'

I shuddered. 'Change the subject.'

He suddenly moved a little closer and kissed me hard. I kissed him back, possibly even harder. It was so fresh, but I didn't know where it might end, or where I wanted it to end. Gradually his kisses changed from hard and savage to soft and teasing, making little light contacts with my lips in one spot after another. It was exciting. We did that for quite a time, then lay with our heads on each other's shoulders. His blanket had slipped down a bit, though I was making sure that mine didn't. I felt the smooth hollow under his collarbone, his skin warm and alive. I nudged it with my lips, making little murmuring noises to it, and rubbed my hands up his arms. I found a little pulse under the skin and concentrated on kissing that. He was humming quietly, I thought, but I wasn't sure if it was his skin or his voice. He played with my hair and the back of my neck, stroking me with surprising confidence. With his long fine fingers he teased my hair out, unravelling a few knots and letting the strands slide across his hands.

'Nice hair,' he said at last.

'It's so oily,' I complained.

'I like it. It feels natural. It's sexy.'

'Thanks.' I laughed.

He must have taken that for encouragement, because he moved his hand down under the blanket for the first time, feeling for my shoulder blades. Oh help, I thought. What do I do here? Dad always used to talk about the thin edge of the wedge, and I was afraid that this was it. I didn't want to stop, but I thought maybe we should, and I thought I might regret it if I didn't stop him soon. But it felt so good. Damn him, I thought, how does he know what I like? I wondered if I was having the same effect on him with my hands, and I experimentally ran my fingers down his side as far as I could get, which wasn't very far. His skin seemed to come out in goose pimples as I touched him, which was quite exciting. I lifted myself a little and touched his left nipple. Steve had taught me that boys' nipples were as sensitive as girls'. Lee's were different to Steve's though. Steve's had been pale and wide, like fried eggs on his chest. I liked Lee's more. They were little and dark brown, like press studs. When I played with the left one it hardened straightaway, so I could strum it and tickle it with the tip of my finger.

'Ai, ai, ai,' he said.

'Is that Thai or Vietnamese?'

'Neither. Universal.'

'Ha.'

My blanket was holding up at the front, just, but was well down at the back, as Lee's hands kept roaming. I lay still for a while, feeling guilty that I wasn't doing more but enjoying his touch too much. My skin had become so heated that I thought his hands would catch fire. I moved back off him a little, but couldn't help playing with his right nipple for a minute, just like I had the left. Then I ran my hand lower, in a long sweeping movement, kissing him warmly as I did so.

'Are you going to be able to stop?' I asked him.

'Sure, sure.'

'You're a terrible liar.'

By moving back off him that little bit I'd given him more room. Trying to look casual, he put his hand under the blanket that was just covering me at the front, at the same time kissing me hard to try to distract me. And I was easily distracted. I let him run his hands over my skin, thinking that what had been fair enough for him was fair enough for me. I rumpled his hair, feeling my face redden as he excited me more and more. Would I be able to stop? Would I want to stop? I already knew the answer to that, as I had done since he first came into the room.

'Oh God Lee,' I said, but couldn't think of how I should finish the sentence. My own hands went further than they should have, down to his waist and beyond. It was as though they had a life of their own. The hell with it, I thought. I'll do it. Last time we'd been in this house I'd spent a lot of time wrapped in a tartan rug: that's when Lee had first called me a caterpillar, a 'beautiful sexy caterpillar'. Now, a caterpillar again, I was emerging from my cocoon of blankets. Lee's hands were at my bum and he was rolling me over a little. I felt up inside his legs as high as I dared, but not quite touching everything. I sneaked a little look though. It was fascinating; such a wild looking thing, so greedy, so determined. I knew Lee was looking at me too, and I was a bit embarrassed. Not very, though. It was obvious that he liked what he saw, and I secretly enjoyed the effect I was having on him.

'Have you got a..?' I asked, turning my head away a little. I didn't want to say the word.

'A what?' he asked.

'You know, a condom.'

'Oh no!' he groaned, 'Ellie! Not that! Not now!'

'OK, OK,' I said, 'that's cool, just as long as you have the baby for me.'

'Jesus,' Lee swore. 'Do you have to?'

'Yes! Can you imagine if I got pregnant?'

He sulked for a minute, then said, 'I think Homer's got some.'

'How many do you think you'll need?' I asked, giggling into my pillow. He started getting up.

'Wait!' I said. 'What are you going to do? You can't just go and ask him for them.'

'I'm not that stupid,' he said, still grumpy. 'They're in his wallet, and his wallet should be in his trousers and his trousers are in the bathroom, drying.'

He disappeared out of the door, shuffling along in his blanket, and I lay there, smiling. I couldn't believe I was actually going to do it. I hoped I wouldn't muck it up and that it wouldn't hurt too much and that it would feel fantastic. I was nervous, but I was still aching all over with the need for him, the longing to feel him against me again. His warm hands had felt fantastic. I gave a little laugh out loud, a laugh of amazement and disbelief and excitement. It seemed ages before he came back, but at last he shuffled in and flung himself on top of me, clutching a couple of the little packets in his hand. With a shy grin, trying to do it as modestly as possible, he got himself out from his blanket and in under mine. To feel our two naked bodies together, skin to skin, was the wildest feeling of my life. I thought I'd been fired up before, but now it was like sparks were shooting off me. Lee had calmed down with the walk to the bathroom, and had cooled down too, but I warmed him by rubbing against him, and felt him quickly react.

'Put it on,' I said at last, nodding at his clenched fist.

He peeled one open and lifted himself off me, looking down so he could see what he was doing. I watched curiously.

'Don't look,' he said, blushing and trying to put his forearm over my eyes.

'Oh,' I said, 'you're so cute when you're shy.'

When he was ready I hugged him to me and nibbled his ear for a minute, before wrapping my legs around him. After that it went OK; not great, but OK. Lee got a bit clumsy, just from nerves I think, and that made me a bit nervous, which didn't help. I wanted to be the great lover, the perfect partner, and I got worried that I wasn't being that. By the time he was really in me he couldn't hold on any longer, and after that he wasn't as passionate; he just wanted to lie there and hold me.

I made him be a bit more creative, until I'd had enough too. I didn't know what I felt then: a mixture of things. I was pleased that I'd finally done it without any disasters, sorry that it hadn't been better, wondering if I'd be completely different from now on. But I enjoyed the cuddling. For about half an hour we lay together, eyes closed, scratching each other's arms and backs with long slow lazy strokes, drifting in and out of sleep.

We were interrupted by a soft knock on the door and Homer's whisper. 'Ellie! It's your turn for sentry.'

'OK,' I called. 'I'll be there.'

I waited a few more minutes, then eased Lee off me. I pulled up a blanket for covering, planning to go downstairs and get some dry clothes from my pack before I relieved Homer. But as I got to the door, I

210

suddenly realised something. Homer had knocked on the door, then called his message through it. He'd never done that before. He always just crashed in and shook me awake. We'd known each other so long we didn't bother with too many polite customs. I turned and looked at Lee, lying there on the bed.

'Lee,' I said, 'why did Homer knock on the door?'

'Eh?' he said, only half awake.

'Why did Homer knock? Why didn't he come barging in like he usually does?'

Suddenly he was awake. He looked at me guiltily. 'Bastard,' I said coldly.

'I couldn't find the condoms,' he said. 'I had to ask him.'

I threw the door open and stormed out, spoiling the effect a bit by tripping over the blanket. I was furious. I didn't want Homer to know what we'd been doing. Once Homer knew, everyone'd know. The only good thing about Lee telling him was that it kept me awake through my whole sentry turn. I spent the time having imaginary conversations with Lee, telling him what I thought of him. Anger's good like that.

Chapter Fifteen

I calmed down eventually with Lee. I could see how it would have happened, his telling Homer, although I still wished he hadn't. But I quite enjoyed the way he hung about, looking so embarrassed and guilty, for a little while anyway. He deserved to suffer a bit.

All in all though, I felt pretty good. A bit sore occasionally when I moved the wrong way, but pretty good. I was watching myself all day, wondering if I had changed, if I was a new person now. But nothing magic seemed to have happened. In one way I was relieved, but in another I was sorry that I'd never be a virgin again. It was one of those steps: once you've taken it, there's no going back.

One thing that I hadn't expected was the sense of being alive that I felt all day. It was strange but nice. I think it was a reaction to all the death and deterioration that had surrounded us for so long. Now I'd done something positive and loving, that wasn't destructive. That made a big change from the way we'd been living. I know babies are a nuisance, and having them is meant to be eleven on a pain scale of one to ten, but

I did have a little daydream about maybe having a few, one day, in fifty years or so.

I just had a feeling that people like us had to keep life moving forward.

The time was to come though when I found myself doing something cold-bloodedly destructive again.

Fi and I were having a prowl that night through the streets of Wirrawee. We were heading for Fi's place. She wanted to see her house, to pick up a few things, and to make herself feel good (or bad) by walking through its deserted rooms. Fi's parents, being solicitors, had heaps of money, and they lived in the best part of Wirrawee, a big old house in a street of big old houses up on the hill. We didn't hurry to get there. We must have been in the mood to take risks. It was early to be out, but we wanted some fresh air. Although it had been raining all day again, and although the streets gleamed with puddles, it wasn't raining when we left the music teacher's house. The cloud was low and that kept the temperature up a bit. We sneaked along for a few blocks, going from garden to garden, so we didn't have to spend much time on footpaths. When we got to Jubilee Park we settled into the band pavilion and talked, looking out across the unmown grass and the weed-ridden flower beds. The first thing that was obvious was that Fi knew what I'd done with Lee.

'How'd you know?' I said.

'Homer told me.'

'Oh, he would! I was so burned off at Lee for telling him. Anyway, I thought you and Homer weren't having too many intimate conversations these days.'

'Mmm, well, it's not like it used to be. But we still

213

get on OK. I don't think he's into long-term relationships.'

'I hardly seem to have talked to him for ages. Most of my conversations are with you and Lee.'

'Must have been a pretty good conversation with Lee this morning.'

'Get out of it! It just happened, OK? Don't give me a hard time.'

'Sounds like Lee gave you a hard time.'

'Oh, excuse me!'

'Was it good?'

'Mmm, not bad. Some of it was fantastic. The actual, you know, was a bit awkward. It'll be better next time.'

'So there'll be a next time?'

'I don't know! Well of course there will eventually. But I'm not saying that I'm going to do it every night.'

'Did it hurt?'

'A bit. Nothing too terrible.'

'It sounds so messy,' said Fi, who always wanted life to be like a magazine. 'Was there heaps of blood?'

'No! It wasn't, like, agony. Some of it, the first bit, hurt, and I was nervous, but after that there were some nice feelings. Lee didn't last long. But I still think it's better for the guy, the first time anyway.'

'Are you sure it was his first time?'

'Yes! He didn't know much.'

'Is he...' Fi went into heaps of giggles, difficult, as we were talking in whispers, surrounded by the damp quiet darkness. 'Is he... how big is he?'

'I knew you'd ask that! I didn't get out a tape measure you know.'

'Yes, but...'

'He's big enough, believe me. I don't know what the average is, but he'd be up to it.'

We both got the giggles then.

At ten o'clock we snuck on up the hill towards Turner Street. It wasn't till we got to the last corner that we had any idea things had changed.

There were about twelve houses in the street and all had lights on. There were even four streetlights. Two houses seemed to have lights in every room but the others were only showing one or two. Fi stood there making little whining noises in the back of her throat, like a puppy that's been hurt. I couldn't believe it. It was like coming on a scene from Disneyland, or walking into Sideshow Alley. It seemed like a kind of fairyland. The only trouble was that for us this was no fairyland. This was dangerous. I pulled Fi back, and we retreated behind a tree.

'What do you think?' I asked her.

She shook her head, tears in her eyes, a sob in her voice. 'I hate them. What are they doing here? Why can't they just go back where they came from?'

We watched for nearly an hour. Occasionally a soldier came out of one house and went into another. We were going to move in closer and have a better look, but as we started we heard a vehicle coming up the hill. We ducked back behind our tree. A large, late model Jaguar cruised past and turned into Turner Street. In its headlights I noticed something else: that there were sentries posted inconspicuously outside a couple of the houses. We were very lucky that we hadn't gone sneaking along there. The Jaguar stopped outside Fi's neighbours', a brightly lit two-storey white wooden house with a high gable. As it stopped, a sentry came trotting out of the bushes and opened one of its rear doors, saluting a man in uniform who got out. Although this man wore jungle

215

greens like everyone else, his peaked cap distinguished him from them. He was an officer, and we began to realise what the houses were being used for. This was the Executive Suite of Wirrawee. Snob Hill was still Snob Hill.

We retreated to the music teacher's house to report to the others but Homer was asleep, and so was Lee, to my secret relief. We were so wrecked ourselves that we didn't wake the two boys. Robyn, who was on sentry duty, was awake, so we talked to her for a few minutes, then headed for bed. I slept with Fi, which saved me from having to make any difficult decisions about my love life, and it wasn't till nine o'clock the next morning that we all sat down and discussed what the two of us had seen in Turner Street.

We sat in a bow window, where we could watch the street, and we talked. It was a good conversation, one of the best we'd had as a group for quite a while. I was lying with my head in Lee's lap, and from there I told the two boys what we'd told Robyn the night before. After Fi added her bit, Robyn started talking.

'I deserted my post for a few minutes last night,' she said. 'The only way I could keep awake was to go for a walk. So I went down to the park at the end of the street and came back again. It's funny, there's something there that I must have been past a thousand times and never noticed. But I noticed it last night.'

There was a pause.

'OK,' Homer said at last. 'I give up. Was it animal, vegetable or mineral?'

Robyn made a face at him.

'It was the war memorial,' she said.

'Oh that,' Homer said.

'Oh yes,' Fi said. 'I knew that was there. I had to put a wreath on it when I was in Year 6.'

'But have you ever looked at it?' Robyn asked. 'I mean, properly?'

'No, not really.'

'Me neither. But I did last night. It was sad. There's so many names on it, with asterisks for the ones who died. There's four wars altogether, and there's forty men who died, just from this little district. And down the bottom there's a message, from a poem or something. It says...' Robyn looked at her wrist and with some difficulty read the lines of tiny writing that she'd jotted there:

' "War is our scourge; yet war has made us wise,
"And, fighting for our freedom, we are free." '

'What's "scourge" mean?' Homer asked.

'It's when something bad happens to you, isn't it?' Fi said to me. 'Something really really bad.'

'Mmm, Attila the Hun, they called him the Scourge of God,' I said, with a vague memory of a History lesson in Year 7.

'Say the thing again,' Lee said.

Robyn repeated it.

'I don't know if it's made us wise,' Lee said. 'And I don't think it's made us free.'

'Maybe it has,' I said, trying to get my brain enmeshed in the idea. 'We're a lot different to the way we were a few months ago.'

'How?' asked Lee.

'Look at Homer. At school he was like Attila the Wog. I mean, honestly Homer, you have to admit, you were hopeless, just lounging around all day with your shirt out, making smart comments. The day this

217

started, you changed. You've been a bit of a star you know. You've had all the good ideas and you've made us do things we wouldn't have done without you. I think you've lost a bit of steam since the ambush of that convoy, but I don't blame you for that. It was an ugly scene.'

'I was wrong about those guns,' Homer said. 'I shouldn't have had them on me without you guys knowing. That was dumb.'

Homer was quite red in the face and looking over our heads. It was so rare for him to admit he was wrong about anything that I bit back the joke I was going to make. In fact he hadn't been entirely wrong about the guns – he'd convinced me of that when we'd argued about it in Hell. But he had just proved how much wiser he was these days. I gave him a wink and felt for his hand, getting a good grip on it. I was now touching the two boys I loved most in the world, and I thought how lucky I was.

'Then there's Lee,' I continued. 'Before, you seemed so bound up in your own life. Violin and schoolwork and the restaurant and not much else. Now, well, you're still a very complicated guy Lee, but you're much more outgoing, and you're very determined and strong.'

'And horny,' Homer added quietly. I gave him a hard slap on the hand. I think Lee gave him a dirty look too, judging by Homer's expression.

'Robyn,' I said, 'you were always strong and you were always smart, so I suppose you haven't changed much. You still stick to what you believe in though, and I think that's amazing. You seem calmer and surer than the rest of us. I think you've got the wisdom that it talks about on that memorial.'

Robyn laughed. 'I'm not wise,' she said. 'I just try to figure out what God would want me to do.'

I didn't know what to say to that, so I moved on to my last subject. 'Fi, I think you've become more free in a way. I mean, you think about your life before, living in that big house, going off to your piano lessons, mixing with the rich and the famous. Now you've been camping in the bush for months, fighting in a war, racing round blowing things up, looking after chooks and growing vegetables... It is a kind of freedom compared to what you used to have.'

'I could never go back to that life,' Fi said. 'I don't want to keep living like this either, of course. But if the war ended tomorrow, I couldn't suddenly start worrying about flower arrangements for Mum's dinner parties, and having the right paper for answering invitations. I don't know what I'd do, but I'd try to find something useful, something that would stop this stuff happening again.'

'Now it's your turn, Ellie,' Robyn said.

'Oh yeah, OK, who's going to do me?' I asked; then, realising what I'd said, gave Homer my best 'Don't you dare' look. I was just in time: his mouth was already opening to say the obvious.

'I will,' Robyn said. She thought for a moment, then began. 'You're better at listening than you were. You're more sensitive to other people. You're brave. In fact I think you're the bravest of any of us. You're still a bit pig-headed sometimes, and you don't like admitting when you're wrong, but you've been a tower of strength, El, you really have.'

I glowed with pleasure. I'm not used to compliments. I've never had a huge number of them.

'I've been braver since that big speech of Homer's

ages ago, down at the creek,' I said. 'I think about that now, when I'm in a scary spot.'

'What speech?' Fi asked.

'You know. When he said that it's all a mental thing. When you're scared you can either give in to the panic and let your mind fall apart, or you can take charge of your mind and think brave. I agree with that.'

'See, that's wisdom,' Robyn said.

'Well, what are we going to do next?' Homer asked. He sat up a bit straighter. 'It's time we did something again. We've had a long holiday. We did nothing with Harvey's Heroes, and it's time we got a move on. Those radio bulletins have been quite encouraging. There's lots of places where people have been fighting back, and the Kiwis have made a difference. We can't let Wirrawee become a stronghold for these scum, and we're about the only people who can stop it happening. So what's it to be?'

'You tell us,' I said, grinning. I knew Homer would already have an idea.

'OK,' he shrugged. 'What Fi and Ellie saw last night gives us our first real chance in a long time. It sounds like they might be using those houses as a headquarters. That's logical enough – they're the best places in town. We need to check it out more carefully though, till we know what's going on. I suggest we spy on them for a couple of days, or however long it takes. And Fi, can you draw up maps of the houses, using everything you remember? And then we'll add to those maps whenever we can.'

We decided that we'd sneak into St John's, the church diagonally opposite Fi's, and use the tower for our lookout post. That was Robyn's church; she knew it as well as my mother knew her kitchen. She was sure she could get in there, through a small window in the vestry that she said was held in place by a brick because the church hadn't had the money to fix it. Using the tower was an unattractive deal in a lot of ways because we'd have to go in at night and stay there till the next night. We'd have to take food and drink and, because there was no toilet, we'd have to take a few containers for emergencies. I don't know what God would have thought of that.

Homer and Robyn wanted to do the first shift and we decided Fi and I would do the next one, then Homer and Lee. But we all went up there that first night to install Robyn and Homer. We waited till four o'clock. That was hardly a problem for us now. We were so used to functioning at night that I no longer felt tired during 3 am and 4 am operations.

We came up to St John's from the rear, climbing over the fence from Barrabool Avenue. It was safer that way, protected from prying eyes in Turner Street. Robyn got the vestry window out with no problems; in fact it had fallen backwards and was resting against its brick. But getting through it was a problem. Robyn had forgotten how small it was. Fi was the only one who had any hope, so Homer lifted her and fed her through, head first. When it came to her hips she had to turn and twist and wriggle. We could hear her giggling and panting, then a thump as she hit the floor head first.

'Ouch,' I squealed. 'Are you all right?'

'Shhh,' Homer went.

'Yes, no thanks to Homer,' Fi whispered back.

She opened the door. We tiptoed in. It was very dark of course, but the thing that struck me most was its smell. It was so musty and dank and cold. Robyn led us out of the vestry and into the main body of the church. The stained-glass windows looked like dark etchings, but some light from the lamps in Turner Street lifted the gloom. I haven't spent a lot of time in churches in my life – we live too far out of town, that's my excuse – but I like the atmosphere in them. They're always restful. I looked around this one, narrowing my eyes to try to see the details. The altar, up in the distance, did look kind of holy. It made me nervous. There was a crucifix, too, on a pillar near me. A square of light from a window crisscrossed the crucifix. I peered closer to try to see the face on it, but it was turned away from me, and in shadow. I didn't know what that meant.

Robyn called us to come into the tower. I walked down the aisle with Lee, wondering if we might do it properly one day. I didn't know what my parents would think of the idea and I knew from something Lee had said to me ages ago that his parents would never want him to marry an Anglo.

As we got to the back of the church Lee surprised me by saying 'I hate these places.'

'Churches?'

'Yes.'

'Why?'

'I don't know. They smell of death. They're like dead places.'

'Mmm. I quite like them.'

Homer and Robyn found little windows halfway up the staircase, which they could use for spying. They made themselves as comfortable as possible. I couldn't help a little nasty thought, which had snuck into my mind like a worm, that maybe the reason

Homer had been so adamant about doing this first day was Robyn's comment that I was the bravest of our group. Homer wouldn't have liked that. In his thinking, guys were always the heroes, always that little bit better than girls.

Maybe that was why I made sure I never let Homer get the better of me.

We'd brought paper and pens, to write down what we saw during the day. We'd been a bit nervous about doing this. Just like with the guns, a long time earlier, we knew the difference between a group of teenagers hiding in the bush and living off the land, and a group of armed guerillas collecting and recording information about enemy movements. We'd seen enough war movies and read enough books to know how that worked. But we found a gap in the stonework of the church tower where we could shove the bits of paper if we got busted, and once dropped in there we figured they'd stay lost forever.

We did want to get a good idea of the movements in and out of the houses, to see what was really going on in Turner Street. Although no one had spelt out details, we all had in mind that we were in the first stages of our next attack. It would be a tough one, our most difficult and dangerous yet, and we had to plan with maximum care.

At five o'clock Fi and Lee and I left the other two to it. They would have a cold and boring and uncomfortable day. Just like Fi and I would have the following day. But back at the music teacher's house we had a pretty boring time anyway. One of us had to keep watch there too – it was just unthinkably dangerous doing it any other way – so most of the time we hung round with the person on sentry, playing Trivial

Pursuit and stuff like that. When Fi was on sentry, Lee and I went off to the sitting room and made out a bit. I wanted to go for it, full on, but Lee seemed distracted. I think the knowledge that we were building up to another attack on the enemy, another chance to get injured or killed, put him on edge. No bloody wonder. I was nervous too. But I seemed able to put it out of my mind better than him. It was strange: back in the old days I got nervous waiting to play Netball or give a prepared speech in English. Compared to that, what we were doing now should have had me in a straitjacket.

Homer and Robyn stuck it out till midnight, which really was heroic, as I realised when I moved in there a few hours later with Fi. But they came back with some interesting stuff. In fact, their notes were so dangerous that it proved how careful we'd have to be not to be caught with them. These houses were hives of activity. There was a fleet of expensive cars – two Jags and three Mercs – and they were coming and going at all hours. At least six different VIPs used them, all in officers' uniforms, all treated with great respect by the sentries. It seemed as if one house might be used as a headquarters and two as living quarters for the senior men and women. The other houses, including Fi's, seemed to be used only by the sentries.

The sentries guarded all the houses, but it was the one used as a headquarters that they guarded most heavily. They changed shifts every four hours. There were four of them guarding the main house, and two each for the others. The soldiers were a real mixture, Homer and Robyn said: some smart and slick, some sloppy and uninterested. 'Most of them don't look like front-line troops,' Robyn said. 'It's like those patrols. The youngest ones look about fourteen, the oldest could be fifty.'

Fi and I settled into the tower just before dawn. It was freezing in there: we had to take it in turns to go for walks round the church every half-hour. We were wearing so many clothes that we looked like Michelin men. Fi made me do aerobics for a few minutes, to warm me up, but it was too hard with all the clothing. There was no action in the street until eight o'clock, when they changed sentries. Fi wrote it down: '8.00, sentries.'

'You should write 0800,' I pointed out. 'That's the military style.'

In each house half of the sentries took up positions at the front and the others disappeared around the back. We could see some activity starting inside the houses too. On the upper floor of the place next to Fi's, a man came to the window dressed only in jocks, and stood there looking out for a minute. Fi collapsed in giggles as the man lifted one arm, then the other, spraying his armpits with deodorant. A woman dressed in a green and white tracksuit came out of another house and jogged off down the street.

It seemed that the officers kept office hours. Maybe that's why they were called officers. Anyway, at five to nine, people started coming out of the houses. Some were just dressed in ordinary soldiers' clothes, but six looked like big shots. One of them was the one Fi and I had seen in the Jaguar. They all converged on a big old brick house halfway along Turner Street.

'Doctor Burgess's place,' Fi said. 'Nice house.'

As the morning wore on it was hard to remember

that we were doing anything dangerous. It was like watching a normal business in full swing. Cars came and went, people hurried in and out of houses, we could even hear phones ringing sometimes when the street was really quiet. Lunch started at 12.30, when people wandered back to different houses. Some sat out in the street in the weak sunshine, eating from little plastic lunchboxes. Delicious smells wafted from kitchens, making our mouths water and our tummies make little snoring noises. Mournfully we turned to our own lunches: Vita Brits spread with jam or Vegemite or honey. It wasn't bad, although I missed little luxuries like butter and margarine. I longed for hot food, and for something with meat, like the meals the soldiers were preparing.

Not a lot else happened until 4.35, and then we saw something that made us nearly swallow our tongues. I was watching while Fi did a few laps of the church to warm herself up. She'd just returned and was leaning against the wall beside me, panting hard. 'Oh Fi, nobody'll buy your fitness video if you don't lift your game,' I said. 'Hello, here comes another car.'

Fi turned towards her window and watched with me as the car pulled up. It was one we hadn't seen before, a Range Rover. 'That's the Ridgeways' car,' Fi said indignantly. She sounded quite outraged, as though this was the most serious crime committed during the whole war.

'Go and make a citizen's arrest,' I said, still watching the car. There was a driver, who looked like an ordinary soldier, and two people sitting in the back. One was another senior officer, wearing a peaked cap, and with gold piping on his uniform jacket. I couldn't see much of the other one.

The car pulled up outside Fi's neighbours', and the two men in the back got out. An archway covered with a leafy creeper topped the front gate of the house and beyond it a winding path through the garden led to the door. This meant that once people went through the gate we only had one more glimpse of them. To make matters worse, the Range Rover had pulled up very close to the front gate. The man in the right-hand rear seat had to walk around the back of the car, so we got a good look at him. But the other man was out of the vehicle and through the gate without us having any view. There was just that moment when he was walking along the path towards the door and would pass between two red-bud trees. I craned to get a good look. Then, with a horrified squeal, I clutched at Fi, who was just beyond clutching range.

'What?' she said. 'What?' She hadn't been looking very hard and already it was too late to see the man.

'Oh God, I don't believe it. Oh my God.'

'What?' Fi asked again, getting impatient, and maybe a bit scared too.

'That was Major Harvey!'

'Oh Ellie, don't be ridiculous.'

'Fi, I swear. I swear to you, that was Major Harvey.'

'Are you sure?'

'Yes, I think so.'

'Well are you sure or do you just think so?'

'I'm ninety per cent sure. No, I'm ninety-five per cent sure. Fi, honestly, it was him. Didn't you even get a glimpse?'

'Well, just a glimpse. It could have been him, I suppose. He was about the right size.'

I leaned against the wall, trembling.

'Fi, if it is him, what do you think it means?'

'I don't know. Oh gosh Ellie.' Fi started to realise the implications. 'Do you think...? Oh no! Maybe... maybe he's just pretending to be with them so he can spy on them.'

I shook my head. Why did I know instinctively that there was something in Major Harvey that would make him incapable of that kind of courage? How did I know that he had some fatal weakness that would always find him out, like water found the weakest spot in a tank, and sheep the one hole in the fence?

I knew though; as surely as I knew that we had unfinished business with Major Harvey.

We kept watching on into the evening, but the man did not come out again. From five to six o'clock, people seemed to finish work and drift back to the other houses. At eight o'clock we saw our fourth sentry change and at ten o'clock we withdrew, slipping out through the vestry door and tiptoeing through the graveyard. I couldn't wait to tell the others what we'd seen. Lee and Homer were asleep but we woke them straightaway. And the five of us spent hours discussing the possibilities. We agreed though: the first thing we had to do was confirm that the man I'd glimpsed really was the ex-commander of Harvey's Heroes.

Chapter Sixteen

We didn't see anyone who looked like Harvey for two days. As far as we could tell the man didn't leave the house for that time, but on the third day, when Robyn and I were in the tower, we saw him quite clearly. The Range Rover pulled up about ten metres short of the gate, so when Harvey stepped into the street he had to walk that distance to the car. As he emerged through the gateway, we got a perfect view: a small tubby man in a dark suit; the only person we'd seen in Turner Street who wasn't in military uniform.

Robyn gazed at me in amazement. 'It really is him,' she breathed.

I'd been starting to doubt my own eyesight and my own memory, and it was exciting to be proved right. I was so pleased with myself that I just stood there gazing triumphantly at Robyn. The Range Rover U-turned and began to accelerate slowly away, still in first gear. I glanced out the window again. Major Harvey, sitting on the left side of the rear seat, as before, was chatting to the driver, an ingratiating smile on his face.

As the car turned out of Turner Street I leaned against the wall of the tower and stared at Robyn.

'That bastard,' I said. 'That...'

'Don't swear, Ellie,' she said, looking uncomfortable. 'Not in a church.'

'All right,' I said, with a big effort. 'All right. But wait till we get out of here. I'll swear like you've never heard. I'll swear like a bullock driver with a team of camels. I tell you what, we're in the right place being in a church, because Judas Iscariot is in the Bible, isn't he, and this guy is a fair dinkum honest-to-goodness Judas Iscariot.'

'But surely he couldn't have... he wouldn't have betrayed Harvey's Heroes... would he?' Robyn asked.

'I don't know.' I tried to think, but I was too tired. 'I just don't know. I don't think he would have set that ambush up at the tank, 'cos if he had, he wouldn't have allowed the spectators. I mean the soldiers obviously had no idea we were above them in the bush. All I'm sure is that if he was on our side before, he isn't now.'

It wasn't till next morning that I figured out the vital clue. I suddenly remembered the conversation with the man in Kevin's machinery shed, when I'd had my reunion with Mrs Macca. In the middle of breakfast, fruit juice dribbling down my chin as I choked on my cereal, I excitedly asked Robyn, 'Listen, what's a chalkie?'

'A chalkie? I don't know.'

'Where's a dictionary?'

'I don't know.'

'Thanks for your help.' I rushed off to the sitting room, where I found an Oxford dictionary and a Macquarie dictionary. But they were no more help than Robyn had been. All they said was that chalky meant having the consistency of chalk. I had a strong suspicion of what it really meant but I needed confirmation. Homer supplied it that night when he got back from sentry go. We were sitting on our own, in the bow window.

'A chalkie? It's a teacher of course; everyone knows that.'

'Is it? Is it really? Well there you go then. The man in Kevin's machinery shed said there was a bloke who used to be a chalkie putting the finger on people at the Showground. He said people were being taken away on his say-so.' I got more excited as I remembered something else. 'Plus, whoever it was, he knew all the people in the Army Reserve. That's a perfect fit for Harvey. A perfect fit!'

When we told the others they all reacted in different ways. Fi sat there white with shock, unable to speak. It was like she'd never dreamt that people could do such terrible things. Lee jumped to his feet, equally pale-faced, his eyes burning. He slammed his fist into the wall. 'He's dead,' he said. 'That's it. He's dead.' He walked across the room and stood with his hands tucked into his armpits, staring out the window, his whole body trembling.

Homer'd had a while to get used to the idea. He seemed almost gentle about it. 'It does all fit,' he said. 'It makes a lot of things clear.'

'Where do we go from here?' I asked. 'If we're going to attack these houses in some way, then what do we want? Do we want to destroy the houses and all the stuff they've got in them? Do we want to destroy Fi's house? Do we want to kill people? Do we want to kill Major Harvey?'

'Yes,' said Lee, without turning round. 'All of the above.' He'd plunged straight back into his psycho

231

state, like when he'd stabbed the soldier. He scared me when he was like that.

'I hate them living in our house,' Fi said. 'I feel like we'll need it disinfected when they leave. But I don't want to wreck the house. Mum and Dad would kill me.'

'Your neighbours wouldn't be too impressed if we burnt down all the houses except yours,' Homer said. 'It'd be a bit unfair.'

Fi looked even more miserable. 'I saw Corrie's house get blown up,' she said. 'I saw what it did to her.'

'Let's worry about that side of it later,' Homer said. 'Let's see whether we can attack these places first. If we can't figure out any way to do it, then there's no point Fi getting upset.'

'You mentioned burning,' I said. 'I don't know if there's any easy way to do that.'

'It's just the first thing that came to my mind,' Homer said.

'Are we going to kill people?' Robyn asked.

'Yes,' Lee said again.

'Lee!' Robyn said. 'Stop talking like that! I hate it when you talk like that. It scares me.'

'You didn't see what they did at Harvey's Heroes' campsite,' Lee said.

'Come back and sit down Lee,' I said. After a moment he did at least do that, sitting next to me on the sofa.

'I think there's a difference between setting fire to the houses, knowing people might die, and deliberately setting out to kill people,' Homer said. 'But the fact is, if we kill Harvey and some of their senior officers, we'll help our side a lot in the war. We could be saving other people's lives. That's a fact, and there's no point even arguing about that. The real question is, do we have the stomach to do it?'

We disappeared into our own thoughts for a minute. I imagine the others were doing what I was doing: searching inside myself to see if I had the guts to kill in cold blood. To my surprise I decided I probably did. Although I hated how this war was brutalising me so quickly, I also felt that it was expected of me, that all the people held prisoner at the Showground – my parents, our friends, our neighbours – would expect it. All the poor harmless nice people who'd belonged to Harvey's Heroes would expect it. Throughout the country people would expect it. Somehow I would just have to do it, and worry about the effects on me afterwards. Strangely, for once I didn't think about the danger to me, about my own safety.

'I'll do what I have to do,' I said.

'And if that means deliberately killing people?' Homer said.

'Yes.'

'Could you put a gun to one of them and pull the trigger?' Homer asked. 'I'm talking in cold blood now. We know what you can do in hot blood.'

Robyn started to protest but Homer cut in quickly. 'We have to ask these questions,' he said. 'We have to know. It's no good going in there and finding at the critical moment that someone can't do what we planned for them to do. That way we'll all end up dead.'

'God, sometimes I wish we'd been taken prisoner like everyone else,' I said. 'Why do we have to be the ones who have to do all this? I don't know what I can do until I'm in a particular situation. But I think I could shoot one of them.'

'OK,' Homer said. 'Lee?'

'I won't let anyone down,' Lee said.

'What does that mean?' Robyn lost her temper. 'Does that mean that anyone who won't kill people is letting the side down? Get real Lee. Sometimes it takes more guts not to do something than to do it.'

Lee didn't say anything, just sat there brooding, ignoring my hand rubbing his leg. Homer watched him for a minute, then sighed and turned to Fi.

'Fi?'

'I'll do everything I can,' she said. 'Even if it means wrecking our house, I suppose. But honestly, I don't see why we need to. They only seem to be using it as accommodation for the peasants. None of the VIPs seem to be using it.'

'Could you shoot someone?' Homer asked.

'No. You know I've never fired a gun in my life. I've practised loading them and aiming them and everything, but I don't want to have to fire one.'

'Well OK,' Homer said. 'But could you push one of them off a roof, or could you stab one, or could you throw a radiator in their bath to electrocute them?'

'I think I could do the last one, maybe.'

'So you could kill someone if it didn't involve you having to come into direct physical contact with them?'

'Yes, I suppose that makes the difference. I could probably even shoot them if I was used to guns.'

'Robyn?'

'What Ellie said made me think,' Robyn said, unexpectedly. 'When she asked why we were the ones in this position, why we hadn't been taken prisoner like everyone else. Maybe this is a kind of trial for us, a test, to see what we're made of.' She stood and walked to the window and turned to face us. 'At the end of it, maybe we'll be judged to see how we've handled ourselves. And I think we'll only pass that test if we've acted with honour, if we've tried our best to do the right thing. If we don't do things out of greed or ambition or hatred or a lust for blood, if we keep testing all our decisions against our own beliefs, if we try to be brave and honest and fair... well, I think that's all that's expected of us. We don't have to be perfect, as long as we keep trying to be perfect.'

'So, what are you prepared to do?' Homer asked.

'I can't answer that in advance. Let's work out a plan and then I'll do all I can to make it work. For the time being, you'll have to be satisfied with that.'

'What about you, Homer?' I asked.

His voice was as steady as his gaze, and he answered: 'I'll fight. I won't back off from anything. Killing women soldiers, well, that'd be hard for me to do in cold blood, that'd be the hardest thing for me. It's not very logical but that's the way it is. But I think I could do it if the need was there.'

We'd each made our statement. We knew now, roughly, where each of us stood. The next stage was to make some plans. We talked and talked. Fi hadn't done the maps she was meant to have, so instead we asked her a thousand questions. Where are the back doors in these houses? Where are the staircases? Do they have verandahs at the back? How many bedrooms are there? Where are the fuse-boxes? What kind of heating do they have? Fi answered all the questions she could but after a while she got muddled and couldn't remember which house had a wine cellar and which had a coolroom.

By then it was time for the next pair to go to the

church, to do a day's watching. We agreed that we had to keep up our surveillance, that we needed more information, as much as we could get.

We maintained the same routine for another three long days, and in the end luck, rather than some grand plan we'd spent the time carefully putting together, seemed to give us the break we wanted. One morning Lee and I sat and watched as a furniture van pulled up in Turner Street. It came from Stratton Removals – Wirrawee was too small to have its own removal business. It drove up the hill and turned around, and parked outside the house at the top end of the street. The soldier-driver left it and wandered off to another house. The truck sat there for a few hours without anything happening. But towards lunchtime an officer came out of the house that we now called the headquarters, and ordered the sentries to him. They obeyed, but they didn't look too excited. He gave them a little talk, then marched them into the end house. Within a few minutes I realised that some serious looting was going on. They started by carrying out a beautiful old dark dining table, that shone in the lukewarm autumn sunlight. Next came six chairs of the same dark timber, with burgundy coloured cushions. After that was a series of paintings in big heavy golden frames, each needing two people to carry it. The officer fussed around, supervising but never doing any actual work. It took a long time, because he was anxious for everything to be handled with the greatest care, but when they'd loaded the paintings he let them go to lunch. No one touched the truck for the rest of the day.

When Lee and I took ourselves off duty and trudged wearily back to our house, I put a plan to the other four. Sitting there all day watching that truck perched at the top of the hill had given me the idea.

'Listen,' I said, 'suppose one of us gets in the truck, lets the brake off, puts it in neutral and jumps out again. The truck's pointing down the hill. It should roll straight down Turner Street and hit that house at the end. Now at that point every man and his dog, and every woman too, comes running. We take advantage of the distraction to sneak into the houses and start our fires. We can take one house each. We should be able to do a bit of damage. And when the fires start, that's another distraction, and we get away in the confusion.'

It was a high-risk approach, but we'd all reached a state of such boredom and frustration that we decided to try it. The biggest advantage was that if it seemed too dangerous in the early stages we could sneak away into the darkness with no harm done. Once the houses started burning it wouldn't be so easy.

We set to work. We grabbed all the inflammables that we could find that would fit into our pockets. Turps, kero, metho and firelighters, and of course matches. We packed all our possessions and hid them in the garden where we could pick them up easily. Our getaway plan was to head right across town and meet in Mrs Alexander's, near the Showground. Last time we'd been there I'd seen two cars in her garage, both with keys in the ignition. I assumed they'd still be there, which would be useful if we decided that a car was our best means of escape.

We synchronised watches. Fi had the job of unleashing the removal truck. The rest of us took one house each, and worked out different routes to get into the back gardens. I chose Fi's neighbours' – the house where Major Harvey seemed to live. Fi's place was spared, only because it wasn't one of the four busiest houses, and we only had four people for the attacks. We left ourselves plenty of time so we wouldn't be under too much pressure: almost an hour and a half for a 3 am attack. Then, with a quick exchange of hugs, we left.

It wasn't until I was getting over the back fence of Fi's neighbours that I really felt fear. Before that, everything had been chaotic, disorganised. But out here, in the cold darkness, knowing that a soldier with a gun was standing somewhere between me and the building, the chill that I felt in the ground seemed to run up my legs and through my body. I got the shivers or the shakes, I'm not sure which, and spent a few minutes trying to will them out of my system. When that didn't work I knew that I'd just have to go ahead anyway. I got over the fence easily enough – it was an old brick wall about a metre and a half tall – and found myself on a mound of compost in a pit in the rear corner of the block. The owner was a very efficient gardener – there was a row of pits, each containing different soils and compost. I'd sunk up to my knees in my pile, so I pulled myself out, shook the stuff off my legs, and started moving cautiously towards the house. There was a dim light inside somewhere; just a night light, I thought. I had about an hour to make a journey of forty metres and that suited me fine. I trained myself to take one step every few minutes and then wait. It was incredibly difficult, even with the fear of a bullet ripping through me. The temptation was to say 'what the hell', and take half a dozen quick steps. But I kept a tight control on myself, and continued to inch along. It was scary, but it was also very boring.

I finished up outside a room that had a laundry look about it. I don't know why laundries always say laundry, but they do. Maybe it's a smell that you notice unconsciously. I huddled there, trying to read my watch face in the darkness. It took ages to work it out, but eventually I was satisfied that it said 2.45. Once I was sure of the time, I spent five more minutes studying the object beside my left shin. It was, I decided, a gas meter and gas tap. Ten minutes to go. I checked out the vegetation beside my right foot. Forget-me-nots. Not very interesting.

I was shivering badly by three o'clock. But this time it was definitely from cold more than anything else. I was genuinely keen for Fi to get the truck rolling; unusual for me. I normally was in no hurry to risk my life.

Three o'clock ticked slowly past. 'Hurry up Fi,' I cursed. I was afraid I was going to start getting cramps. Five past three and the road was as quiet as a hayshed. Ten past three, and nothing. I couldn't believe it. I wondered how long I should wait before giving up. We hadn't worked that out. New sentries, fresh, wide-awake sentries, came on at four o'clock, and I wanted to be well gone by then. At 3.15 I stood slowly, hearing the little clicks in my knees, feeling the strain in my hammies. I'd decided 3.20 would be my deadline and at 3.24 I acted on that, beginning a retreat that was almost as slow as my arrival. By the time I got to the back wall it was 3.40. I paused in the compost pit for a few seconds, wondering if I was doing the right thing, then scrambled over the wall and set off at a jog for the music teacher's house.

Homer was already there, in a frenzy of worry. 'What the hell do you think's happened?' he kept asking. 'What do you think?'

'I don't know,' I kept answering, very helpfully.

'Do you think anyone would go straight to Mrs Alexander's?'

'Not without their swags.'

Just after four Robyn arrived. 'Nothing, no sign of anyone,' she reported.

At 4.30 came Lee, and at last, at 4.45, came Fi. She was distraught. 'The truck was locked!' she blurted out as soon as she saw us. 'It was locked!'

I laughed. There was nothing else to do. Such a simple thing, and we'd never thought of it. I hadn't seen anyone lock it during the day, but I hadn't been watching especially.

'I couldn't think!' Fi sobbed. 'I couldn't smash the window because of the noise. I kept waiting for one of you to come, but nobody did.'

We were all exhausted, probably emotionally as well as physically. When I said we had to keep watch from the church for another day I got no support at all.

'Oh no,' Fi groaned. 'It's too much.'

'We've done enough for one night,' Robyn agreed.

'Do it yourself,' Lee snapped. 'I'm going to bed.'

'All right, I will.'

I was sure it was important. They watched sullenly as I got my gear together. No one said a word as I left the house. But I could hear them through the window, starting to argue about who'd do the first sentry duty. I pushed the window up and put my head in, to get the last word.

'Keep it to a whisper, guys. Sound travels a long way at night.'

I knew it'd be a lonely day in the tower of St John's, but I didn't mind. I had a sleep for an hour or so when I got there, which left me feeling stiff and sore, but when I'd recovered I spent the day just watching and thinking. Not a lot happened in the street. The truck was moved down to the next house and had a baby grand piano loaded on it, and then to the next, where it collected a couple of rugs and a dresser. By then it was too far down the hill to give us any hope of trying to stampede it again. We had to come up with a better idea.

I saw Major Harvey emerge from his house at 9.30. The Range Rover had arrived and was waiting for him. He got in the back of the car, on his own except for the driver, and the Range Rover U-turned again and drove away. I wondered if he was going to the Showground. Maybe it was my parents he'd be interrogating today.

When he returned, just after four, he got out of the car and went into the house, but this time the driver got out too, and went to another house, leaving the Range Rover parked in the street. It was still there when I gave up and stole back through the darkness alone, at about ten o'clock. But by then my knowledge of the sentries' habits, and the smell of cooking food which had been making me drool all evening, had given me an idea. That time spent crouched behind the house in the cold early morning hadn't been wasted.

The others fussed over me when I got back. I think they were feeling guilty. I was so tired that I accepted it without protest. And when I told them my idea they accepted it, almost straightaway. It was like the previous night: we were desperate for something that would work and so were clutching at any old straw.

What I wanted was to cause an explosion that would rattle windows in Los Angeles, that would make the San Andreas Fault seem like a minor mistake. My idea was based on the memory of our gas heater in the TV room at home. There was one thing I'd learnt in infancy about that heater – if you turned the gas on and it didn't ignite straightaway, you had to get it off again fast. If you waited a few seconds, then lit another match, you'd nearly lose your face. It was amazing how fast the gas poured out.

If that could happen so fast, what would be the effect of leaving on three or four heaters, full bore, for thirty minutes? And then striking a match? A huge, huge bang, that's what.

So that was the main part of the plan. But Homer and I made them go through everything carefully and closely. One thing had made me nervous during our failed raid and that was the feeling that we hadn't spent the time planning that we normally did. We'd left too much to chance.

So this time we worked out careful timetables, based on our succeeding or our failing. And we decided to collect five bikes and take them with us, so we could get to Mrs Alexander's garage faster if necessary. That left us with just one problem to solve. I'd known all along it would be our biggest one. The problem was the fuse. I'd suggested laying a trail of inflammable liquid, like we'd done when we'd destroyed the bridge with the petrol tanker, but I'd always known that was the weakest part of the plan. And sure enough, the others ruled it out straightaway.

'The sentries'd smell it,' Homer said. 'We've already got one risk with smell, although they should have their windows shut on these cold nights. But we don't need another risk.'

Lee solved the problem. He'd been sitting in silence for half an hour but he suddenly leapt to his feet, giving me a shock. He didn't actually yell 'Eureka', but we got the general idea. 'Go into any houses you can find open,' he commanded, 'and bring back toasters. And electric timers. Don't come back till you've got one each. And don't ask questions. There isn't time. We can still do this tonight if we hurry.'

'And while we're at it, get the bikes too,' Homer said, as we stirred our tired bodies into life. I'd lost track of the last time I'd had a proper sleep but I was operating on autopilot now.

I went with Fi. We were moving a little more confidently around the town. There were two other areas, apart from Snob Hill and the shopping centre in Barker Street, that were lit each night. We assumed people were living there and we kept away from them. But the rest of the town, the dark streets and silent houses, seemed to be left alone these days. We never saw patrols in them. It seemed like the soldiers were confident that they had Wirrawee under control. They'd probably caught everyone except us.

'Well,' I thought grimly, 'if we do what we want to do tonight, we won't be safe in Wirrawee for a long time.'

Fi and I got into four houses, getting four toasters easily enough, but having trouble with the timers. But in the last house we struck a jackpot. There were timers in almost every room, each controlling a radiator. Seemed like a very organised person lived there.

By two o'clock we were back at the house, each

243

with our little collections and each wheeling a bicycle. Robyn had a pump, which we all needed, as most of the tyres were quite flat. Lee hadn't been able to find a timer, so Fi and I solved that problem for him. But Lee did have a pair of pliers, and with those he gave a demonstration of what he wanted us to do. It was very simple and very clever and had a very good chance of success.

When we were satisfied with his plan he used his pliers to cut the filament in each toaster and made us practise setting the timers. By then it was three o'clock and time to go. We set our timers, quickly repacked our swags and saddled ourselves with them. We were taking them with us this time, so we could make faster escapes.

We'd chosen the same houses as the previous night. I had Fi's neighbours', Robyn had the next one, which we thought was also being used as offices, then Lee took the next – Dr Burgess's house – which was obviously the main headquarters. Opposite that was a big new brick house where a lot of officers slept, and Homer had chosen that. Now that Fi didn't have to take a truck out of gear she was free to attack a house too. She bravely offered to do her own but we talked her into going to the one at the top of the hill, which seemed to be more heavily used. Of course there was every chance that hers was going to be damaged by the blast, as she knew.

I followed the same course as the previous night, climbing the brick fence and trekking through the compost pit. I was clutching my toaster; a timer was making a bulge in one pocket, and a torch in the other. We had to be in our positions by four o'clock, so again I had enough time to be able to move slowly and carefully. But I guess I was sick of being so careful, so disciplined all the time. After taking five minutes to move six steps I finally lost my cool and moved ten metres in one rush, to hide behind a lemon tree. I thought by doing so much it'd make the rest of the trek less monotonous. But it nearly killed me. I was just about to leave the tree and take my next step when I heard a snap of wood. It sounded horribly like the tread of a human foot. I hesitated, then crouched and waited. Sure enough a moment later a beam of light shone across the garden. It traversed the plants in deadly silence. I crouched even lower, scrunching up my eyes, waiting for bullets to come tearing into me. Do you hear the bullets before you die? I wondered. Or does it all happen so fast that you feel them and die without even hearing the noise? I forced myself to open my eyes and twist my head slightly, to take a little look. I half expected that the sentry would be there, looking down at me, with rifle poised. But there was only the torch beam, continuing to explore, at this moment quite a way from me and shining on a rose bush. Then it was turned off. I realised straightaway what a stupid position I'd put myself in by my impatience. If I moved any time between now and four o'clock I risked being heard. If I didn't move I'd left myself quite a distance to get to the house when four o'clock came. Time was going to be tight enough anyway. I thought about it for ten minutes and decided on a compromise. I'd move to a position where I could see the sentry, and then decide my tactics.

I moved with excruciating care. With excruciating pain too, after being curled up like a frightened guinea pig for so long. I nearly got the giggles when I wondered how I'd explain the toaster if I were caught. 'I had a sudden craving for toast, and I was looking for a power point.' I kept shuffling along, taking little sneak looks every step or so, until at last I could see the sentry. He or she – it was too dark to tell – seemed to be facing out into the garden still, as though watching and listening. Just my luck to get one of the efficient ones. I tried to get a look at my watch but it was too dark here to tell the time.

We had arranged everything for the sentry change at four o'clock and now I didn't know how close four o'clock was. My only hope was that I'd hear the new sentries arriving out the front, for the changeover. There was quite a little ceremony that took place for the changing of the guard. I'd watched it so often now that I knew the script. The new ones marched up the street to the Burgess house and halted there. Then the person in charge blew a whistle and the different sentries emerged from their positions, made their reports, formed a line and marched off to their quarters, while the new ones split up to go to their different posts. It only took a few minutes, but it was those few minutes we depended on.

I thought that if the sentry could hear the whistle then I should too, so I stayed frozen where I was and waited. I thought that I'd be there for ages but after only ten minutes I heard the scrunch of marching feet from the road. The sentry heard it as well, and suddenly lost her attentive attitude and walked off to the corner of the house. She paused there, waiting for the whistle. You could tell she wasn't allowed into the street until she heard it, but she was hanging out for the signal. I'd guess that every house had a guard poised at its back corner, waiting for the moment of freedom. Four hours of boring duty in the middle of the night would have that effect.

I heard the distant trilling of the whistle, and the sentry was gone, without a backward glance. I didn't have time for any more caution. I stood straightaway and walked quickly to the back door. These sentries were going to be in a heap of trouble tomorrow, if they survived. My biggest fear now was the door itself. If doors were locked we'd agreed to use our discretion: either to give up, or to wrap a hand in our jumpers and punch a pane of glass out. But Fi was sure they wouldn't be locked. Her theory was that most of the people who lived in Turner Street were so security-conscious that they'd all have deadlocks, like on her house. For the soldiers to get into these houses in the first place, they'd have had to break in. That meant, that unless the doors had been repaired, they'd still be unlocked – and unlockable.

It was a very logical theory and for once logic worked. When I turned the handle of the door and pushed, the whole door nearly fell off. It had been smashed open, then stood up again and propped against the doorframe. 'Onya Fi!' I grinned, hoping the others were going as well as me. It was so dark that I had to use the torch; I fished it out and put my hand over its lens and switched it on. In the dim pinkish light I saw a row of boots and knew I was standing in the back porch. It was just the way Fi had described it.

I moved fast, straight through to the kitchen. With a tiny thin ray of torchlight I found the stove. One glance was enough to make me feel sick. It was electric. That meant I'd have to search further, take longer. I hurried through into the dining room, sweat starting to rush out of my pores. Here I found what I wanted: a gas heater. I turned it full on, and jammed the timer and toaster into a power point, throwing the switch on. I'd set the timer to an approximate time, as we all had, in case we were too rushed to fine-tune them. Now, I didn't know if I had time or not, but I was too scared to think about it, and to be honest, too scared to care. But I did check the broken filament in the toaster: if the two broken ends weren't close enough together there'd be no spark and all this would have been for nothing. Gas was gushing into the room and I was trying not to breathe it in. The smell was terrible. It was frightening how quickly the gas rushed out. I moved the ends of the filament a little closer together, put it down gently, and ran into the sitting room. Another heater here, good. Turn it on. Is there time to check the rumpus room? And the study? Yes. Well, one anyway. The rumpus room. Into there on fast feet, and another quick search with the covered torch. And yes, lucky lucky, a third heater. I switched it on and scrambled for the back door, desperate to get away, full of desperate fear that the new guard would be in position. I could smell the gas even at the back door. I couldn't believe how it was spreading. I got to the door and took a quick peek out. I couldn't afford to take any more time, to show any more caution. I propped the door up again behind me and scurried for cover. Scrunch, scrunch, scrunch. That was the sentry's boots on the gravel, coming around the side of the house. I dived like a footballer, landing under a bush with tiny leaves and tiny flowers, but banging my knee on a rock as I did. Oh, that poor knee. Every time I hit anything it seemed to be with that knee. I stuffed my fist in my mouth in agony and lay there with tears smarting my eyes. At the same time I couldn't help noticing how sweet and fragrant the bush smelt. It seems crazy to have been aware of that, but I was.

I let myself have a few seconds under the bush, but I knew I had to move. With the rough job I'd done on the timer, the whole place could go up much earlier than I'd planned. I crawled out from my cover and began another interminably slow hike through the garden to the back wall. I gave myself ten minutes, but I was terrified there'd be an explosion before that. Sweat was streaming down my face, as though I'd run five k's. I kept picturing the timer suddenly throwing its switch on, the rush of electricity into the toaster, the sparks flying from the end of one broken wire to the other, the gas erupting in a sudden huge blast...

At the compost pit I ignored my knee and hauled myself over the wall, then did a kind of limping run down the lane. I went straight to the bikes and with wild joy saw Fi, holding a bike with each hand.

'What are you doing?' I hissed. 'It's too dangerous to wait here.' But I grinned at her.

'I know,' she said. 'But I couldn't bear to go off on my own.' And I saw her perfect white teeth gleam back at me from her grubby face.

I grabbed the bike and without another word we pushed off. As we did I heard running feet behind me. I looked round, startled, but hopeful. It was Lee, panting hard.

'Let's get out of here,' he said.

'Good line for a movie,' I whispered. He gave me a puzzled glance, then remembered, flashed me a smile, and took off. Inside a second he was five metres ahead of me. Fi and I had to pedal hard to catch up.

It took us ages to get to Mrs Alexander's. We had to

go such a roundabout way, and most of it was uphill. But as we were finally dismounting outside her garage, the hill opposite seemed to catch fire. I've never seen a volcano, but I imagine that's what it'd be like. There was a kind of 'whoosh' and flames shot into the air like a Roman candle. A moment later a thunderclap of sound hit us. At exactly the same time there were two more eruptions. We couldn't exactly see the houses but I saw the roof of one lift into the air and disintegrate, and the next moment all the trees around them caught fire and were blazing fiercely.

'Golly gosh,' Fi said, gazing in awe. That was about the strongest expression she ever used.

The roar of the fire was so loud we could hear it from our possie. A wind of energy from the explosion suddenly came through the garden like a wall, bending trees and plants over and buffeting us. Small dark shapes blipped past me. They seemed to come from nowhere: birds fleeing from the blast. The whole of one side of Wirrawee was gradually being lit up. There was a hellish red glow in the sky; I could almost smell the burning.

'Quick,' Lee said. 'Let's move it.'

We rushed into the garage. At least this time we had some light, from our torches, unlike the last time I'd been in that garage, groping around looking for matches, and in desperate danger.

'I hope Robyn and Homer were well out of that,' I said. There was no time for more talk. I threw open the door of the nearer car, clambered in, and turned the key. There was a weary grinding sound.

'Oh God,' I said. 'Flat battery.'

Lee leaned into the other car, a ute, and tried that, with the same result.

As he stood up again Robyn came bursting into the garage, puffing and wild-eyed.

'Are you all here?' she asked.

'Not Homer. And the cars won't start.'

'Oh help,' she said, and disappeared outside again, to look for Homer, I imagined.

I tried the first car again but the weary noise got more and more tired, until it became just a faint murmur.

'It'll have to be the bikes,' I said to Lee. We ran outside and retrieved our bikes from behind a shed, where we'd dumped them. I couldn't help stopping to look at the furious fires raging on the hill. There were lights on in every occupied part of Wirrawee, and we could see the headlights of many vehicles converging on Turner Street. And I could see two fire engines trundling out of the Showground.

'We've got one thing going for us,' Lee said. 'If we've wiped out a lot of their officers they mightn't have anyone smart enough to take charge or give orders.'

I nodded. 'Let's take advantage,' I said. 'What about Homer? Can we leave him a note?'

Robyn came over, out of the darkness, wheeling her bike.

'I'll wait for him,' she said.

'No, Robyn, no, it's too dangerous. Please Robyn, don't do that.'

She paused. Then we were all saved by a voice out of the night.

'Anyone for toast?' said Homer.

'Stay on your bike,' I said quickly. 'The cars are both stuffed. Where's Fi?'

'Here,' came her little voice.

'Let's go, famous five.'

Chapter Seventeen

Daylight came too fast, catching us when we were still a long way from my place and from the faithful Land Rover. We made an emergency decision, to swing off the main road and into the nearest property, the Mackenzies'.

It was only the second time I'd been here since a jet had destroyed the house, in our full view. We'd watched from the shearers' quarters as the house had exploded, so many weeks ago. Seeing it again, in the cold, grey, miserable light of dawn, made me feel better about blowing up half of Turner Street. I felt sorry for the owners of those houses, but I knew we'd probably done the enemy more damage there than in all our previous operations put together. And it was at least a little repayment for the way these people had smashed the lives of the Mackenzies, bombing their house and shooting their daughter: Corrie, their daughter, my friend.

The others went straight on up to the shearing shed but I wandered through the ruins of the house for a few minutes. Already some little weeds had taken root and were starting to spread. Angrily, I pulled them out. Maybe I was wrong. They were life, in their own way. There was little else of it around. Nothing among the ruins was undamaged. Every piece of crockery was smashed, every saucepan warped and bent, every piece of timber splintered and scarred. I looked in vain for something that was unmarked. At least my teddy bear Alvin, a little scrap of love, had survived the Harvey's Heroes' massacre.

I did find one thing though, as I turned towards my bike and started walking away from the house. Poking out from under a brick was something that gleamed silver. I pulled it out. It was a letter opener, long and thin and sharp, with a short crossbar as a handle. I pocketed it. Maybe one day I'd be able to use it. I thought of it as a weapon. It never occurred to me that one day I might use it to open letters. But I did hope that maybe one day I'd be able to return it to its owners.

'Ellie!' a voice screamed.

Startled, I looked up. Robyn was waving at me from the shearing shed. 'Plane!' she screamed.

I realised then that there was a low buzzing noise in the background that I hadn't consciously noticed. Maybe I'd been too tired. But exhaustion was pumped out of my system by adrenalin as I ran for my bike, stumbling over bricks, feeling the ache in my knee becoming a sharp pain again.

I ignored the pain, fumbled to pick up the bike, wondered if I would lead the planes to the shed by riding towards it, but realised at the same time that there was no other cover, and so pedalled like mad straight at it. As soon as I was in its shadows the others grabbed me and hauled me into the old building. I lay on the floor sobbing for breath. The noise of the plane swept straight over our heads and kept going. I lay there, my face in the dust, wondering if it had seen me, if it was going to return. I thought of it as an evil creature with its own eyes and its own mind. I couldn't visualise the humans who were sitting at its controls, directing it.

The roar of the plane faded again and I let Robyn help me to my feet.

That was the start of a terrible day. We were proud of what we'd done, but before long we were scared too. We began to realise that whatever and whoever we'd blown up must have been bigger, more important than we'd ever dreamed, ever thought. Planes and helicopters prowled the sky constantly. Their endless buzzing, like angry chainsaws, seemed to seep inside my brain, till I didn't know if they were in my head or in the sky. After a couple of hours we were so nervous that we left the shearing shed, hid the bikes, and went up through the trees into the hills. Not until we were holed up in thick bush did we feel safer. We had no food, except for a packet of dry biscuits that Homer had brought, but we preferred to starve than go into the shooting gallery of the open country.

As we sat there we at last had a chance to tell our stories. It was exciting to compare notes, and it helped take our minds off the endless snarling of the aircraft. I told them my experiences first, then Robyn described hers. She'd taken the next house to me, which we'd thought was a less important office building. But she hadn't been able to get in.

'The door was locked,' she explained, 'so as soon as the sentry marched off at four o'clock I broke a window. I tried to do it gently but it was quite a way above my head, and the whole pane fell out and smashed onto something inside the house. The noise! It was unbelievable. I was starting to panic but I thought I still had time, so I tried climbing up to it. There was a drainpipe running down the wall that forked in opposite directions, so I got up on that. I started stretching to the window to grab the sill, and the pipe broke under me. That made even more noise than the window. I'm sorry, but I chickened out then. I got the shakes and convinced myself that I didn't have time to get in. Looking back, I think I probably could have done it, but all that noise had freaked me out. Then I realised the broken pipe was leaking water all over the ground. It just seemed like everything was against me. I propped the pipe up and set off for the place next door to see if I could help Ellie, but I ended up getting caught between the two sentries coming back, so it took me ages just to get away to the lane. So, I didn't do anything, I'm afraid. You guys can have all the credit.'

Lee had also met a locked door. Maybe they'd locked the buildings they used as offices but not the ones they used as residences. But Lee had one advantage: Fi knew Dr Burgess's house almost as well as she knew her own, so she'd been able to give him a good detailed plan. When he found the back door locked he ran straight to the coal chute, opened it, slid down into the cellar, and from there up into the house.

'Dr Burgess was always talking about putting a lock on that,' said Fi looking smug. 'He was hopeless about security. Dad always said that's why he'd never get burgled.'

Lee had found a gas stove and three gas heaters, so with those on full blast he would have caused quite a bang. I asked him if he'd had any problems getting away, and he just shrugged, looked up into the trees, and said 'No.' I didn't know what that meant. Why couldn't he look at me? I had a horrible feeling that there might be more blood on his hands, on those long graceful musician's fingers.

Homer had got into his house easily, but had found no gas appliances at all. When he left he decided to wait a few blocks away, to see if anything happened.

'You love doing that,' Fi said. 'You did it when we blew up the bridge.'

'He's a mad bomber,' I said.

'This was even better than the bridge,' Homer said. 'It was massive. There was one explosion, then another one, a huge one. Maybe they had explosives stored there. You should have felt the shock wave. It was like this gale suddenly hit me. Wow! And the noise! I can't believe it. There were a lot of secondary explosions too. We did something great this morning. We took on something incredibly hard and brought it off. We're heroes!'

I thought how strange it was that to destroy something, and to kill people, was a great achievement, and I thought how much easier it was to destroy than to build.

'How'd you go, Fi?' Lee asked.

'Oh, I just burrowed away through the garden like a little rabbit,' Fi said. 'I took forever getting to the house. And when I was finally about a metre away from the back wall I realised the sentry was asleep. So I could have walked in whistling and she wouldn't have woken up. I was a bit worried because it was ten to four, and I thought she'd miss the change of shift.

But she had one of those watches with an alarm, so just when I thought I'd have to go over and wake her up, the alarm went off. The whistle was only a few minutes later. She staggered to her feet and marched away. I think she'd been drinking, because she had a bottle that she put in her pocket as she went. As soon as she'd gone round the corner I shot into the house. I did the gas stove in the kitchen and a heater in the breakfast room, but I was too scared to do any more. And I didn't check the timer, just plugged it in and hoped it was all right and left it there.'

'So did I,' I confessed.

It turned out that Lee was the only one who'd checked his timer.

'They would have been all right,' Homer said. 'We'd set them pretty carefully back at Ms Lim's house, and everything ran according to the timetable. The houses did all explode so close together, so maybe one set the others off, or maybe there was an ammo store, like I said.'

In the middle of the afternoon a ground patrol came through the Mackenzies' property. They were in two four-wheel drives, a Toyota and a Jackaroo. I recognised the Jackaroo. It belonged to Mr Kassar, my drama teacher at school. He'd been proud of that car. Although we felt safe enough for the moment, in the thick bush, our great fear was that they'd find some clue to show we'd been there, and then they'd call in back-up forces. We watched intently as they searched the area. The funny thing was that they were so nervous. They kept their rifles in their hands, they stuck close together in little groups, and they kept looking anxiously around them. 'It's only us,' I wanted to call out. 'We're only kids. Don't get too carried away.' But of course they didn't know that. For all they knew, we were professional soldiers, highly trained killers. For all I knew, we were. Maybe that's what we'd become.

One thing was for sure, if they ever caught us, and could identify us as the ones who'd done all this stuff, we were gone. We were dead. I don't mean that just as a saying. I mean that it would be the end of our being alive, of our breathing, of our seeing and thinking. We'd be dead.

The soldiers went on up to the shearing shed. They approached it just like in the movies, moving forward in little rushes, covering each other all the time, kicking the door open. It made me think how lucky we'd been to beat them so many times. We did seem so amateurish, compared to them. I don't know though, that could have been an advantage. Perhaps we had more imagination, more flexibility of thinking, than them. And they were just employees, carrying out someone else's orders. We were our own bosses, able to do what we liked. That probably helped a bit.

It reminded me of a daydream I'd had often when I was younger. It was the world-without-adults daydream. In my dream I'd never quite figured out where the adults went but we kids were free to roam, to help ourselves to anything we wanted. We'd pick up a Merc from a showroom when we needed wheels, and when it ran out of petrol we'd get another one. We'd change cars the way I change socks. We'd sleep in different mansions every night, going to new houses instead of putting new sheets on the beds. It'd be like the Mad Hatter's tea party, where they kept moving along the table to the next place, rather than doing the washing-up. Life would be one long party.

Yes, that had been the dream.

Now I would have been hysterically happy to hand over the reins of the world to adults again. I just wanted to go back to school, to study for uni, to mess round, to watch TV, to do the bottles for the poddy lambs that I used to whinge about when I was feeling lazy or was on the phone talking to Corrie. I didn't want all this worry, all this responsibility. Most of all I didn't want this fear.

In my daydream we weren't chased all over the countryside. We didn't spend our time looking over our shoulders. We didn't have to kill and destroy.

The soldiers finished in the shearers' quarters and ambled back to their vehicles, looking more relaxed. I assumed they hadn't found any giveaway clues. But maybe that was just their trickery. Maybe they knew now that we were nearby, and they were just acting casual, to put us off guard. I don't know whether the others thought that too. We didn't discuss it. We just sat there all afternoon, staring through the trees, out across the paddocks. No one spoke. No one slept, either. We were all tired, tired in a bone-aching, sore-eyed way that made me feel a hundred years old.

At last the light started to fade. The rabbits came popping out of their burrows, looking around nervously, hopping a few steps, nibbling their first mouthfuls for the evening. I was shocked again at how many of them there were. It made me worry about the land, that no one was looking after it properly. I hoped the colonists had a few clues about how to do it. Better to have them look after it than to have no one.

As the rabbits spread out we began to talk. There was a little stirring of relief, that we looked like surviving the day, that we should be OK for another night. We talked quietly, without emotion. I think we'd run out of feelings for the time being. We talked about what we should do next, how to keep ourselves safe, how to act for the best. We were all very calm. We agreed that before we returned to Hell we should pick up more supplies. The more the better, as this could be our last chance for a while. We could try to replace things we'd lost when Harvey's Heroes were blown apart, and we could try for more food and clothes. As long as the heat from our Turner Street attack was on, we wouldn't be able to come out of Hell.

There was a property that we hadn't yet visited, about five k's south of Homer's place. It was a place called 'Tara', that belonged to the Rowntrees. Mum and Dad didn't like the Rowntrees much – Mr and Mrs Rowntree had been more interested in parties than farming, according to Mum and Dad. They'd separated a year ago and were in the middle of a divorce. It was a big property, three times the size of ours, but I didn't think the colonists would be there yet. It was too far from town, and in some hilly country that would be hard to defend.

So, at ten o'clock, we cranked up the bikes and cranked up our legs and rode over to my place. We picked up the Land Rover there. We still had a Ford carefully hidden up on Tailor's Stitch, which we used occasionally, to keep it ticking over. But I preferred the Landie because I'd been driving it for so many years. It was like an old friend. As usual it coughed into life. It always sounded tired, but it always started.

We chugged over to 'Tara', going slowly, because I didn't know the road. There was a manager's house which we thought we'd check later, if there was time, and the main house, about a k away at the end of the drive. It was closer if you took a short cut across the paddocks, but again, because it was dark and wet, I didn't do that. Instead we crept up the drive, between the two rows of huge old pine trees, until we were halfway along it. Then Lee and Robyn walked on up to the house to make sure there were no intruders.

When they signalled us forward, with a wave of torches, we drove up and parked at the front door. It was quite fun, in a strange sort of way, to stickybeak around other people's houses. I liked seeing how they lived, what they owned, how they arranged each room. So Fi and I had a good poke around. It was a nice place. They had beautiful furniture, all big old dark antiques. Must have been worth a fortune. The soldiers would be here one day with their removal trucks, no doubt about that.

Of course they'd been here already though. They'd been everywhere, except Hell. Drawers were open in the bedrooms, and things chucked around. In the sitting room the glass cabinets had been emptied and one of them was broken. There was glass all over the floor. Someone had gone through the grog cabinet, leaving it bare. The music system had been looted too, because the speakers were still there and you could see where the player had been. They hadn't bothered with our old record player, back at my place. Ours must have been worth all of twenty bucks. The Rowntrees' one would have been something special.

Food was our main interest, and we were rapt to

find half a dozen big salamis in the pantry. We were always hanging out for a change of diet. There were two cases of Pepsi, loads of chocolate, and some chips that were getting a bit stale. The Rowntrees seemed to live pretty well. Not many cans, except for soup, plus three of salmon, which I don't eat. But there were plenty of odds and ends, like two-minute noodles and packets of smoked oysters; enough to fill a couple of overnight bags.

We searched the other rooms quickly, grabbed a few pieces of clothing and some sleeping bags, and Fi and I filled our pockets with expensive toiletries. My old daydream had almost come alive for a moment. Lee came back from the study with a pile of big fantasy novels, and it was time to go. I jumped in the driver's seat. Fi was sitting beside me; Homer and Lee were in the back seat; Robyn was stretched out in the back, having made a bed for herself with blankets and clothing we'd taken from 'Tara'. I had the feeling everyone would be asleep before I reached the bottom of the driveway.

'All aboard for Hell,' I said. 'Please fasten your seat belts and extinguish all cigarettes. We'll be cruising at an altitude of a metre above road level, and at speeds of up to 40 k's per hour. Weather conditions for Hell are expected to be wet and cool.'

'Except in Lee's tent, where it'll be hot and steamy,' Homer called out.

'He hopes,' added Fi.

I ignored this childish behaviour and put the car in first. Away we went.

As we neared the bottom of the drive Homer called out again. 'There's something funny over there,' he said.

'Funny peculiar or funny ha ha?'

'Funny peculiar.'

I slowed down a bit and tried to peer across the paddock in the direction he was pointing. It was too difficult to do that and drive at the same time, so I asked him, 'Do you want to stop?'

'No, doesn't matter.'

'Yes, stop,' Robyn called out suddenly, in a strange voice, like someone was twisting her throat.

I hit the clutch and brake and the Landie rolled to a halt. Robyn was out the back door and running.

'What is it?' Fi asked.

'Over there,' Homer said. 'Near the dam.'

I could see the reflecting water of the small earthen dam, and the dam wall itself, but that was all. Perhaps, though, I thought I could see an odd dark shape to the left of the dam and slightly below it. Then I heard a strange sound, a weird, unearthly sound, that brought all my skin out in bubbles, in an instant rash of fear. My scalp burned. I felt like small insects were crawling through my hair.

'Oh sweet Jesus,' said Fi. 'What's that?'

'It's Robyn,' said Lee.

The sound was not a screaming or a crying, more a wailing. The sort of keening that you hear in documentaries about other countries sometimes. I jumped down from the Landie and ran round the back of the vehicle towards the dam. When I was about fifty metres away I began to recognise that there were words to the noise she was making. 'Too much,' she kept saying. 'Too much. It's too much.' It was almost like she was singing it. It was the most horrifying sound I've ever heard, I think.

When I reached her, I'd intended to grab her, to

hold her, to calm and comfort her. I could hear the others coming a bit behind me, but I was the first one there. But when I did reach her, and my eyes saw what she had seen, I forgot about holding her and instead stood wondering if anyone would hold me, or if I'd just have to comfort myself.

Before the war I'd seen a lot of death. You get used to dead bodies, working on a farm. You never like it; sometimes it makes you sick, sometimes you rage against it, sometimes you mourn for days afterwards. But you get used to the ewes killed by foxes as they're giving birth; the lambs with their eyes picked out by crows; the dead cows who are bloated with gas till they look like they might float away. You see myxo'd rabbits, roos caught in fence wire, tortoises that you've run over with the tractor when you're down at the creek filling the furphy. You see ugly death, dry death, quiet death, death full of pain and spit and blood, and intestines torn out with flies laying maggots in them. I remember one of our dogs that took a poison bait and became so frenzied with pain that he ran full speed into the side of a parked truck and broke his neck. I remember another old dog that was blind and deaf. We found his body in the dam one hot day. We think he went in to cool off and couldn't find his way out when he'd finished his swim.

Chris's body was different. It should have been like the others, like the corpses of animals. He'd been there a few weeks, like they often were before anyone noticed them. Like them he had been attacked by predators: foxes, feral cats, crows, who knows? Like them the earth around him told the story of his death: he lay ten metres from the overturned ute, and the rain had not been able to rub out the marks that his hands had made as he gouged at the soil. You could see where he'd been thrown, how far he'd crawled, and you could tell he'd lain there a day or more, waiting to die. His face still stared at the sky; his empty eye sockets gazed up as if searching for the stars he could no longer see; his mouth was locked open in an animal snarl; and his back was arched in agony. I wondered if he'd tried to write anything on the ground beside him, but if he had, it was no longer readable. That would be so like Chris, sending messages that nobody else understood.

It was hard to think though that from this body and inside this head had once come wonderful messages. This stinking ugly body had once written 'Stars love clear sky. They shine.'

Beside me Robyn had stopped wailing and was now on her knees, sobbing quietly. The others were still behind me. I don't know what they were doing, just watching, silently I think, too shocked to move. I looked over at the wrecked car. It was easy to see what had happened. It was the Ford four-wheel drive that I'd thought was safely hidden on Tailor's Stitch. It had tipped on the slope beside the dam. It had slid downhill as it rolled. Half a dozen cartons of grog had spilled across the ground. Broken bottles and empty boxes were scattered everywhere. Some of the bottles still looked intact. I couldn't help thinking what a stupid thing it was to die for. And I couldn't help wondering what figure Chris would have blown in a breathalyser when he took that short cut across the paddocks.

It seemed like every time we came back from a major hit against the enemy we lost one of our friends. Only this time the enemy hadn't had anything to do with it. Not directly, that is. And Chris had been dead quite a while before we'd gone and attacked Turner Street. A lot of things had killed Chris. Us leaving him alone in Hell was one of them.

We stood there some time without saying anything. Surprisingly, without being surprising, it was Robyn who at last took charge. She walked back to the Land Rover and returned with a blanket. She still hadn't said a word. She spread the blanket out beside Chris and began to roll him onto it. She sobbed and hiccuped as she worked. A constant shaking, like a wind, was blowing through her, and made it hard for her to do it neatly, but she wrapped him up quite firmly, not gently or nervously like I would have done. But her actions, so deliberate, caused us to start to move. We gathered around the body and helped Robyn finish her task, wrapping Chris securely, tucking the blanket in at his head and feet. Then with Fi holding a torch to light our way, Robyn and Homer and Lee and I took a corner each and carried Chris back to the Landie. We made room in the back and dragged him in, clumsily, knocking and banging him around, although we were trying our best. We were just too tired. Then we got in the car, wound the windows down because of the smell, and drove on. No one had said a word. We hadn't even discussed what to do with the body of our friend.

Epilogue

We haven't left Hell for about a month now. It's hard to be sure exactly – I've lost my sense of time a bit. I don't have a clue what day it is, for instance, and I wouldn't know the date to the nearest week.

It's cold, I know that much.

The planes and helicopters kept coming over every day after we got back. I think they suspect we're hiding up in these mountains, because the choppers seemed to spend a lot of time patiently searching, moving slowly backwards and forwards, like giant dragonflies. It was hard on us. We had to be very sure that everything was concealed from the air and we had to keep under cover all day. It's been OK the last week or so though. I can't remember exactly when the last one came over. It gives me quite a thrill to think what damage we must have caused in Wirra-wee that night. A thrill that's three-quarters fear, but definitely a thrill.

But we may have had one failure. I didn't realise until Homer said something yesterday that there were no vehicles parked in Turner Street when he snuck across it to get to the house he tried to blow up.

As far as he can remember, anyway, but he says he's pretty sure. That leaves just a little doubt in my mind about Major Harvey. The Range Rover had been sitting in Turner Street when I left the church. I did want to get Harvey, and at the moment there's no way we can check whether we did or not.

We brought back some fresh batteries, so we've been able to listen to the radio a bit more. Things have bogged down a bit in most areas. We don't seem to have lost any more ground, but we haven't won any back either; and in lots of the best farmland, like our district, they seem pretty confident. The radio says a hundred thousand new settlers have moved in and there's heaps more with their bags packed, just waiting to come. The Americans don't talk about us much on their news now, but they've given us a fair bit in the way of money and equipment. Planes in particular. They send all the stuff to New Zealand – that's where everything's being organised.

The Kiwis have been pretty gutsy. They've sent landing forces over and they've fought hard in three different places, and they've won back some important areas, like Newington, where there's a big Air Force base. They haven't been near us though. The only action around here was at Cobbler's Bay. We heard a lot of planes go over three nights ago and Lee and Robyn both thought they could hear bombs way in the distance. In the morning, when I snuck up to Tailor's to take a look, there was a lot of smoke hanging over Cobbler's. So that was good.

It's not over yet, that's how I look at it.

I guess we'll have to try to help out again soon, too. I hate the thought, but there's no choice really. It's going to scare the crap out of me, because it's going to

268

be so much harder. I hate to think what changes we'll find. More colonists and tougher security, for two. It's a worry.

Last night was the first time anyone mentioned it. Lee said, 'When we go out again we should have a crack at Cobbler's ourselves.'

No one else said anything. We were all eating and we just kept our heads down, shovelling the food in. But I know what it's like. One cockatoo takes off from a tree, and suddenly the air's full of white birds. Lee just became the first cockatoo.

Lee and I are like an old married couple these days. We're so used to each other, I guess. We're good mates. But we're not like an old married couple in some ways – I like my space too much for that. I prefer sleeping alone – not that I sleep much. I'd feel a bit suffocated sleeping with someone every night. But we've made love five times now. It's nice. I like the way my body starts off feeling tingly and excited in one spot and then gradually it spreads and spreads until I'm freaking out all over. The only worry is those condoms. They're not that reliable; ninety-something per cent I think. When this is all over I sure don't want to roll up to Mum and Dad and hand them a baby. And another thing, I don't know what we'll do when Lee's supply runs out. There's only four left.

Maybe that's the real reason he wants us to take another trip out of Hell.

Fi told me this morning that she wants to do it with Homer, which had me choking on my Cornies. I never thought Fi would be game. I think it's more that she's jealous of Lee and me maybe, because she and Homer really don't have that kind of relationship any more. But there's not a wide choice of partners down here. And she's not having Lee.

The only other thing I have to write to bring this up to date is about Chris. And what I put won't be very logical. I'm so mixed up in my feelings about it all. We brought him down here and buried him in a nice spot: a hollow between some big rocks, about halfway between our tents and the spot where the creek runs into the bush. There was a soft piece of green grass there, almost like turf. Of course when we started digging we found that the softness didn't go far down. It was just a surface softness. Inside was all hard and rocky. In the end it took us three days to dig the deep hole that we wanted. We weren't too organised about it. Whenever we felt in the mood we'd wander over and do a bit more. We put him in there at dusk and covered him up straightaway. That was the worst part. That was just awful. I still get weepy when I think about it. When it was filled in we stood around for a minute or two but no one seemed to know what to say, so after a while we drifted away to our private spots, to sit on our own and think. We weren't able to do for our friend what we'd been able to do for the soldier we'd thrown in the gully in the Holloway Valley.

There's always a flower or two on the grave though. Every time anyone goes for a walk they bring one back and stick it there. The problem then is to keep our last lamb from eating it.

It makes me wonder if the Hermit's body is here somewhere in Hell too. It'd be funny if they were both here, because I think they were probably alike in some ways.

Anyway, that's not the illogical part. The illogical part is the way I feel about it all. About Chris. I miss him and I feel terrible that he died like that and it seems so unfair and such a waste. But I feel other things too, guilt especially. Guilt that we left him on his own, that we didn't try harder. When he was in one of his moods we usually gave up and didn't make an effort to humour him out of it. I think we should have done more. And I feel angry, angry at him. Angry that he was so weak and didn't try harder. Angry that he was such a genius but didn't do enough with it.

Sometimes you just have to be brave. You have to be strong. Sometimes you just can't give in to weak thoughts. You have to beat down those devils that get inside your head and try to make you panic. You struggle along, putting one foot a little bit ahead of the other, hoping that when you go backwards it won't be too far backwards, so that when you start going forwards again you won't have too much to catch up.

That's what I've learned.

There's a rustle in the grass to the left of my tent. Some little night creature, probably hoping to raid our food. Same as us, I think, searching around the countryside, trying to avoid the predators, just finding enough to keep ourselves going. I can hear Homer snoring, Fi calling out in her sleep, Lee wriggling into a new position, Robyn breathing steadily. I love these four people. And that's why I feel bad about Chris. I didn't love him enough.

They will carry me to the field
Through the wreaths of mist
Moist on my face,
And the lamb will pause
For a thoughtful stare.
The soldiers, they will come.
They will lay me in the dark cold earth
And push the clods in upon my face.

Also by John Marsden from Pan Macmillan

Tomorrow, When the War Began

Ellie and her friends leave home one quiet morning, wave goodbye to their parents, and head up into the hills to camp for a while; seven teenagers filling in time during school holidays.

The world is about to change forever. Their lives will never be the same again.

Would you fight? Would you give up everything? Would you sacrifice even life itself?

Tomorrow, When the War Began asks the biggest questions you will ever have to answer.

'The reader is unwittingly flung headlong and gasping into the plot . . . the images created are so vivid that they stay wlth you long after the book is reluctantly closed on the final page'
MELBOURN HERALD-SUN

'. . . a story to be read at full pelt – I could not put it down – and then returned to, for a second and third more thoughtful savouring'
AUSTRALIAN BOOKSELLER & PUBLISHER

'. . . an enlightening book about growing up and discovering who you are'
SUNDAY TELEGRAPH

The Third Day, the Frost

Live for what you believe in . . .
Die fighting for it.

The third day comes a frost . . . a killing frost.

The enemy spreads across the land, cold and relentless. They invade. They destroy. They kill.

Only the heroism of Ellie and her friends can stop them.

When hot courage meets icy death, who will win through?

In 2000, *The Third Day, the Frost* won Germany's Buxtuhede Bulle for the best book in the world for young people published in the previous two years.

'This is a real *Day of the Jackal* stuff and, if you want action, adventure and heart-stopping danger, *The Third Day, the Frost* delivers'
SYDNEY MORNING HERALD

'. . . a high octane adventure . . . unputdownable'
AUSTRALIAN BOOK REVIEW

'. . . tense, exciting and, most importantly, realistic, I wish I could read this series again for the first time'
SUN-HERALD

Burning for Revenge

The world is on fire. The world of Ellie and her friends has been set alight and is in flames. No-one will come out of it unscathed.

Burning for Revenge is scorching: the hottest book you'll ever read.

A sensational novel from the series that has transfixed millions of readers worldwide.

'Once started, this book is hard to put down. It should carry a warning "Don't start it at night unless you are an insomniac"'
THE CATHOLIC WEEKLY

'You will not be able to put this down until the last page has been turned – and even then you will be left breathless, thirsting for more!'
QUEENSLAND TIMES

'. . . if you pick up this book to dip in you'll find that you are galloping along with the narrative, unable to extricate yourself until those final words'
AUSTRALIAN BOOK REVIEW

'As addictive as the earlier books in the series and guaranteed to attract even more readers'
ILLAWARRA MERCURY

Darkness, Be My Friend

Nowhere to run, one place left to hide.

Darkness is the friend and enemy of those who hunt by night. And for those who hunt by night there can be a darkness of the soul, a darkness of the heart. Ellie has to defeat an inner darkness if she is to defeat the outer one. This is the engrossing story of her brave and bold struggle.

'. . . another enthralling tale of survival from one of the country's best-loved children's authors'
MERCURY

'A tale of gripping intensity and blinding fear, it will have your adrenaline rushing, your head pumping, the blood roaring in your ears and your fingernails bitten down to the quick'
QUEENSLAND TIMES

'This is a book that is hard to put down . . . it's gripping in its intensity and its intrigue. It's Marsden at his best!'
GEELONG ADVERTISER

'. . . check your heart rate as you read'
THE AGE

The Night is for Hunting

Hunting and being hunted.

Sometimes life seems to offer nothing more than a chase to the death.

The fight to survive has never been fiercer.

But as they wage war, Ellie and her friends still find time for other things: friendship . . . loyalty . . . even Christmas.

If only they can withstand another night.

The Night is for Hunting is the sixth volume in the award-winning *Tomorrow* series.

'. . . elevation of adventure literature to heights that are only achieved once or twice in a generation'
SFSITE.COM

'It is without a doubt the best series for younger readers that an Australian writer has ever produced'
DAILY ADVERTISER

'Adventure in a world where the characters must fight and survive – a powerful mixture and a tale very well told. *The Night is for Hunting* is another winner by this top-selling author who knows how to write for young people and what makes them tick'
GEELONG ADVERTISER

The Other Side of Dawn

This is a story of courage and adventure, of a tiny group of teenagers engaged in a struggle in which everything is at stake: their families, their friends, their countries, their lives. For them, there can be no turning back, no surrender. Too much rests on their shoulders, too many lives are at stake. They must go on . . . to life, to death, to the unknown.

You will never forget the brave hearts of Ellie and Homer and their friends.

A sensational novel from the series that has transfixed millions of readers worldwide.

'I feel, now that I have finished the series, something is missing. I wish I'd never read the series, so that I could discover it all now'
SARAH LAIN, UNITED KINGDOM

While I Live
The Ellie Chronicles

We were halfway up the spur when we heard it. Homer and Gavin and I, just the three of us . . . I'd say there were fifteen shots in the first volley, evenly spaced, lasting about twenty-five seconds . . . All the way down the spur I'd heard the scattered shots, getting closer as I got closer, and all the way down I tried to think of reasonable explanations for them, and I couldn't think of a single thing that made sense.

Wars never end. They go on loudly or they go on quietly. They grip you with bulldog teeth.

The town of Wirrawee is emerging from war, slowly. School's back in, Juicy's is open for coffee, farmers are bidding at the cattle stores.

Ellie Linton at last gets what she longed for and what she fought for, to be back on the farm with her parents.

But it's not the same. A new nation is on the other side of the new border. Suddenly the war is about to explode into Ellie's life again. The effects are devastating. The consequences will change her forever.

While I Live: The Ellie Chronicles is the first book in a new series featuring the immensely popular Ellie Linton, heroine and narrator of the *Tomorrow, When the War Began* series.

'. . . a brilliant, spirited, wonderfully written, extraordinary book . . .'
SUNDAY TELEGRAPH

Incurable
The Ellie Chronicles

The second book in *The Ellie Chronicles*, following *While I Live*, the post-war series featuring the immensely popular Ellie Linton, heroine and narrator of the *Tomorrow* series.

I held my line. I knew from the war, if not from shooting rabbits, that we were safe enough for the first moments. It is too impossible to hit a target like us from a helicopter that's rocking and rolling and trying to find its target. But maybe this guy had new equipment or maybe he was a brilliant shot or maybe he was just plain lucky. Bullet holes tore through the ute like a huge metal-punch was suddenly and roughly slamming a simultaneous line of them from our rear to our front.

Ellie Linton is a survivor.

Survival is an art form. Ellie is a survivor because she's honest, loyal and incurably brave.

And sometimes she's lucky.

What happens to survivors when their luck runs out? If they're incurably brave, they have a problem.

The border clashes are getting worse, the Liberation Front is becoming more daring and her young ward's terrible secrets threaten Ellie's hopes and hard work . . . even her life.

The war may be over but battles rage in every direction.

These are battles Ellie cannot avoid.

Packed full of action and human drama, John Marsden delivers another fast-paced adventure that will thrill old fans and new readers alike.

'Marsden is a master storyteller'
THE AGE